FALL
GUY

T0314591

Also by Liz Reinhardt

The Brenna Blixen series:

Double Clutch
Junk Miles
Slow Twitch

FALL GUY

LIZ REINHARDT

Definitions

FALL GUY
A DEFINITIONS BOOK 978 1 782 95123 0

First published in Great Britain by RHCP Digital,
an imprint of Random House Children's Publishers UK
A Random House Group Company

CreateSpace Independent Publishing Platform edition published 2012
RHCP Digital edition published 2012
Definitions edition published 2013

3 5 7 9 10 8 6 4 2

Penguin Random House is committed to a sustainable future for
our business, our readers and our planet. This book is made from
Forest Stewardship Council® certified paper.

MIX
Paper | Supporting
responsible forestry
FSC® C018179

Printed and bound in Great Britain by Clays Ltd, Elcograf S.p.A.

Set in Palatino

Definitions are published by Random House Children's Publishers UK
61–63 Uxbridge Road, London W5 5SA

www.randomhousechildrens.co.uk
www.totallyrandombooks.co.uk
www.randomhouse.co.uk

Addresses for companies within
The Penguin Random House Group can be found at:
global.penguinrandomhouse.com

THE RANDOM HOUSE GROUP Limited Reg. No. 954009

A CIP catalogue record for this book is available from the British Library.

To my Ma, who never doubted for a single second that I could do everything I have done and is still waiting expectantly for more. Your ferocious love has forced me back up every time I've been knocked down, and I'll never be able to express how much I appreciate that. I love you.

Evan 1

My grandmother's pearls slide soft and cool against the skin of my neck as I twist them nervously.

I always imagined myself touching them just before I walked down the aisle on my wedding day, their gold hue complementing a snow-white wedding dress that showed a tasteful amount of skin and hugged me in all the right places.

I had no idea I'd get to wear them so much sooner, and for such an embarrassing reason.

This morning my grandmother inserts the necklace's little gold hook into the eye-shaped clasp and presses it tight, her dry fingertips light and gentle on my shoulders, the softly sweet, rich smell of her perfume reassuring in my nostrils.

'Ninety per cent of this entire ordeal is how you look, sugar. Keep that backbone straight, but don't you dare even think one solitary saucy thought. You don't have what it takes to keep that temper off your face.'

I glance up at her reflection in the gold-framed

mirror of my dressing table, and guilt gives a long, silent scream at the back of my brain. There are lines between her ash-blonde eyebrows I can't recall being there before I became a permanent fixture in her daily life. Her smile strains across her face and her blue eyes, the same icy blue as mine, are dull with worry.

Granddaddy stands in the doorway and clears his throat, too much of a marrow-deep gentleman to feel comfortable entering any lady's room while she is dressing. Gramma helps me slide my arms into the navy and white seersucker jacket that gives me an aura of demure sweetness.

'I'm ready, Granddaddy. You can come in.'

Shame shudders through me like a tiny tropical storm bashing underneath a bell jar. Granddaddy walks up to me, the sodden heaviness of his steps making guilt prick my eyes like a relentless wind.

'Well, darlin', you look a picture. No man in his right mind, judge or not, could see a young lady so beautiful and fail to realize this is all just a big misunderstanding.'

His breath wheezes from his mouth in labored gasps. August is an uncompromisingly hot month in Georgia, and the humidity makes his lungs constrict. It's painful for Gramma and me to see Granddaddy operating at less than his usual cyclone-riding-a-galloping-mustang energy level.

'I'll be fine. No matter what the judge decides.' I pressure my lips to curve in a perfect, patient smile that is an undeniable family heirloom, passed down from my grandmother like a birthright. Composure in the face of any obstacle is just how the women of our stock deal with things.

'I can't believe that boy's family wasn't willing to make peace over this whole . . . misunderstanding.' Granddaddy's bright-white mustache quivers with rage. 'I understand a family's connection to their land, but it was just a bunch of damn nut trees.'

Gramma squeezes his elbow and runs her hand in relaxing circles on his forearm. 'Come and let's have some sweet tea. Kailyn made a big batch before she left last night. Come on, now. Evan needs to get a move on, or she'll be late.'

'Shouldn't we go with her?' Granddaddy demands for the hundredth time, and my heart squeezes with love for him.

It's beyond sweet that he's so focused on me and my crazy dilemma, especially considering the fact that Kailyn's sweet tea is usually enough to tempt that man away even from golf, his primary obsession.

'No, Granddaddy. This is my own mess, and I'm going to take care of it all by myself.' Before he can protest, I hike up on my toes and pop a kiss on his cheek and on my grandmother's, making a registered effort to avoid looking either of them directly in the eye. 'Plus that, we have a strategy we need to stick with. I show up with you, and the judge assumes I think I can get myself out of this using my name.'

'You should be able to.' He rubs the spot just over his heart with short, firm strokes of his fingers, a tic that always rears its head when he's particularly annoyed.

I'd worry, but his doctor says he has the heart of an ox.

'I'll be just fine,' I reassure them both, turning away from their worried faces.

I keep a firm hold on those breezy, confident words like they're my life-jacket in a shipwreck, because I don't feel nearly as confident as I sound.

I run my hand down the shiny banister of the curved staircase that leads into the gleam of our crystal-filled hall, my feet tripping lightly over the marble tiles before I burst through the large oak front door into the heat, so stagnant the air feels heavy and dead. I slide into the car and head to court early.

I manage to hang on to my cheery forced optimism all the way to the courthouse doors, in through the metal-detectors, and right up to the doorway of my assigned courtroom, but that's where my confidence explodes like a water balloon dropped from thirty stories up.

I'm positive the splash of my shattered courage should be audible, but no one gives so much as a quarter glance my way.

Lawyers with scuffed briefcases, a man with slicked-back hair and a clip-on tie, and a woman in saggy sweatpants rolled at the waist walk by, but no one notices me skulking in the corner.

My gold watch flashes, warning me not to be tardy and not to make a bigger, more complicated mess of this than I already have.

I'm tempted to call my best friend, my lifeline, Brenna, but what would she say? She'd make me go in, and I *can't do that*.

So I sit on the chilly slate floor, not worried about the wrinkles setting in on the sheath dress Gramma pressed for me this morning. I bury my head in my clammy hands and resolve to stare at the tiles until I manage to convince them to open wide and ingest me whole.

A voice punctures through my self-pity and fear. A smooth, obnoxiously confident voice with the undercurrent of an accent I can't place.

'Are you nervous?'

The words are overly familiar, like he's backstage with me before a big recital or at my shaking, heartbroken side at that second when I've realized my mother disappeared on another bender.

I focus on the polished shine of his black boots and try not to admit that his voice is a sweet caress, despite my brain sounding warning bells.

'I'm fine. I just ... needed a second. To sit.' It may be the most idiotic thing I've ever uttered, but I refuse to back down from my resolve to sit on this floor.

For a second.

Like I said.

The boots shift slightly, and I realize he's leaned over to open the door of the courtroom. A woman thanks him in a high, nervous voice.

'You're welcome, ma'am.'

My head whips up at the 'ma'am'.

Not that I haven't heard that word spilled like sticky sweet syrup from a thousand mouths of a thousand boys who've been born and bred to use it every day.

There's something about *this* boy, the way that word slides off *his* tongue, buoyed with cautious respect and elegant pleasure.

Like he loves saying the word.

Like his lips weigh the worth of it.

I crane my neck, and he's looking down at me with half a twisted smile, his hand extended. I put my freshly manicured fingers into his, rough with calluses, and he coaxes me to stand up with a gentle tug, so I'm suddenly nestled too close to the lean, towering height of him.

'Have you had long enough? To sit?' The questions are sweet, but his lips have a twisted curve that makes my heart double-beat to the tune of one word: wicked.

I smell him: it's a smell that's not part of the deep, salty musks of this area. It's clean and fresh and sweet. Something foreign and intoxicating – like clover, wet with a sheen of overnight dew.

'I've had long enough.' I pull my hand from his, reluctantly, and press my palms down the front of my skirt. For an instant, the wrinkles smooth out, but the second I take my hands away, they spring back. I can't keep the *tsk* of my tongue locked in my mouth.

His laugh scatters a little too loud for this dim, serious court hallway.

'Hey.' He says it informally, like we've known each other forever, and I move a step back to keep him out of my physical territory while the imprint of his big laugh twines through my neurons. 'You can get away with them.'

His eyes are blue, but not glacial frozen blue like mine. They're like sun-warmed blueberries, dark denim-blue, well-deep and framed by overlong jet-black lashes. He blinks slowly, and his lean, chiseled face is relaxed and calm despite its cut lines.

'Get away with what?' I keep my voice coolly unaffected.

Eyes trained on me, he leans over, and whispers.

'Wrinkles. Stains. Tears. You're too pretty to bother worrying about any of that. The first thing people notice is your face. Once they notice that, there's really no noticing anything else. Trust me on this one.'

He tilts his head to the side, indicating that we should go into the courtroom, and I notice that his short, dark hair is newly cut, expertly done.

'That's the worst pick-up line I've ever heard,' I tell him, but a tiny shiver of appreciation jolts through me, like that magical fragment of a second when a snowflake lands on your tongue, perfect and whole before it melts into oblivion.

'I'm not trying to pick you up.' His eyes are dancing – a jig, the robot, the macarena – and I work to keep my lips in a neat, straight line. 'Judge Schwenzer is a stickler for being on time, and we're two minutes away from being late.'

He swings the door open, and I do my best not to be too obvious in my admiration of the clean lines of his muscles through the thin cotton of his button-down. I notice a tattoo etched on his skin, just peeking out from his cuff. I can't see what it is.

'After you, m'lady.'

Then he smiles, my nerves unfurl in a long, smooth

spin, and I walk into the hushed courtroom with tiny sparks of silvery light flickering on the outsides of my eyes. It's probably from nerves. It's probably because I didn't eat breakfast. It's absolutely not because this irritatingly over-familiar hustler is trying to pick me up in the hallway of a courthouse.

I clamp down hard and quick on my judgment. I'm here for trespassing and unintentional arson. He's probably here to argue a speeding ticket.

I murmur a 'thank you' and panic petrifies my legs and leaves me blocked in the doorway. He nudges me in, takes my hand as if I'm some new kid he's been assigned to lead around on the first day of school, and pulls me to a long wooden pew-like bench, where we sit.

I run my fingers over the red-leather portfolio cover I'm holding onto for dear life. Other people have their court documents clutched in their fists or in cheap ten-cent folders, but I have fancy taste in accessories.

Mystery Guy has nothing in his hands. Unlike the other people in the courtroom, he's not sitting ramrod straight or fidgeting. He looks perfectly relaxed.

I bet it was a speeding ticket. He probably thinks just showing up will get him out of it.

I flip my cover open, glance over all the damning evidence pitted against me in black and white, then snap it shut again.

The judge enters the courtroom, and we all jump to our feet – a sheepish unit of criminals. Law breakers. Deviants. Sweat coats both my palms.

When Judge Schwenzer finally sits and we settle back down, she attacks the files on her desk. From her shellacked hair to her sensibly hideous glasses, she's all business, and I feel my heart sink.

This woman would never splurge on a red-leather portfolio cover for her incriminating court documents. This woman will hate me on principle.

I catch the guy looking at me. Not sneaking a look, no flirty attempts to maybe establish eye contact; just plain, open looking. When I put all my efforts into staring him down, he gives me a clear, wide smile and winks, one slow, lazy flick of an eyelid laced with all those gorgeous lashes. My heart races again, and I turn my attention stubbornly to the front of the courtroom.

Which is a mistake. Judge Schwenzer is chewing some poor girl apart over a charge for driving under the influence of alcohol. Apparently this isn't her first. And just when she's finished reducing the girl to a blubbering mass of tears, she picks up the next file.

'Winchester Tobar Youngblood.'

The guy stands and says, 'Excuse me,' before he flashes me one more cocky smile and walks with sure confidence to the judge's bench.

Judge Schwenzer's lips are already compressed

flat and mean, a line she's daring anyone to cross.

'Winchester, the charges against you involve disturbing the peace and public intoxication. How do you plead?'

Shock jars my eyeballs right to the front of the room, though it makes no sense at all for me to be shocked. I do not know him, no matter how strangely intimate our little court hallway rendezvous felt. Sweet manners, a few open smiles, and a wink aren't enough to establish a man's character. But maybe he's not—

'Guilty, Your Honor.'

I'm admittedly a poor judge of guys, but the disappointment I feel over this particular guy is uncanny.

Judge Schwenzer also seems ... not so much disappointed, but disbelieving.

'I don't buy it, Mr Youngblood. The officer filing the report said the man he observed was shaggy and unkempt. In all the times you've come before the court, you've never looked that way.'

Winchester bows his head with deference. 'My mother told me I should always get a haircut before an important court date, ma'am.'

That is a perfectly reasonable explanation. And, honestly, it makes no sense for the judge to question something so easily explained. Why didn't she think of it?

'The officer also noted that the man he gave a citation to had a tattoo on his forearm. Very distinctive. A Pegasus.' Her eyes are sharks-with-lasers intense, and they're trained right on Winchester.

He rolls his sleeve up and holds his arm out for her to see, out of my line of sight. His words are low and even – almost meditative.

'A pooka, ma'am, not a Pegasus. No wings.'

I need to see that tattoo. It's like a foil-wrapped birthday present I'm not allowed to open.

The judge closes her eyes behind those steel-framed glasses and lets out a sigh heavy with frustration.

'That tattoo looks very fresh.'

'My skin takes a long time to heal, ma'am.'

His voice remains even-keeled and patient, and that just seems to dig like splinters into Judge Schwenzer's ass.

She puckers her lips, shakes her head, and swipes her pen. 'Five thousand dollars, probation, and community service.' She glances up from her paperwork. 'Winchester?'

He looks up at her, and there's a long, silent exchange of facial tics and stares before she says, 'This is me giving you one final chance. One. Don't throw it away. The next time you're in this courthouse, I will not exercise leniency.'

Silence rocks between them for a few counts.

'Thank you, ma'am,' Winchester says and turns to go.

I watch his confident swagger all the way to the back of the courtroom, but I never get to see him leave, because Judge Schwenzer, angry as a warthog that's been poked with a sharp stick, calls my name next, venom practically dribbling over the syllables that fall from her mouth.

Winch 1

With girls, it's all in the eyes.

That's how you can tell, how you know if a girl's going to be some doe-eyed princess you have to tiptoe around until you can unlock what she wants you to find or an eye-rolling vixen ready to run just for the fun of having you chase her.

Blue, green, brown, hazel, amber, gray: I can remember the eyes of any girl who caught my attention, even after her name and number are long-forgotten memories.

I asked her if she was nervous, and it was like a thousand icicles shot out of those eyes to murder my pick-up attempts in cold blood.

There's a saying, 'Cold hands, warm heart'. In my experience, a better indicator of a girl's heart is her eyes.

This girl's are arctic, but I read beneath them, and could see that the cool exterior is nothing but a cover for a hot temper that burns underneath. I've got a head for gambling, and I'd be willing to bet everything I have that she gets emotional as hell, probably throws tantrums and sets things on fire.

I've got warm eyes, but my family always talk about how I'm a cucumber, cool and collected, never letting anything rattle me. That's why I have the job I have. That's why I do the things I do. I don't buckle under pressure. Ever.

I know she's watching me when I'm in front of the courtroom, and when Judge Schwenzer gives me another wrist-slap round of community service and a serious warning, I also know I have to get the hell out of Dodge.

That girl with those eyes and those curves and that voice, like slow sex during a summer storm, runs way too hot for me to mess with. Especially now, when every damn thing in my world is spiraling out of control, and I'm the only one who can grab all the ends and hold it together.

I have my hand on the doorknob when Judge Schwenzer calls a name.

'Evan Williams Lennox.'

The judge's voice is tight and bland, like a puke-colored rubber band stretched until it's about to snap. But the name ... there's no way it can be that girl's, with her heirloom pearls and her little preppy court uniform.

No girl that high class could be named after whiskey. Evan Williams just happened to be my favorite brand, too.

I turn my head and see her walking up, and I don't even remember taking a seat, but all of a sudden, my ass is back on one of those shiny benches, focusing on the front of the courtroom as old Schwenzer puts the girl through hell, spits her out, and drags her back for more.

'Ms Lennox, could you explain to me how exactly it was an *accident* that you wound up burning down some of the oldest trees in the entire state of Georgia?'

Behind her old-lady glasses, Schwenzer's eyes are bright with glee. She must come from an ancient line of executioners who really enjoyed their profession.

'It was an accident because I never meant the trees any harm, ma'am. I was only trying to burn some personal items.'

That damn voice is hot and husky in my ears. I know I should leave now, but again, I hold back, just for one more minute.

'Burn some personal items? On someone else's property? You're lucky you didn't set the entire house on fire, Ms Lennox.' She raises her eyebrows and scans the charges. 'I have half a mind to let you spend a week or two in a correctional facility.'

The girl lets out this soft little gasp, but I know

Schwenzer's bluffing out her ass. 'But I won't. This time. Your record has been clean so far, and I imagine this was the result of a night of carelessness. But you caused serious damage, and you have to accept punishment for that. You will pay the owners of the property for the damages, you will pay your court fines, and you will be spending your free time for the next few weeks in community service. Don't let me see you here again.'

Judge Schwenzer waves a hand to dismiss her, and the girl picks up the papers, looking like she'd rather die than begin the long walk of shame from the bench to the doors. Those cold eyes don't even flutter in my direction when I hold the door open for her.

I follow the sweet curve of her ass as she races to the outer doors, her red heels clicking on the tiles so fast, I'm sure she's about to trip and face-plant any second.

Every cell in my brain tells me that the smartest thing I can do is get my paperwork in order, pay my fine, figure out what community service I'll have to wrestle through this time, and get the hell away from this girl and this whole crazy day.

But I'm not really thinking with my brain when I follow her outside. She's already across the parking lot, about to key the paint around the door lock of a silver Lexus because her hands are shaking so hard.

I stand a few feet away so I don't spook her more.

'Evan?'

Her name feels good in my mouth, and I like the shocked and pleased look in her eyes when she hears me say it.

'Oh. Hi. I have to . . . uh, I have to get home now.' Her voice is thick, and I keep my eyes on hers, waiting for the tears.

They don't come.

'You have to visit your parole officer. Schwenzer went light on you. Don't piss her off.'

The words are technically a warning, but I don't say them that way. It's just information, just something for this pretty girl to think about before she blows her own foot off with a shotgun by leaving in this sleek little ride without finishing her paperwork.

And, maybe, part of me hopes I'll get a few more minutes with her before I head back home and force myself to forget her forever.

She lifts one foot a couple inches off the ground and lets her shoe slide off her heel and just hang there, half off, half on.

'Does it take long?' Her voice is sweet and rough at once, like sugar would be if you rubbed it on your skin.

For some reason, that shoe hanging off her foot makes my brain cloud over and I want . . . I want a thing I definitely can't have with this girl. I stuff my hands in my pockets, a reminder to my stupid body that this is a hands-off situation.

'Not too long. Follow me.'

I smile at her, at first just to show her she has nothing to be freaked out over, but when she rolls this tiny, shy smile my way, I can't hold back the weird surge of something deep and fucking good that spills through me. I feel like whistling. And I also feel like I should run in the opposite direction.

Fast.

Instead I stay by her side, catching the scent of cotton candy and magnolia, and just a little undercurrent of ash.

'You looked so relaxed.' Her voice is jittery and she jangles her keys in her hands in a quick, nervous rhythm. 'In the courtroom, in front of the judge, you looked like you didn't care what happened to you.'

She flicks her eyes in my direction and twists those classy pearls at her throat.

I have this second where I wonder what she'd look like in just that necklace and nothing else, but I rein it in so I can answer her.

'I'm used to being here. And I was a little nervous. I'm trying not to get any jail time on my record. But I've been in front of Schwenzer three times this year, so she's about done with my ass. I have no clue why we got off so light.'

I'm about to joke that maybe old Schwenzer got lucky last night, but I'm not going to push it with this girl. We're already closer than I meant to get, and I'm not sure how we got where we are.

'Maybe she got laid last night.' She bats her lashes at me, and hits me with a smile that's as brutal as a sucker punch.

I want to say more, keep this banter going, ask her what she's doing tonight and for the rest of the weekend and the week after, but I bite my tongue.

That's what I'm good at: staying cool, no matter what. This girl is already loosening everything I worked so hard to tie tight, and I can't afford to lose it now.

In the parole office, I make sure that once I tell her what to do and who to talk to, I don't look directly at her again.

It's not exactly an easy task.

I can't remember the last time a girl made me sit up and pay attention the way this girl does. Even though I'm trying to keep my eyes on some boring-as-hell article in *Sports Illustrated*, I can't help but notice that her skirt is riding up, giving me an eyeful of smooth, tanned thigh.

Some slick-haired jackass across from her is

undressing her with his meth-bleary eyes, and I give him the fuck-off snarl that always sends guys with no backbone scampering like little bitches.

She crosses and uncrosses her legs, and my eyes follow the line of her thigh down to her ankle and along the curve of her arch, watching as her red high heel slides on and off the back of her foot, driving me insane for reasons I can't put my finger on.

'Evan Lennox.'

Jan calls her name and crooks one finger, the nail painted some crazy bright orange. Jan is one of the good people, and I relax knowing that Evan will get an OK assignment. Maybe she'll get stocking at the food pantry or sorting at Goodwill. Jan won't give a newbie the shit details like road pick-up or mortuary clean-up.

At least I hope she won't.

I'm starting to sweat it for the girl by the time Kevon calls my name.

'Man, what're you doing back here?' His voice is too loud and jolly for parole. He should be one of Santa's elves or an aerobics instructor.

I shake his hand and refuse to wince when he almost takes my arm out of its socket. I'm glad to see him, but I wish he'd stop screaming in my ear so I could eavesdrop on Jan and Evan.

'Drunk and disorderly, eh? Doesn't sound like you, Winch. You sure it was you, now?' His smile is so wide

I can see his gold teeth, way in the back, but his dark eyes go serious. 'Look, kid, I like you. I really do. But just because Schwenzer has a soft heart when your name comes on the docket doesn't mean you're safe. This is three, man. Strike three. I can't believe you didn't get time. Lucky, that's what you are. But you can only ride that so far.'

He pauses and puts his hands flat on the desk. 'Hey. Hey! You listening to me?'

All I can hear is low murmurings, but Evan sounds upset. It's not my business.

It's really not my business.

I know Jan is fair, and it's probably just a case of a rich girl stamping her little designer heel over the fact that she has to rub shoulders with people at a home-less shelter or something.

Only I don't really believe Evan would be like that.

Not that I know her.

Not that I should even be thinking about it, because she's not mine to think about that way.

I've got bigger, more important things on my plate.

I make sure I don't even glance her way, but Kevon is pretty hard to trick. He looks past me, not even bothering to be discreet, and raises his eyebrows.

'All right. I'll let you off the hook for being dis-tracted. I can't blame you for wanting to look at her instead of me. Winchester Youngblood, heartbreaker.'

I shoot him an irritated face that I'm hoping communicates my desire for him to shut the hell up before she overhears, but my look only gets him going. 'Oh, look at you, my man! Temper, temper. All right, I'm not made out of stone. Give me a second.'

I think Kevon must have serious family connections to have landed this job, because this guy is the biggest pain-in-the-ass parole officer ever, and I can't imagine how he got this legit government job when he acts like he's auditioning for some cheesy sitcom.

Why can't he just stamp my papers, take my check, and let me go on my way? He has no business meddling in this girl's life, but there he goes, off to Jan's desk to shake hands and probably tell Jan how nice her crazy hair looks or some crap so he can wheedle out the information he wants.

Funny how when he's around me, he talks like there's a megaphone attached to his mouth, but now that he's over there with Evan, I can't hear a damn thing.

A few minutes later he walks back like he owns this sad little office, his smile smug as a fool's. I try not to look over, but I hear Evan thank Jan and say goodbye, then those sexy heels click on the floor, and I have to punch and jab at my urge to jump up and follow her out, beg for her number, take her on a date . . . at least take one more look before she's out of my life for good.

Like he can read my mind, Kevon asks, 'You wanna run and get that lady's number? I'll wait.'

'I don't need to get involved with a girl like her, Kevon. Can we get this party started? I have places to be.'

I slide the papers over so he can sign and notarize everything, pissed off that he got me to lose my temper and snap at him.

I never do that. I take a lot of pride in the fact that I can keep things cool. It's my job.

It's my life.

It's who I am.

'You sure do, boy-o.' He stamps and staples my paperwork with a grin that I don't trust on instinct and sends me on my way.

Her silver Lexus is gone when I get to the parking lot, and I tell myself that's a good thing. The last thing I need to involve myself with is an ice-eyed girl named after whiskey with a talent for setting things on fire.

By the time I pull onto the highway, I accept the fact that Evan Williams Lennox was just a blip on my radar. A sexy ass blip, but a blip I have to forget.

Evan 2

'So you didn't even wait to get his number?'

My best friend, Brenna, a love-obsessed romantic down to the pulp of her sweet little heart, is on the line.

I expected to be lectured a little bit because I burned down part of an orchard and got a crap-load of fines and weeks' worth of community service, but all my friend cares about is the specific shade of blue his eyes were and what, exactly, he said to get me off the floor and into the courtroom.

Sweet, soft, indigo and 'Are you nervous?' for the record, but there is no record, because this guy was just some guy I bumped into at court who is basically an irresponsible drunken brawler.

Not that I can talk.

'So how do you know he wanted to give me his number?'

I'm hanging up green plaid skirts and egg-yolk yellow blouses, my daily clothing staples now that I'm enrolled at St Anne's School for Catholic Girls, the only school that would take a girl with my dubious criminal record and lukewarm grades. I hate the uniform with an intensity that makes me gag, but wearing it is my penance.

And it hurts so much more than kneeling on dried peas for hours ever could.

'Did you wear your navy sheath-dress?' Brenna demands.

I hang the last complexion-destroying blouse and move to my bed. This is an unnatural state of affairs for me. I'm usually a slob and a half. But I can't put Gramma and Granddaddy through any more bullshit.

'Sweetie, it doesn't matter what I was wearing. But yes, I was. And he is a criminal. Why can you not grasp that?'

Brenna laughs in my ear. 'No offense, but you're a criminal, too, Evan. That doesn't mean you really did anything so bad. And it definitely doesn't mean you can't flirt a little. Look, I'd try to encourage you to date some respectable geek, but St Anne's is all girls and you haven't mentioned a single, solitary guy in months. Months! What shoes did you wear?'

I throw all my make-up in my violet-embellished bag and snap it closed.

'The red heels.'

My ears burn.

The line is quiet for a few seconds as Brenna processes her shock and amazement.

'Evan? You wore the hot-sweet-magic-sex heels? The ones we got in New York City? The ones you swore you were going to wear on your first date with The One? Do you not see what a sign this is?'

Brenna is dangerously close to squealing and I'd bet the last tube of my favorite mascara that she's dancing around in her gorgeous little room, hugging herself like she just watched my fairy godmother change me into a princess for the ball.

'Calm yourself, girl. I wore those shoes because I gave up on all that nonsense. I figured I'd wear them on the one day I knew for sure I wouldn't meet anyone life-changing.'

I step out onto the balcony off my bedroom and listen to the hiss and hum of a million insects busy in the deep green of the garden below.

'But you met *him*.' Brenna refuses to be thwarted.

'OK. I wore the heels and met a guy who was, I'm not gonna lie, hot as hell. But also a criminal. And also did not give me his number or ask for mine, so there is nothing – listen to me now, Brenna Blixen – *nothing* going on. At all.'

I lean over the balcony and pull a magnolia flower close, rubbing the waxy petals with the tips of my fingers.

'You're going to see him again. I know it. I can *feel* it. Those shoes are hot-sweet-magic-sex shoes. They work.'

Her laugh is gleeful and happy on my behalf, so I don't roll my eyes at her.

But it's hard to resist the temptation.

I steer the conversation on to other things, like Brenna's sexy-sweet boyfriend, her crazy, over-loaded, over-achiever school schedule, and her design business, which has expanded to include bumper stickers and pins.

I love listening to her chatter. Gramma said that one of her biggest disappointments is that I didn't meet someone like Brenna sooner.

Someone who could have helped give me direction.

Someone who could have kept me from doing what I do best: crash and burn.

I'm sad to let the lone ray of sunshine in my otherwise cloudy world go, but I have to say goodbye to Bren and start getting ready for day one of community service. I have such a towering pile of days to complete, I'm not even going to count.

I pull on jeans, a T-shirt and boots, and pull my hair into a ponytail.

Simple.

OK, maybe the jeans are perfectly butt-hugging and low-riding enough to still be sexy, and the T-shirt is gauzy and cut in just a deep enough V to give me a sultry feel, and the boots have a tiny heel and are a gorgeous dark leather. But I wear a uniform every single day to school. There's no way I can throw on any old thing, even to do community service. This outfit is the plainest I can manage.

Gramma and Granddaddy are at one of the dozens of golf tournaments they spend all year attending, so there's no one to say goodbye to as I hop into my car and drive to the site.

I'm not exactly sure what I'll be doing, but they told me to dress for potentially dirty work. Which I half listened to.

Sweat slicks my palms and makes my hands slide over the steering wheel as I drive past favorite restaurants, stores and salons. My weekends won't be spent indulging my wild material-girl side or driving to the beach house to polish off a bottle of something sweet and numbing, and then sleep it off with the sound of the crashing waves in the background.

I will be servicing my community each Saturday for all the hours of my morning and most of my afternoon, and by the time I'm done, everyone else will be in the middle of their weekend benders.

Anyway, I can't get involved with that stuff any more even if I wanted to. Since I broke up with my disgusting pig of an ex-boyfriend, I moved across town from my old neighborhood, changed schools in my senior year, and dabbled in reckless criminal mischief, so I've blown any chances for local friends.

The only person who loves and accepts me is Brenna, and she lives in godforsaken New Jersey and is deaf to my pleas to move to the more hospitable and sunny South.

I'm alone here. But, given my record for going apeshit when I have an audience, that's probably a good thing for me.

I pull up to a little office in the backwoods of nowhere and grab my paperwork. I have to have it signed by the foreman, or whatever they call the officer in charge of watching all of us criminals. When I get inside, there's a little desk where a woman in uniform is checking off names and giving out tasks. I give her my name and she squints at the paper for a moment.

'Evan Lennox?' she double-checks.

'That's me.' I clutch at the paper in my hands nervously and chew my lip. Did I somehow manage to screw things up already?

'You'll be painting today.' She eyes my outfit. 'We have smocks you can change into.'

My cheekbones feel singed. 'It's OK. These are work clothes.'

It's not a lie. My work clothes just happen to be very fashionable.

'Suit yourself. You'll start in the station room, around the corner to the left. You've painted before, I assume?'

I nod, and this time my answer is a complete lie that I pray won't bite me in the ass.

'Good. There are several guards who will be patrolling the premises regularly. Stay on task or your service card won't be signed, and you'll have to make today up. If you need help, come to this office or give a holler.'

She shoos me away with a wave of her un-manicured, unbejeweled hand, and I go around the corner and to the left.

The door is open and there's a radio blaring. I can hear the rhythmic sweep and clack of a paint roller. I guess I'll be working with someone else.

I walk in the doorway and a huge drip of light blue paint blobs on the dustsheet at my feet. I step over it and almost crash into . . . *him*.

'Oh! What are you doing here?' I demand stupidly as he stops rolling paint on the walls and stares at me, naked shock all over his face.

'What am *I* doing here? What are *you* doing here?' His mouth pulls tight, a bowstring just before the arrow flies. 'Un-fucking-believable, Kevon,' he mutters, and he eyes me from the top of my ponytail to the tip of my inappropriate footwear with a look that is definitely pissed off and annoyed.

'Excuse me?'

I feel stupidly overdressed and unprepared for even this simple day of painting, and now the one person who was slightly nice to me on one of the most embarrassing days of my life is being a complete and utter ass, and it's caught me off guard.

I immediately hate myself for having had a crush on him, and I hate him with instant, total fury. If he couldn't bother to be nice when he saw me, he could have at least been neutral and not made me feel like an out-of-place idiot.

Anger settles on my tongue like a hot pepper, and one bite is all it will take for me to access the spicy heat.

'I just, uh, didn't expect you. Didn't expect to see you. Again.' He tosses the roller into the tray and paces, running a hand over his short black hair. 'This is . . .' He looks up at me, those deep-blue eyes scanning my face the way honor students speed-read before an exam. He clenches his teeth so hard his jaw twitches, and then announces, 'I should sign up for another duty station.'

I crunch down on the pepper of my anger and my temper flares. I want to keep cool, but I lash out blindly – every insecurity about this crazy day bubbling to the surface, so I can't keep my emotions in check.

'Sorry it's such a huge issue to work with me. You know, where I come from, judging someone based on their clothes is considered a really shitty thing to do. I may dress well, but that doesn't mean I'm useless.'

I stalk a few feet closer to him, so angry I should be able to jump right in his face. But something about him stops me.

He's perfectly still, perfectly quiet and cool, but there's a dangerous edge in those warm blue eyes. Like a volcano, dormant for so long you forget how vicious it can be until it explodes.

'It's not your clothes. It's not that I don't think you can work.' His voice is low and deceptively sweet – candy from a stranger I know I shouldn't take. 'It's just not a good idea if we work together. Nothing personal.'

But his eyes, half deep-blue velvet, half dark-blue diamond, tell me loud and clear that his declaration is a bald lie. This is entirely personal, and I decide to throw my stubborn pride out of the window and plead my case.

Which is weird for me.

I don't plead my case to anyone. Ever. And especially not to guys.

But there's something about Winchester. Something that makes me run boiling then frigid, something I'm attracted to and can't stand at the same time.

And part of me wants him around, needs him even. For practical reasons.

And another part of me wants him for other, less practical reasons.

Reasons that have to do with the energy that crackles between us in this room. Energy that's waking up something in me that's been dormant since way before I axed my ex.

I put a placatory hand on his wrist and our eyes both snap down to it before I pull away, the tingle of his skin's warmth still on my fingertips.

'Look, I'm in enough trouble right now. I'm just trying to keep my head down and get through this damn day. If you hate working with me after today, feel free to talk to the warden or whoever the hell manages this stuff. But please don't make me look bad right now. I promise, you won't even know I'm here.'

To prove my point, I walk over to the tray, pick up the roller, sop up some paint, and roll it along the wall.

Paint gushes out of both ends of the roller and leaves long, sloppy dribbles on either side, but I play it cool and act like that's what I meant to do all along.

I roll another long stripe of paint as far up as I can reach and bend down to get all the way to the bottom. The paint isn't going on as thickly, so I dip the roller again and make another squishy line.

I feel his heat when he walks up behind me, like I

have my own personal human sun radiating warmth against my back.

'You're making a mess.' I can hear his smile curved against his words.

I push the roller back up and down the wall, and it sputters with an uneven gush of paint. 'Why don't you do your thing and leave me to do mine?'

'Because if I let you keep going like that, my "thing" is going to be redoing your paint job. Give it here for a second.'

He holds one hand out, and I stare at the long, strong fingers that I imagine doing a whole slew of naughty things before I hand the roller over.

He squats down in front of a tray and points. 'The idea isn't to soak up as much paint as possible and smear it on the walls.' He coats the roller with a steady backward and forward motion. 'You want to reapply more often and make uniform coats. Also you want to paint in a big W-shape. Like this.' He picks a clean area of wall and rolls a clean, effortless W.

I should be watching his technique, but it's hard to focus when the coiled muscles of his back bulge against the stretch of his threadbare T-shirt. He repeats the lines, saying something about even pressure and blend, but I'm a little obsessed with the way his arm muscles stretch and contract.

When he turns back to check on me, it's like he

can read on my face how completely I'm not paying attention to his instructions. He shakes his head and directs a reluctant smile at the grisly blue paint. My mouth goes a little dry. I love that smile.

I want more of that smile.

'You want to try?'

He holds the roller out and breaks through my thoughts, which have strayed to his mouth, and what else it might do, other than smile.

That mouth could do so many incredibly hot things to me.

I take the roller from his hand and make a W that must meet his approval, because he gives me a nod and goes back to his own wall. We work in silence for a few minutes, but I am not doing well with refilling my roller. He made the whole thing look so damn easy, but I slop way too much paint on it over and over again, and soon the wall is a runny, streaky mess.

I'm chasing trails of blue paint with my roller and attempting some damage control when I feel him close behind me. I go completely still and wait until he's inches away from my back.

'Can I show you?'

His voice twines in my ear, and his breath moves a piece of my hair escaped from my ponytail, causing a shiver to run up and down my spine.

I nod and his arm wraps around me, his hand

closes over mine on the roller handle, and his chest presses to my back. My heart does star jumps.

'Like this. Easy, OK? You keep trying to press the paint into the wall. Relax and let the roller do the work.'

He leads me through the process one more time, and this time I can feel the exact amount of pressure he uses and how lightly he applies the paint.

I also feel the hard wall of his chest, the way his hand envelopes mine, the steady, strong thud of his heart at my back. He still has that clover smell that makes me think of spring and sex. Sex outside, sex under the stars, sex with someone strong and confident and honest as hell.

My hand shakes under his, and when he pulls away, I make a jerky lunge to the paint tray so I can inhale the chemical smell of the paint and push back these insane thoughts about this boy and sex so good it's making my knees knock just imagining it.

Winch 2

I need to get outta this damn room and away from this chick before I get both our asses in trouble.

But she asked me not to make a big deal about our assignment, and it's not like they wouldn't ask what the problem was. And then I'd have to tell them . . . what? That the girl they assigned me to work with is giving me a hard-on, and I want to take her on a date then get her naked in my backseat? Even though I know damn well what a bad idea that would be.

So I kick the crackly old-as-dirt radio up a notch and paint like there's a gun to my temple and keeping the roller moving is the only way to still the trigger. The effort of staying away from her pumps so much adrenaline through me, I don't give a shit if she makes a total slop mess of her walls. I can repaint them in a few minutes, no problem, with all this excess energy.

And she is making a mess. I'm not annoyed.

I'm turned on. I'm desperate to be with her, and just

as desperate to get away. So I snap a little, even though I don't mean to.

'You're doing the same thing as before, and now you're dripping paint all over the place. Hey, why don't you try edging? I'll do the rolling, OK?'

I point over to the paint bucket and smaller brushes, and she curls her lip at them in a frustrated grimace, showing the sharp white points of her teeth.

'I don't think I'll be any better at edging.' She puts the roller down and heads to pick up the can.

I try to ignore how perfect the curve of her ass is as she bends to pick up the can and brush. I want her. Bad. The realization hits me like a fresh wave of paint fumes, making my head blur and spin.

But I have no business wanting this girl, so I say what I need to say to give her a hard shove in the opposite direction from me before I make a huge mess when I know better.

'Well, there's no way you could possibly be worse.' I roll my eyes at her shitty job, even though I know she's working as hard as she can. I feel like an asshole, but I push through. 'No doubt about that.'

The sharp clatter of the brush falling to the floor whips me around. Her lips are all trembly, maybe like she's about to cry. I feel like a jackoff for being un- necessarily cold to her, but it's what I have to do. If I don't hold this girl at arm's length, I'll pull her so she's tight against my body, start kissing that sweet mouth, and won't be able to stop until we're both naked and panting.

No girl's made me think anything so out of control in a long time, and I roll faster to get this damn job done and get my ass as far away from the sugary smell of her as I possibly can.

I just hope she doesn't cry. I'm not good with crying girls.

But there are no tears.

'Fuck you.'

The words are clear out of her mouth, and I realize now that the wobble on her lips is all about fury.

'Excuse me?'

Even if I have been a little bit of a dick, I'm not big on being told to fuck off by anyone, especially not girls who are born and bred thinking they're better than I am.

'Maybe you got paint in your ears?' she suggests, her voice as sugar-sharp as her smell, like candy just about to burn. 'I told you to fuck off.'

She pops one paint-flecked hand on her hip and gives me a pursed-lip, raised-eyebrow pissy face that pings my irritation.

I let out a short, hard laugh, but I know damn well my smile isn't hiding the aggravation pumping through me.

'Look, I'm not one of your prep-school tutors, all right? My job isn't to tell you how perfect every damn thing you do is. You suck at painting. But I get it. I'm sure it's hard to do physical labor when you're worried about keeping your nails and hair perfect. But if this room doesn't meet spec, we do it again. Meaning *I* do it again, since you obviously can't. So get back to work, and try not to do such a shitty job this time.'

Harsh, I know, but this girl isn't from my world, and it will all be easier if I let her see what a dick I can be and how completely wrong we are for each other, no questions. Next session, she'll be the one who requests we don't work together, I'll get the work done twice as fast, and I can go back to life as usual, without ridiculous thoughts of this sexy, out-of-my-league girl clogging up my brain.

That perfect mouth is hanging open, her cool blue eyes are totally round, and her breathing is so hard, I can see her chest rise and fall. The urge to yank her over to me is strong as hell, but I put a lid on it and get back to business, determined to do my job and ignore her as much as I can for the next few hours.

My ears register the whip and spatter a split second before my skin feels it. I reach one hand to the back of my neck, and my fingers are coated in light blue paint that's leaking in a slow line down my back and pooling at the waistband of my boxers. Paintbrush fisted in her hand, eyes hurling me a dare I can't resist, this girl is upping the stakes quick.

'What the hell do you think you're doing?' My voice is soft and smooth, and I hope she doesn't take that to mean I'm above getting her wise ass back for throwing paint at me.

'Putting you in your place. Were you raised in a barn? Where I come from, men don't talk to women the way you just talked to me.' She points at me with the paintbrush. 'You know what's really hysterical? That day in court, it was your good manners that made me like you.'

I can instantly tell she regrets saying that by the way she bites her bottom lip and darts her eyes to the side.

'I'm not gonna apologize for telling you the truth, especially when it affects how long I'll be in this hell hole. By the way, I have very good manners. But I only use them when I need them.'

I pick up the roller and nonchalantly walk her way. She backs up one step, two. 'And I only need them around people who earn them, not snotty spoiled brats who expect everyone to worship at their feet.'

She holds her small hands up and her scowl deepens.

'Don't. You. Dare.'

Her eyes flip to the roller in my hand, and she turns

to run the few feet she can away from me. I take aim and smack the roller right against the sexy curve of her ass, leaving the entire seat coated in baby-blue paint.

She whirls on one heel, eyes ethanol-flame blue, and I expect more paint flicked my way, but she smiles at me instead.

'Thank you, Winchester. You're right. I do need to cut in closer to the ceiling.'

I nod and back up, finally sensing the presence of someone else in the doorway. I'm pissed off I was so preoccupied with her, I didn't keep my guard up.

'What's going on in here?' The female officer who checked us in narrows her eyes at me. 'Everything OK?'

She directs the question right at Evan, not caring if I catch her implication.

I can guess exactly how much those designer jeans I just ruined cost, and I'm getting ready to have my ass thrown under a speeding bus all because I let myself act like an idiot. Not that I don't deserve it. Just because I have a thing for her doesn't mean I have to provoke her like I did. But that's the thing: this girl makes me lose control, and losing control isn't an option.

'Everything is fine.' Her smile is bright and toothy, the kind of smile that commercial producers would kill for. That smile could sell huge amounts of shampoo or toothpaste or cans of lentil soup; it's that hot.

When the officer looks directly at the paint on her ass, Evan giggles. 'I sat in paint. I'm such a klutz. Luckily Winchester has been helping me out, so I'm not making a total mess of things.'

There's a long couple of seconds when I'm sure the officer is going to call our bluff, and I'll have Kevon on my case for causing shit on my first day on site, but it doesn't happen.

'I'll be back to check on you two.' The officer gives a jerky nod, then leaves us alone.

I pick up the roller and, for a few minutes, there's just the sound of her brush sliding across the wall and my roller clattering as I make giant Ws.

She didn't have to cover for me.

The music blares, and some lame summer dance song comes on. I glance over my shoulder, and she's swaying her hips from side to side, bopping her head to the tune, just chilling when she could have been pouting in a royal little temper tantrum.

'Evan?'

She stops rocking her hips and turns slowly, her face gorgeous, but clear of any emotion at all. I miss the glow she got when she was about to lose it.

'I, uh, want to apologize. I lost my temper. I shouldn't have talked to you like that. I deserved to get hit with paint. And I deserved to have you throw me to the wolves. I have no idea why you didn't, but thank you. I know you don't want more trouble. And I should be thinking the same way.' The words choke and sputter out.

The corner of her mouth lifts in the tiniest trace of a smile. 'I've got a pretty shitty temper myself. Don't worry about it. We gotta get through this, and I know you just want this room painted and it looks like crap, but I'm doing my best.'

She shrugs and one sleeve of her T-shirt slides down. Her shoulder is tanned. Her bra strap is red. And I stop my brain from going too wild imagining what she'd look like if I peeled that shirt off, unhooked the bra and let it slide down her arms.

'Winchester?'

The sound of my name pops me out of my dirty daydream.

'Winch,' I say and stick my hand out. 'We've never really introduced ourselves, right? Everyone calls me Winch.'

She nods and smiles, then grabs my hand and gives me a handshake that would make any hardcore CEO proud.

'Evan. Nice to meet you.'

I don't want to let go of her hand. It feels tiny in mine, and the skin is ridiculously soft. I'm dying to know what those hands would feel like in places I better stop thinking about if I'm going to last a few more hours with her.

And suddenly I realize how stupid I've been. Because I didn't keep my damn cool, I went from kind of hitting on her to being a total tool. And now we're at some kind of shaky friend level when the only thing I needed to do was keep things distant.

So much for that plan.

'Winchester.' I love the sound of my name from her mouth. 'I've never met anyone with Winchester as a first name.'

She perches her fine painted ass on the ladder and slides the paint brush along the edge of the ceiling with careful, even strokes.

'My grandparents made their money in illegal arms dealing.' I finish the wall I've been working on and move to the next one.

I expect the mandatory girlie scoff or for her to ask if I'm serious, but instead she says, 'My family made most of their startup money during Prohibition.'

My lips tug up at the corners in reaction to what I know other people probably don't notice about her.

'Evan Williams Black Label is my mother's favorite bourbon,' I tell her and watch the color slide over her cheekbones and up to the roots of her dark hair.

'Yeah. That.' She laughs, a cool, loose sound. 'I tell

people Evan is a family name, and it is. But it didn't come from my grandma. It actually came from what my dad poured for everyone in the waiting room when I was born.'

Swapping family stories is a fucking slippery slope, and I should know better. But the words slide out before I can remind myself of all the reasons why I should hold them back.

'It's a good bourbon. My mom always says it's under-appreciated, and she knows her whiskey.'

Her smile is warm and smooth like a shot knocked back on a hot night, and it loosens my tongue the same way.

I tell her a little piece of my history I've never shared with anyone outside my family before. 'My mother said she stared at my father's Winchester revolver the entire time she was in labor, and thought about getting it off the wall and shooting him with it a few times. I was a ten-pound baby.'

Her laugh this time is brighter and a little too loud.

'Ten pounds! Your poor mother. No wonder she wanted to shoot your dad. How did they get a gun into the hospital?'

She moves a dark shiny strand of hair away from her face with the back of her wrist.

'I was born at home. All of us were. My family is kind of old school that way, and they all hate hospitals.'

I'm done painting this wall, but I have a really nice view of her back and the curve of her neck. I have a weakness for girls' necks. Evan's is perfect, long and graceful, and I have this insane urge to bury my nose at the crook and breathe in deep. I wonder if she'd moan if I kissed her there.

'All of you? How many Youngbloods are there?'

She looks over her shoulder and gives me a smile that's less toothy than the one she tricked the officer with and way wider and sweeter than the one she threw me a little while ago. It knocks the wind back down my throat.

I recover in time to strangle out an answer.

'The world is crawling with Youngbloods, and all the worst ones are related to me. But as far as siblings go, I'm one of five.'

'Five.' She tilts her head to one side. 'Are you the oldest?'

I shake my head.

This is detailed. This is already more than I usually tell anyone outside our circle. But this community service is only a few weeks long at the most. Evan and I don't cruise in the same circle. The only place we'll ever connect is here, so why not? Why not let her get a peek behind the infamous Youngblood family curtain? I'm so used to protecting this information at all times, it feels traitorous to share. It's also a little like a weight's being lifted off my back, like I'm not burdened with every single asinine family secret they demand I keep.

It feels good.

'I'm second oldest. Remington, my brother, is a year older – he's twenty-two. Benelli, my little sister, is two years younger than me, and the twins are Colt and Ithaca. They're five years younger.' I roll extra paint on the wall that's already completely coated. 'You?'

'I came after three miscarriages, one stillborn, and probably a good half a million in fertility treatments. Once they had me, they called it quits.' She wipes her hands on her jeans absent-mindedly, leaving light blue finger smears at her hips. 'Um, it looks like we're almost done in here. Wanna look busy when the officers come around and stretch this out?'

She takes a little pot of lip stuff out, spreading it on her sexy lips with the tip of her finger, using slow strokes that make my mouth dry up.

Did I want to spend all day in a sweltering little government building painted dirty sky-blue, smelling paint fumes so strong they were making my head spin?

If Evan Lennox was with me, then the answer was a clear and definite 'Hell yeah.'

Evan 3

I had a hard time falling asleep the next Friday night.

That was never a problem before I moved in with my grandparents because I was usually so blitzed after beginning my Friday drinking binge during last period study hall that by the time night came, if I was even aware that it was night, I was so out of my mind sleep wasn't a conscious thing. I knew I'd fall onto some couch or bed or pillow on the floor and black out until I woke up to a huge hangover. This I invariably cured with a long day at the beach wearing dark sunglasses, nursing Bloody Marys while I got a nice toasty tan, and letting the crash of the waves dull my pounding headache.

But I'd cleaned up my act after the arrest, and now my Friday nights are all about laundry, homework, painting my toenails, tidying my room, cleaning underneath my laptop keyboard with Q-tips . . . if I didn't deserve every boring second, plus a million more, I'd feel pretty damn sorry for myself.

But there is one bright spot in my week.

The irony of my situation doesn't escape me. The girl who used to be the life and soul of the wildest parties, now excited to go to community service?

But, of course, it's not nearly as wholesome and simple as it sounds.

I get out of the shower early Saturday morning and dress in a hurry. I pull out the pair of jeans with the blue backside, turn them in my hands, and contemplate the person I've been looking forward to seeing all week long.

The crackling paint is a dirty sky-blue, so far from the deep blue of Winch's eyes, it seems impossible they're in the same color realm. No amount of scrubbing would get that paint out, and Gramma is completely perplexed about why I don't just toss them.

'Sweetie, they are useless. I wouldn't even want you to work in the garden in them.' She shakes her head and clucks her tongue at the stain Winchester Youngblood delivered with his paint roller, while I run a hand over that crackly dried blue paint and resist the urge to smile like a fool.

I pop a kiss on her cheek to hide my grin.

'Gramma, when do I ever work in the garden? I'm doing this community service thing for weeks, though. It's probably not a bad idea to have a pair of work pants for next time.'

Even work demands style, as far as my gramma is concerned.

'Bad enough they have you doing all that work when we pay taxes to feed and support the incarcerated while they laze around like they're living in the lap of luxury. They should be giving this heavy labor to the criminals and letting you kids volunteer with the arts or at schools or religious institutions. It's ridiculous. And if you have to go, you can at least look clean and neat.'

Her silver bob sways backward and forward with her nod of conviction.

I put on a clean pair to mollify her, kiss her and Granddaddy, and fly to my car, ready for the day, eager as a kid at the beach ignoring the burn of the hot sand on her feet in her haste to get to the waves.

Eager for a day of muscle-tiring, bone-deep ache-inducing labor in some old dump.

With Winch.

Brenna texts me.

Brenna: Ready for your date with criminally hot McHottie?!?! Get it? It's a pun! Get it?
Me: You're such a dork. And don't be a halfwit.
Brenna: Are you rushing to see him NOW? Sweaty palms? Butterflies in your stomach?

Me: Can't text. About to drive.

Brenna: LOL!! I KNEW IT!!

I pull in at the dilapidated building that is looking much less dilapidated with every hour of work we chisel into it, and I feel puffy-chested with pride. I'd accomplished things before: written papers, completed projects, aced exams, but I'd never worked with my hands, turning something ugly into something gorgeous using my own sweat and talent. Well, using a ton of criminals' sweat and my very-limited-but-slowly-increasing talent.

When I walk in, the officer in charge, Officer Rannick, points me in the direction of one of the rooms we'd painted last week.

'They finished the floors and the precinct had some file cabinets sent over. Unfortunately, they tipped some of the drawers out. You just need to fish though the files and put them back in alphabetical order.'

'OK.' So today will be an easy day compared to the grueling grind of last week. I go through the door and my eyes nearly evacuate their sockets. 'Oh shi . . . z,' I amend as Officer Rannick frowns.

'Go ahead. You can handle it.'

She opens the door wider, and I stumble into a roaring, heaping, sliding typhoon of papers that has absolutely no rhyme or reason that I can decipher. My eyes race around the cluttered, paper-filled room, and I feel like I've been buried in sand up to my neck, weighed down by the millions of individual grains.

But if I'm going to be balls-to-the-wall honest with myself, this deluge of paper spiraling in every direction isn't what makes my heart drop.

Winchester isn't here.

I edge a pile of documents aside with my toe and consider that he might just be late. I put my back to a huge filing cabinet and push off with my feet to move it and rationalize that maybe last week was just a fluke. There is no reason to expect we'd be assigned together every single time.

The cabinet slides against the wall and gives me a tiny square of space to work in, and I pick up a few manila folders and put them back down, shuffle some files into a heap, and stare at the overwhelming paper whirlpool threatening to suck me down. I put my hand to my mouth, praying I won't cry and smear my lovingly applied eye make-up down my face.

A light knock at the window makes me jump and skid on the files and folders, and I can't help the upswing in my heart when I see his face, all soft blue eyes and wry smile.

I throw up the sash and say, 'Hey, slacker. You having a picnic out there?'

'I'm on weeding duty.' He leans in and looks around, making an eyeball pit stop on me from the top of my hair to my designer-booted toes. 'I thought I had it bad today. They stuck you with some crazy pile of shit.'

'Agreed. At least I'm not in the heat.'

Not that the stuffy little room with its tiny, rusty fan is much better than being outside under the blistering sun. And I'm not saying I wouldn't be happy to sweat under said blistering sun if I had Winchester Youngblood to keep me company.

After our paint fight last week, the hours we spent together slipped by too fast, and by the end, I felt like a little kid regretting the dip of the sunset at the reluctant end of a perfect day.

It was clear he was attracted to me, sneaky though he thought he was with all those long looks he threw my way when he assumed I wasn't looking, like he was a big bad wolf and I was some fairy-tale maiden flouncing down his path. But I could also feel that he was pulling back, trying to stomp that out. And that's why I'd let my temper cool when he acted like such a lowlife douchebag. Once I thought about it, I realized it was all an act and wondered why.

And the only answer that makes sense is that he felt a spark between us, and it scares him.

But nothing scares me. Not since I fucked every

single thing in my life up anyway. What do I have to be scared about?

Well, maybe he scares me a little. I have a shitty track-record with guys, and there is this gnawing fear that this is just another disaster waiting to happen, which is why I lied to Brenna. Or tried to lie to Brenna. But that little prickle of fear isn't enough to keep me from hurling myself towards this potential craziness with complete abandon.

It feels scarily good to free-fall when I'm with Winch. I've been treading carefully for months now, and it goes against my natural grain.

'I don't mind working out here.' He jerks a thumb at the ground, choked with weeds, and pulls me back to reality. 'I'll hammer this out in no time. My grand-father used to make us weed as punishment when we were kids. I'm pretty damn quick.' He glances around at the hills and valleys and oceans of paper and files. 'You're swamped. Wanna hand when I'm done?'

'Are you implying that you need to do my work and yours?'

I lean out the window, and our faces are so close I can see the starbursts of navy around his pupils.

He twines a piece of my hair around his finger. He tries to look nonchalant, but the tight draw of his lips hints at all the tension he's working to hide. His voice drops and he angles his face so close to mine, I can smell the sweet mint on his breath.

'I'm implying that if I have to kill myself to get through this damn weeding so I can come inside and spend the day with you, it would be cool if you'd let me.'

And there it is. The pull that always dances my way and yanks me tight after any push. Last week started out all about distance, but eventually slid us closer, and this week seems to be about nothing but closing until there's no space left between us at all.

I take the reins and hold tight so my voice doesn't flutter too much.

'I will be cool and let you, as long as you don't get in my way.'

He takes a baseball cap out of his back pocket and pulls it low over his eyes, and I tip the brim up with my finger and watch the smile commandeer the bottom half of his face.

'Work fast,' I whisper.

'Will do. And I'm not making any promises about staying out of your way. I never had any fun at these community service things before you came around. You can't ask me to avoid the only person I actually like hanging out with.'

He picks up a rake that someone left tossed on the ground and leans against it, the pull of his tanned muscles making my mouth water.

But it's his words that make my heart boomerang. It's all casual right this minute, but maybe it's the first taste of something more, something exciting.

'You know, you don't have to go breaking the law if you want to spend time with me. Most guys just ask me on a date. Not that I always accept.'

I prop my elbow on the sill and hold my chin in my hand, batting my lashes suggestively.

His spine snaps up and the dark blue of his irises deepens closer to black. 'I'd better get to work or I'll be out here all day.'

I watch him rush toward the far end of the plot he needs to weed, as I smother the indignation pressing against my lips.

I pick up a few files, determined that I will tackle one paper at a time, no matter how long, hard, and grueling it is. While I sort Abbots from Babcocks, I also work very hard to keep my mind from wondering why Winchester didn't take me up on my offer.

I tend to be the kind of girl who lets whatever's on my mind explode out and ignite everything around me, which accounts for some of my recent trouble. I just can't let things lie. I could soothe my ego and tell myself that he was just being shy, but a guy as good-looking and charming as Winchester Youngblood doesn't have a shy cell in his body.

I glance out of the window. His shirt is already

getting soaked with sweat and clings tight to his shoulders, showing off the lean curl of his back as he heaves weeds out of the dirt with rapid, almost frantic yanks.

Because it's hot outside and he wants to finish quickly.

Or because he wants to finish quickly and come in and help me.

Then why the hell not ask me on a date? I sort through a whole slew of Babcocks with half an eye before I find some Conways and make a neat stack, A, B, C. Maybe I misread the signals, as usual.

Suddenly I wonder if the most obvious reason is getting tossed to the side like mental junk mail: maybe he has a girlfriend.

That would be a game stopper because I would never even run my finger over home-wrecker territory. My best friend, or the-bitch-I-thought-was-my-best-friend-before-I-met-Brenna-and-realized-what-that-term-actually-means, screwed my ex-boyfriend just before he and I broke up.

I slam the few files I've sorted into a drawer with a crash that shakes the entire metal structure and wonder if I still hate her more than I realize. I caught her and him together, and seeing the two of them having sex made it feel like she drugged me, cut my heart out with a scalpel, took a bite, and sewed it back in. Rabin was such a bastard, and I was almost waiting for him to crush me. But Mackenzie? I'd opened up to her more than most people in my life.

Letting her get close had been one of my biggest mistakes, but I refuse to let the way she hurt me shape how much I open up to other people. Brenna helped me get over what Mackenzie had done and wound up being one of the best people to ever enter my world.

I believe in jumping over past hurts and letting love in. I try to believe, anyway, and am trying, even as images of Mackenzie and Rabin flash through my head and cause me to slam another drawer closed.

'What did that filing cabinet ever do to you?'

Winch's voice has me spinning around, and I make a mental note to keep the corners of my mouth tugged slightly down. I have things to figure out before I start snapping tons of smiles his way. The instant after I think that, I feel the upward inch of a grin I have to force back down.

'That cabinet is taking the blame for all these stupid files. Are you coming to help with this mess?'

He shrugs and gives a half-smile. 'Officer said I can do whatever I like. I haven't decided.'

I may love his company, but I'm sure as hell not letting him know that.

'You know, you kind of stink. It might be hard for

me to work with you so close.' Despite my resolve not to smile at him, one creeps on my face.

'Rolo said he needs help outside.' He leans against the doorframe and crosses his arms over his chest, which makes his biceps bulge. 'Say the word, and I'll leave.'

'Winchester Youngblood, you do whatever your little heart desires. It doesn't matter to me one way or the other.'

To grand-slam my point home, I flip through a stack of papers and stare at them intently, moving my lips like I'm talking to myself about important filing issues and have no interest in what Winch decides to do.

Meanwhile, my ears are pricked for his response, and I'm hoping he's going to pull closer instead of pushing away.

'All right. If you don't complain about my man-stink, I won't complain about having to do paperwork.'

He heaves off the door and starts to move closer to me. When I catch him taking a discreet sniff under his arms, my smile stretches so wide, it hurts my cheeks.

I slide the files into a cabinet drawer, close it with one hip, and crook my finger his way.

'What?' he asks, but his voice is low and husky.

I crook my finger again and he maneuvers around the papers until we're a foot or two apart.

I lean forward until there isn't more than five inches between us.

'Hot, sweaty man is one of my all-time favorite smells.' I watch his pupils dilate and feel a thrill pirouette down my spine. 'Now come help me find the rest of the Ds so we can finish this filing, and I might just take you to my favorite pizza place when we're done.'

Winch 3

I should have gone out and chopped wood or whatever the fuck it was Rolo needed help with, because
being this close to Evan isn't going to work.

And, to top it all off, she asked me out.

I avoided answering because I know what I want to
answer isn't what I should, and now we're both working like two busy-ass ants in a hill, trying not to crash
into all the awkwardness hanging in the space
between us.

'Did you find the other Fischers?' she asks and leans
over to sort through some papers on the floor.

She leans from her waist, her long, sweet body
folded in half, and I notice her feet are always pointed
toe out, like maybe she's a dancer. She definitely has
the body for it.

'No. Just a whole hell of a lot of Harris files. That
family needs to send one of their kids to law school,
'cos they're gonna have legal bills like you wouldn't
believe.'

'They probably shouldn't let hardened convicts like us flip through all this private information.' She fans herself with one of the folders and bats her lashes my way.

'The judicial system in the low country leaves a lot to be desired. I'd bitch about it, but it's probably why a career criminal like me is sorting files with a first-time offender like you when I should probably be making license plates and lifting weights at state.' I smile at her. 'Yeah, definitely no complaining on my end.'

My breath slams through my lungs when her laugh rings out, loud and happy, filling this stuffy, dirty room with something so good I never want to leave it.

I push that thought out of my head. This wasn't supposed to have gone as far as it did. I should never have knocked on the glass when I saw her this morning, all my fears that she'd been reassigned put to rest. I should have walked right past her when she was sitting there, slumped on the floor, that day at court. She probably would have bailed if it wasn't for me interfering.

She would have missed her court date, and by the time she got reassigned, my community service would have been almost over, and I wouldn't be stuck thinking of a way to dodge this date I want to go on with her so badly, but can't.

I just can't, and it's too complicated to explain why to her, even though I want her to know all the reasons why more than I've ever wanted anything before. I want to tell her . . . everything.

But that's not a possibility.

'Winch?'

She's got her head bent over some papers she's sorting between her fingers, so I almost don't hear her say my name.

Which would be a shame, because I love the way my name sounds, coming out of her mouth.

'Yeah?'

I hand her over some files and her eyes meet mine, all cool and sweet like a snow-cone in July.

She grabs the files and her fingers run over the skin on my hand.

'About later? The pizza thing? It's cool if you don't want to go. Or can't go. If you have a reason . . . you can tell me if there's a reason that it would be a bad idea.'

She looks down at those folders like they're gonna tell her the secrets of the world, and I'm so shocked by this direct hit, I have no clue how to juggle it.

'There is a reason—' I start to explain, and her look of pure horror and embarrassment cuts me off.

'I'm sorry. I mean, if it seemed like I was coming on to you . . . I sort of thought you might . . . that there might be someone. It makes sense! And I never asked. And it's not like you led me on. Actually it explains a lot.'

I've never seen her just tripping over her words like this. Her cheeks are bright pink, and she's holding her eyebrows up high, like she's trying to keep all her crazy emotions in check.

When she looks directly at me her eyes are so fiercely honest, I feel like I took a boot to my ribs. 'I had that happen . . . I was cheated on. And I would never, ever do that to someone else. I mean, I'd never put someone in that position.'

She was cheated on? What fucking loser would cheat on a girl like her? And why is she bringing up . . .

'What?' I ask, but my confusion clears up as soon as the word is out of my mouth.

Cheating? She must think I have a steady girl. This is the perfect time to go with it. It would explain so much without me coming off looking like an asshole. It's my chance to walk away, no strings, and know that she doesn't hate me.

I'm ready to agree with her entire misunderstanding.

But I open my mouth and say, 'Evan, I don't have a girlfriend.'

Relief floods her eyes and she lets all her breath out at once. 'Oh good. That's so good. I was feeling like such an ass since I asked you.' But the relief blots out as soon as she realizes there's still some reason I didn't say yes. 'And you still don't have to go, of course. It was just a friendly invitation, OK? No pressure. But if you have something else, some big reason, it's OK.'

She slams the drawer shut with a little too much force again, and I pull close to her like she's an industrial magnet and I'm a heap of scrap metal.

I should let it lie, should let this whole thing fizzle out before it blows the hell up in my face. I look at her so I can tell her, honestly, without being a pussy, that I can't, and I fully intend to stand firm and just spit it out.

But all my stupid intentions crumble under my feet.

The look in her eyes is the perfect cocktail of self-assured sexiness and vulnerable worry, and it brings out my swagger.

'I'm not letting you buy me dinner. We'll go out, but it's on me.'

Her long hair sways back and forth when she shakes her head.

'I asked you. My terms or nothing.'

She bites her bottom lip a little to stop the smile.

Even though every logical brain cell in my skull screams at me for doing it, I take a giant step over the line of good fucking sense, and land my ass flat in no man's land with my next brilliant statement.

'I've never let a girl pay for a date before, and I'm not starting with you.'

She files a few folders, and I keep my hands busy making piles of paperwork without really seeing what I'm doing, because I'm waiting on her answer.

'No one said this was a date, Winch. Let me pay, and we don't have to go there.'

Her voice is smooth and, to anyone who isn't paying close attention, it would sound like she's completely in control. But I've spent hours watching this girl and trying to figure out what exactly makes her tick. I know she's playing cool.

I should lose her. Drop this. Let it go.

I keep giving myself this same damn speech, then I let myself drift a little bit further. This is just trouble waiting to happen, but it's been a long time since I got into any trouble of my own. I've been so busy picking up the pieces for other people, and being around Evan, I've started realizing for the first time in a long time how much I want something for me.

Something that's all mine.

It occurs to me that she can be mine, at least for a little while. No one else has to know. It's stupid. It's risky. But I want this to work, even if I know it can't, really.

I reach over and pull the folder out of her hand, tug her to me so we're eye to eye. I watch her throat move when she swallows and the way her lips tremble, and I have to stop myself from kissing her here and now.

'I don't do things halfway. Come out with me on a date. I pay, and we go wherever you want.'

Her lips part. She's got a tiny overbite, and it makes her lips puff out, like an invitation. 'Are you sure?'

I rub my thumb over her knuckles just to see if her breath will catch, and my jaw clenches when it does. The things I'm going to do with this girl . . .

'Never been more sure in my life.'

I check the gold watch my dad gave me, passed from his grandfather, a reminder of who I am and exactly what I'm supposed to be doing.

Taking Evan out is not on that long, complicated list of who I'm expected to be, but, right now, I don't give a damn. 'We've got twenty minutes before this shift is over. I'll be back to get you then, OK?'

I pull my hand out of her grasp and walk backward to the door just because I love the way she looks, and I don't want to stop looking yet. Her eyebrows furrow low over her eyes.

'Where are you going?'

'Some mean-ass girl told me I stink. I'm going to wash up.'

I grin at the out-of-focus look on her face and wonder if her brain went *there*, to hot, soapy showers and slippery naked bodies. Because that's exactly where mine went.

Luckily all I get is a cold, sputtering rinse at the hose with some anti-bacterial soap I found in the bathroom. I need something chilly and uncomfortable to jar me out of my current insanity.

'Hey, man. How'd you get to spend your day tailing that sweet honey in the office?' Rolo's come to rinse off too, and I'm torn between feeling sorry for the overworked ape and wanting to slam my fist into his face.

'Luck, I guess.'

I shrug as the frigid water runs down my shoulders and over my arms. I bend at the waist so I can rinse my head and armpits before I hand the hose to Rolo.

'She's hot as hell. Put a good word in for me, OK?'

His grin is easy, and I have to tell myself to relax the fist I'm making.

'She's my girl.'

The words sit sure and steady in the air between us, and the extent of how true they are shocks through me like a bolt of electricity from a Taser.

Rolo holds his hands up, surrender-style.

'All right, cool. Sorry, man. I thought you were still with Lala. I didn't know.'

Lala. I haven't been with her for a few weeks, but I know she'll be pissy if she hears I'm with someone else. I don't need the drama. And I don't need anyone in my family finding anything out yet.

Or ever.

'It's cool, man. Look, could you just not say anything? Lala's still a little sore over our whole break-up, and I don't want to mess things up with Evan.'

I know Rolo doesn't want to cross any lines with me. He was there when I fought all three Rahn brothers after they attacked Remington. It was a bloodbath, and hardly any of that blood was mine.

'No worries, no worries, man. Lala's always had a nasty temper. She won't hear shit about it from me.' His eyes shift down to the hose in his hand, still dribbling icy water.

'I appreciate it.' I give him a nod and set out to my car so I can put on some deodorant and throw on a clean shirt. I stuff my sweaty shirt into the trunk, then pick up the garbage on the floor of my car and toss it back there too, chewing my brother out under my breath when I notice that he left a half-empty bottle of Jack Daniels on my backseat.

Sometimes, I swear to God, it feels like Remy wants me to get arrested.

The car looks good, I smell good, it's all good, and then Evan walks down the steps towards me, and good gets so much better.

'Hey, slacker, they need you in there so they can

sign you out!' she calls, shading her eyes with her hand.

I can tell she's dolled up for me a little, and it feels damn amazing. Her dark hair swings down her back instead of in its high ponytail, long and straight almost to her waist, where it goes a little curly. Her lips are colored a deep shade of pink, but she doesn't need the lipstick, or any make-up really. I've never seen a girl who looks so beautiful when she's dressed plain, hardly done up. The sun is behind her, and I take in every curve, every long, sweet line of her, and the excitement pumps through me so strong, it makes my mouth go dry.

I want this. I want her. And it's been a while since I wanted anything this much.

'You wanna wait in my car?' I point to the open door.

'What about mine?' she asks, walking closer every minute, her long hair picking up and blowing a little in the breeze.

I have to ball my fists to stop from reaching out and yanking her closer, crushing her to me.

'We'll come back and get yours later.'

I wonder what will happen in all those hours between when we leave and when we head back to get her car. The possibilities make the blood rush fast through my body.

'What if I snoop through your stuff?' She tosses her hair behind her shoulder and her eyes tease me.

'Snoop away. I got nothing to hide.' I hold my arms out wide and know my smile is all cocky confidence, even if my words are the world's biggest lie.

I hate selling her on a scam. I hate starting things this way. But I'm already taking a dumb risk just going on this date with her. I have to keep myself protected.

I jog in and get my papers signed, and when I come back out, she's leaned back all comfortable in the passenger seat, and I'm ready to be anywhere, alone with this girl who's daring me to put my hand to the fire and feel the heat for the first time in I can't remember how long.

Evan 4

It's been weeks since a Saturday night consisted of anything other than sitting on my bed and contemplating the complete shit my life has become.

This Saturday night, I'm sitting in Winch's low, gunmetal Mustang, the window rolled down, my eyes squeezed tight, my lungs drawing in the smoky rich smell of backyard fires lit up in time for the sunset and the salty tang of the ocean just far enough away to hold a sense of adventure.

I don't ask where he's driving or what we're doing, because the sweet freedom is made even more delicious when it's twined with the unknown.

Winch holds the steering wheel with one hand and props the other arm on the open window, his shoulders squared and tense.

'I won't be upset if this isn't really a date.' I hang my head out the window and catch the reflection of my huge black sunglasses in the wing mirror.

'What makes you think it isn't?' He looks sideways

and his smile is just about to unfurl into a laugh. At me.

'I get this feeling like you don't really want to be out tonight. With me. Like you aren't sure if this is such a good idea. And it's OK. I'm mostly excited to get the hell out of my house. So if this . . . doesn't go anywhere, you don't need to worry.' I stretch both arms over my head and love the way my muscles loosen. 'I'm used to being with guys who aren't sure they want to be with me.'

The edge of laughter fades and his smile twists into a hard scowl. 'Sounds like you were with pricks.'

'Pricks, dicks, fuckheads, assholes, douchebags, and all your basic garden-variety loser. Darling, you name an unsavory character from around here and chances are I made out with him. Or worse.'

I tilt my sunglasses down and play-act a cheeky smile that makes the steel bands of a migraine start to take hold at my temples.

'You're happy about that?' His words are forged out of iron.

I give a shrug that's supposed to seem careless, but feels like I'm trying to shrug the coils of a venomous snake off my shoulders.

'I'm not happy or unhappy. I have truly terrible taste in guys and have gotten screwed over by more than I can count, but I like me a bad boy. Stop giving me that look! I'm young. This is the time in my life when I'm supposed to experiment and get burned.'

'Getting burned is one thing.' He rolls his neck like he's trying to release the tension in his muscles. 'Spending time with guys who treat you like shit is another. You dated Rabin Francis, didn't you?'

Rabin's name scratches against my ears like a wire brush on an old metal pan. I wished I had never mentioned my shithead ex-boyfriend to him.

'So?' I snap, pulling my sunglasses off my face in frustration.

'So, he was all over the news for assaulting some dancers.' There's a long pause, and the next words out are more growls than actual syllables. 'Did he do anything like that to you?'

His lips curl back and his eyeteeth glint, like a wild animal about to jump for the jugular.

'No! I mean, nothing that bad.' I dig my heels into the floorboards and breathe through my nose to slow the words that are struggling to burst out of my mouth. 'Nothing like that. And I can handle myself, OK? I broke up with him because he cheated . . . well, he also got arrested. And things had been escalating, so I had to get out sometime.'

Sweat dampens under my armpits and coats my palms. I feel gross. I feel trapped. How did it all flip so quickly? I wanted easy and sweet and fun, and this is terrible and so freaking wrong.

'That's a lot of excuses. How long did you put up with him for?' Winch's words snarl out of his mouth.

My gut twists.

'Look, like I said, it was my choice. OK? Mine. I decided to date him because he was hot and wild and I wanted to be around him. I decided not to date him because he was also an asshole and did some seriously stupid things. But a lot of guys I've been out with have been like that. So . . .' I shake my head. 'I guess I can just chalk it up to the fact that there's something about me that loves an asshole, and something about assholes that gets off on yanking my chain.'

I'm so close to tears, my eyes feel like they've been chemically burned. My throat is reduced to a tiny alley that just lets my panicked breath crawl and stumble in and out.

Winch's hand fists over the steering wheel. 'I don't know who's stupider. You or them.'

Magma-hot anger bursts through me and makes me see bright silver spots in front of my eyes. 'Well, that's fucking rude.'

'Rude my ass. It's honest and you need to hear it from someone. Don't brag about the fact that guys treated you like shit, Evan.' His voice is a midnight cannonball into a winter-frigid lake, and the chills that rush up and down my spine leave me shaky. I want him to just shut up but his voice continues to pummel me. 'You think it's cute? You think it makes you badass?'

'Pull over.' My voice bounces the words out so hard, they border on a stutter.

'No way.' He accelerates slightly and pulls down streets even I don't know, and I've roamed Savannah since I could toddle. 'You wanna see badass? Do you? 'Cause I can take you places where guys are fucking animals, Evan. Animals who don't give a damn. They scare the shit out of *me*, and I'm not a pussy by any stretch of the imagination. And if you end up with one of them because you think it's cute to date fuck-ups . . . I don't even want to think about what could happen. It isn't a game, Evan. It isn't a goddamn joke. It's serious, and you should take it seriously.'

I grip the handle of the door and tug, but Winch swings the car to the side of the road and brakes before I can thrust it open.

The night is filled with happy groups of friends walking to bars, the low hum of a million insects, the roar of the engine of some sporty car showing off as it buzzes past us down the street, and a promise of wild fun that only the late, lazy yawn of summer can hold.

I wish I could stop the shivers that rip through me and enjoy all of this beauty instead.

'I'm getting out,' I say in a slow, firm voice. 'This date is so over. I'm going to call a cab and get dropped off at home. I'll be perfectly safe, but you're a fucking jerk, and this date is over.'

I open the door and slide out, and for a second Winch does nothing at all, which makes relief and sadness tango cheek to cheek in my heart. Then his door opens and slams shut, hard enough to rock the car back and forth.

I walk fast, glad that I wasn't wearing the dangerously adorable sex-kitten heels I'd usually put on for a Saturday-night date downtown. Winch's boot-steps trail me.

'Go home, Winchester. This date is over!' I glance over my shoulder and shoo him with a flick of my fingers.

His mouth tightens. 'I'm not letting you walk through this part of town alone. *I'm* not an asshole.'

His implication burns like acid in the back of my throat. 'Actually, aren't *I* the best judge of that, asshole? And I've been walking around Savannah by myself since I was in middle school, so get lost.'

I'm so busy mouthing off I don't notice an uneven paving slab and half trip. I would have been perfectly capable of catching myself, but Winch is right next to me, his hand cupped under my elbow, and I'm pissed off that I need his assistance for even a second. I plan to shake his hand off and run far away from this miserable failure of a date. But once he has his hands on me, he grips too tight for me to get away.

'You're hurting me,' I hiss as he turns me to face him.

'I could never hurt you as bad as you hurt yourself,' he answers with chilly calm.

A tiny voice inside my head screams in his direction, *How could you know that?*

We stand on the sidewalk, and I attempt to yank away from him, but it's pointless, so I focus on his gorgeous, glowering face, cursing my bad luck in picking yet another control-freak douchebag. His hands slide down to my elbows and then open up, letting me go, and he shoves them firmly into the depths of his pockets.

'If I let you wait with me while I call a cab, will that be good enough for you?' I press my hands palm-to-palm in front of me, prayer style, and his glower deepens. 'What? What do you want then?'

He kicks at the ground. 'I want to rewind tonight. Start over. Make it right.'

'I've given a lot of guys second chances when I shouldn't have. But you know all about how *stupid* I am when it comes to relationships, right?'

My voice whips out and smacks the lazy night air. His eyes, so dark denim-blue, feel like they're soaking up the puddle of all my crazy emotions.

'Fair. But I only got pissed off because . . .' He trails off and shakes his head. 'If I try to explain, I'll fuck up more.' He pulls his hands out of his pockets and grabs mine by the tips of my fingers. 'Give me five minutes.'

He smiles, and it's beyond contagious; it's viral. My lips tug up despite my efforts to keep stone-faced.

He holds up one hand, fingers apart. 'That's all I'm asking for. Five minutes, clean slate, then you decide what you want from this night. Fair?'

I shake my head and sigh. 'I guess.' I slide out my cell phone. 'It's 7:38. You have until 7:43.' I set the alarm and purse my lips at him. 'You're on a timer, monkey boy. Dance for me.'

He holds his hand out to me, and it takes me two beats, maybe three, before our fingers are threaded together and we're clean-slated, wounds licked for five short minutes.

He starts walking, and I keep pace next to him. He clears his throat. 'First minute I saw you? I thought you were trouble.'

My laugh tumbles out before I can stop it. 'When I first saw you, I thought you were cocky.'

He nods. 'Not too far off the mark.' His fingers squeeze mine tighter. 'You were sitting on the floor, and I thought you had great hair, you know? Shampoo-commercial hair.'

'Shampoo commercial, huh?' I bump my shoulder against his. 'Do you write sonnets? Because you've got what it takes to make a girl's heart melt.'

'Sonnets, huh? I've never written one before. But I'd give it a try for you.'

If he was still teasing, I'd have winked or pretend-sighed, but the half-crook of his eyebrow lets me know he's serious, and the idea of him toiling over some long, complicated poem for me turns me on so hard and fast, I feel a telltale heat between my legs.

'But it was when you looked up that I knew I was in trouble. That face ... So damn gorgeous, and so furious. I thought I was gonna charm you and all that, make you see what a nice guy I am and get you to fall for me a little. And you looked angry as hell. I felt like ... I felt like I was finally looking at someone who could understand all the crazy shit I feel every day.'

I stop walking and stare at him, the way his eyes seem to pace back and forth, the lock and release of his jaw, and I want to kiss him so badly, it's embarrassing. Especially considering what a rude bastard he was a few minutes ago.

My problem is always falling too hard, too fast, without listening to the warning bells ringing clear as day.

I can't tell if they're ringing right now, but they've

rung so loud for so long, I might just have become deaf to their noise.

'I know I said I wouldn't try to explain why I got so pissed off, but you deserve an explanation, even if you only give me these five minutes, then never talk to me again, OK?' He cups one palm against my face and runs his fingertips along my cheek, the sharp focus in his eyes suddenly blurred. 'You're tough. And that is so unbelievably attractive. But there's this softness in you, too, and I know it's not a piece of yourself that you put out there for everyone. But I love when I get glimpses of it.'

He drops his voice. 'I was a dick ... I *am* a dick, because I liked you the minute I saw you. And when you told me about the other guys, how they fucked you over, I swear to God, I never felt more like kicking some ass, Evan. And part of me felt ...' He slides both hands to my shoulders and holds on tight. 'Part of me felt like I'd better be damn sure I'd never do anything like that to you. So I was pissed off at them and pissed off at me, and a little pissed off at you for not realizing that you're worth so much more than that. That you should never, ever let anyone treat you that way. So I'm sorry. I really am. Trust me, that little outburst wasn't in the plan.'

Goosebumps run up and down my arms and legs, I feel hot, and the blood rushes quick and deafening in my ears. 'So, there was a plan?'

He nods, his mouth twisted to the side. 'A good plan. Slick as hell, romantic, the whole nine.'

'You messed that up big time.' My voice wobbles. The cell phone in my pocket lets out a soft tone, marking the end of our five minutes.

Winch pulls me closer, and the entire world funnels into the space between the two of us. 'It was chicken-shit of me to want to be slick instead of honest. But I'm glad you gave me a second chance, Evan, even if being honest might have fucked it all up. You deserve honesty. And I wouldn't rush this under normal circumstances, but I respect that you might beat it now that I got my five minutes. I'd never forgive myself if I didn't at least try.'

His hands run up along my neck, and he tips my face to his. I can smell the sharp tang of his aftershave and the underlying salty sweat from his long day working in the sun. I snake my arms around his waist, and my knees wobble when he locks his hips to mine. He nuzzles my neck gently, and breathing deeply I press against him.

He moves his mouth up my neck, across my cheek, and finds my lips with a desperation that shocks me and knocks a moan out of my mouth and into his. The fingers of his one hand slide through my hair and his other hand dips down to the small of my back, pulling me tighter and locking me closer.

My mouth opens and his tongue slides in. His kiss isn't the mix of lazy and confident I was sure it would be. It's all crazy passion and possessiveness, like he knows that if he snares me with a kiss I can't forget, I won't be able to walk away now that our five minutes is up.

The alarm on my phone tones its reminder again, but all I can think about is the hungry pull of Winch's mouth, the strong cage of his arms, and the fact that even when the alarm I set is ringing a warning in my ear, I'm powerless against a bad boy and his hot kisses.

Winch 4

I don't know if I ever kissed any girl the way I'm kissing Evan, like a maniac, on the curb in the middle of Savannah. I can hear her damn cell-phone alarm beeping, and I'm scared as hell she's going to turn and walk out of my life. Not that I'd blame her. I acted like a douchebag, and I deserve whatever she wants to throw my way.

I usually hold back when I'm first with a girl. I'm usually thinking about the whole situation, analyzing it to check that it's good, but also making sure that I have half an eye on everything going on around me.

This is nothing like that. I think a bomb could have gone off next to us, and I wouldn't have noticed. She tastes better than I could have imagined she would, sweeter and darker, with the unexpected bite of her teeth on my lip that makes me yank her closer and kiss her deeper.

When I pull back, her eyes are wide, icy circles and her lips are fat and bruised from my mouth on them.

I want to say something suave, something to convince her not to leave.

I have nothing.

She opens her mouth and says, 'Do you want a hamburger instead of pizza?'

Maybe I should be worried she isn't more into the kiss, but I'm just happy she isn't going anywhere. I rush around to get her door, drive like crazy to the nearest Five Guys, and feel like I don't breathe until she's standing at the register with me, eyes squinted at the menus overhead, one hip slanted close to mine.

'I'd like a bacon cheeseburger, lettuce, tomato, grilled onion, grilled mushroom, mayonnaise, ketch-up, mustard . . . and relish. No! No relish. Please. And thank you.' She looks over at me like she's going to ask a question, then looks back at the poor guy behind the counter. 'And a bacon cheese dog. And Cajun fries, please.'

'I'll have what the lady's having, and we'll need two sodas,' I tell the guy, who is trying to call out the colossal order to the girl cooking the food. I pay and follow Evan to the fountain, where she's getting a root beer. 'There's gonna be more topping than burger on your burger.'

'Yours too.' She dunks a straw in the soda and swirls it around to get rid of the foam on top. 'You ordered the same as me.'

'I didn't want to cause mass confusion in the kitchen. I figured it would be easier if they just had to remember one crazy order twice.' I get a Coke and lead her to a table. 'Plus that, I'm not picky about food, and I have a feeling you know how to order a good meal.'

'One of my many talents.' She sits back in her chair and smoothes a piece of long, dark hair between her fingers. 'I'm not sure we should be on this date. I'm not sure this is such a good idea.'

'It's not.' I watch her eyes and lips shift down.

She balls up her straw wrapper and flicks it across the table at me. 'Why are we here then?'

'We met in court. I don't think we qualify as good decision-makers.'

I'm trying to keep things light, but she looks more and more restless, and I realize this date is still on probation, no matter how crazy-amazing that kiss was.

Before I can think of some way to show how our being together on this date makes sense, our number gets called and I go and bring our heaped piles of food back to Evan, who's wriggling with excitement like a little kid.

Lala, my ex, smoked and chewed a lot of gum, which tended to translate into her never being hungry. That was true for most of my exes, so I'm not really prepared for Evan's undisguised enjoyment of this monstrous burger. Or how much it turns me on.

She closes her eyes and chews slowly, moaning a little around her mouthful of food.

'Oh. Oh my sweet baby Jesus. Even if we never go on another date, I will always remember this burger fondly.'

The way she relishes every bite of this food makes it hard for me to take my eyes off her and pseudo distracts me from the fact that she maybe said we wouldn't be going on any more dates.

'Seriously? All it takes is one burger to make a horrible date with me worth it?'

'It's an amazing burger. But I have a food history with them anyway.' She points to the burger, gushing ketchup and mayo and all kinds of extras out of the bun, and shakes her head. 'My dad has a gambling addiction. Whether his horses won or lost, he always took me out for a burger. At first, it would turn my stomach if it wasn't a win. But, after enough losses, I figured out that I'd tear my stomach to shreds if I worried like that. So all I concentrated on was the burger. Now it's one of those foods I can eat no matter how awful I feel.'

She takes another huge bite and keeps her eyes on the napkins she has balled in her fist.

I imagine her as a kid, wolfing down burgers with stubborn determination. A weird kind of pride jumps to life in me at her being that courageous in what had to be a pretty shitty situation with her father. 'All right. I get that. In a screwed-up way, it makes a lot of sense.'

She leans her head to the side and narrows her eyes at me. 'Really? Because I think it's kind of strange.'

And, because I've fucked up so much on this date, I take a big step forward and loosen the disguise I wear for everyone else. Because she makes me want to strip away the stupid mask I hold up for everyone else and just be honest. Be myself.

For once.

'It's my thing to be cool,' I start. She gasps out a laugh, biting her lower lip to stop it in its tracks. 'All right, smartass, not in front of you, obviously. But generally, I keep my cool. I . . . handle things. When shit gets crazy, gets out of control, I step in and sort things out. So I get exactly what you're saying. Sometimes I gotta drink when I'm not thirsty or stay up when I want to sleep or laugh with a big group of idiots when I want to sit in a dark room and just think.'

Saying it is like ripping the curtains down and throwing the windows open in some, secret room I've been trapped in for years. My heart runs crazy laps around my chest.

'Are you a secret agent?' she demands, wiping a smear of ketchup from her mouth and leaning across the table towards me, her eyes laughing.

I think about how what I do was part of what made Lala and all the girls before her so hot for me. I wonder if it would turn Evan on if she understood more. Or if she'd run the other way, as fast as she could.

I crumple up my hamburger wrapper. 'Uh, no.'

She dumps the fries out on a spread of napkins in front of us. 'Superhero?'

'You met me in court.' I drag a few fries through the ketchup and watch her chew and wonder.

'A misunderstood superhero?' she asks between bites. When I don't say anything, she presses, 'Like Magneto?'

'You like the X-Men?' I try to tone down my total shock.

I'm aware that there are tons of girls who do like the X-Men, but none of my ex-girlfriends ever did. Evan is completely different than any other girl I've ever been with in every possible way, and I love it.

I'm shocked just how much I love it. I thought I knew exactly my type when it came to girls, but it winds up I had no idea. Or maybe I just don't have a type; because I can't imagine anyone else like her, and I can't imagine wanting to be with anyone but her.

She looks surprised. 'Of course. *Everyone* likes the X-Men.' I remember Lala whining through the last X-Men movie we watched and choose to ignore Evan's inaccuracy and listen to her maniac explanation instead. 'Magneto will never be a villain in my eyes. Never. What happened to his mother, what he went through, it made him who he is, and excuses his crimes, I don't care how extreme they are.'

It's just a comic book. She's talking about a comic book, not me, I remind myself as I wrestle with the urge to grab her and kiss her hard. I can hardly stay in my chair.

'So you think people can do bad things for good reasons?' I press, and I'm relieved she doesn't seem to notice how suspiciously anxious I am for her answer.

'Of course.' She pauses, fries held in midair, thinking it through. 'Yes.' She nods, more convinced every second. 'It happens all the time. And I'm in no place to judge. I'm always doing stupid things for stupid reasons, and I should know better.'

I'm twisting her innocent confession and making it into something that applies to me and the idiot decisions I've been making for the last few years. The ones even I can't really come to terms with. She's talking about Magneto and her little accidental foray into arson.

This has nothing to do with the lifestyle I live and the sacrifices I have to make and keep making.

She won't be able to accept it because even I have a

hard time with it, and I have no choice but to do what needs to be done, like it or not.

Guilt and hopeless frustration rip through me like a wild-dog pack on the scent of a kill.

'You ready to get outta here?' I ask, and she wordlessly sweeps the few scraps of leftover food and garbage into a pile. I throw it out, and we head to the car.

'Is this date over?' she asks when I have her door open.

Her feet hang half off the curb and she rocks back and forth.

'Completely your call.'

I hold still, one hand on the car door, one on the roof, every nerve tensed to keep from kissing her right into the car, into the backseat, kissing her until it goes a lot damn further than kissing.

She sucks her bottom lip in and chews on it, and I have to hold back a groan because I want to suck on that lip. I want to suck on her.

'I want to stay with you longer.' It's so blunt, she can't possibly mean for it to be a come on, but I'm so turned on, I'm about to make a dent in my car from gripping it so damn tight. 'I have to be home by midnight or my grandparents will freak out. But that's hours away. Can we go somewhere?'

'Yeah. Yes. Of course.'

I should kiss her. I want to, but this moment is damn close to perfect, and I don't want to mess with it. So, instead, I get in the car and we go.

The beach is half an hour away. I'd take her to my family's rental, but Remington has been holed up there in a booze-and-pot coma for weeks.

She interrupts my thoughts, 'My grandparents have a house right on the ocean.' I nod and she programs the address in the GPS for me, then warns, 'As long as we don't get crazy, we can hang out there.'

'I'm not the fire-starter,' I point out, and regret it instantly.

Nothing like setting everything to rights just to piss her off a second later.

Her laugh starts out low and deep in her throat and bubbles through the whole car.

'Accidental fire-starter, asshole.' She punches my shoulder and gives me a glare that's offset by a wide grin. 'At least, lighting up the orchard was an accident.'

The sound of her laughter makes me comfortable enough to ask, 'So, what were you burning that night?'

She presses her hands over her eyes and moans, 'It's too embarrassing.'

She's kicked off her boots and peeled off her socks, and now she puts her little feet with glittery-red-painted toenails on the dashboard.

I usually have a set-in-stone rule that no one puts anything on my dashboard, especially feet. But for this girl, I'm willing to make major exceptions.

'Tell me. I won't laugh at you,' I promise, watching as she gathers her hair up on top of her head and into a messy bun.

'I'll tell you mine if you tell me yours,' she sing-songs, letting all that hair swirl back down around her shoulders in long, sexy pieces that brush into the deep V-neck of her shirt and the soft press of her tits.

'Mine?' I push the pedal to the floor, speeding past the clumps of marsh grass and white sandy dunes, then let up and relax. I need to keep cool, keep my head, but it's not easy with her around. 'Mine isn't exactly mine. It's complicated.'

She picks her foot up and points at me with her toes, making the glitter sparkle.

'Everything with you is complicated.'

I try to smile, but it's panicky. She really has no idea just how true that is.

'Well, *I'm* an open book,' she continues. 'I was burning a pile of crap from my ex-boyfriend. He spent the summers with his grandparents, so I wanted him to see the bonfire and me and understand what a dumb-ass he was and what he lost when I dumped his sorry ass. I know, it was totally melodramatic, but I was a little bit drunk and really emotional that night, so I'm not apologizing for it. Anyway, of course, I forgot that he was partying with his stupid friends since he just got out of jail and all. So it was just his grandparents, but his grandfather had put all this pesticide down that morning, and apparently it was super flammable. And I might have been a wee bit drunker than I felt, so I wasn't any help in putting it out.'

She covers her face completely with her hands.

I imagine those old proper biddies waking up in the dead of night to this gorgeous drunk maniac setting their orchard on fire, and I can't help laughing, and she laughs behind her hands, and then she drops them and looks over at me, and we're both laughing like two idiots. I can't remember the last time I laughed so hard.

We pull into the driveway of her grandparents' beach house, and I'm still laughing when I get to her door. She jumps out and half falls into my arms.

I love the feel of her against me, the long line of her back and the soft curve of her ass.

Suddenly we're not laughing any more.

'Your eyes are like blueberries,' she says and brushes her fingers over my eyebrows.

'Do *you* write sonnets?' I test pulling her closer, and she moves my way, standing in her bare feet on the toes of my boots.

'I'll write one for you. And come to your window.

And read it underneath. Where do you live?'

Her voice is a hushed whisper, tugging at something wild in me that I've been keeping on a tight leash up till now.

'I . . . it's complicated,' I fumble.

She pushes her mouth close to mine and runs her hands up and down my back, first on top of my shirt, then underneath. My skin jumps under her hands and my breath holds fast in my lungs.

'What isn't complicated with you, Winchester Youngblood?'

Her mouth reaches up to mine, and the taste of her kiss is as slow and hot as a long swig of grappa. My hands are at her waist, a safe place to stay while her tongue twines with mine in a rhythm that makes me want to grind against her.

It's safe, but I start to hate safe when there's so much of her I want to know, need to touch. The burned sugar smell of her makes my head spin and my entire body freak into overdrive. I try to keep calm, but I'm powerless against the pull of her.

I move my hands up slowly, matching the sweet slide of her tongue on mine, and my fingers dip in at the small of her back, climb along the indent of her spine, press through all her unbelievably soft hair, and rest on the twin juts of her shoulder blades, pulling her closer.

She licks and sucks at my lips, and I back her to the outside wall of the house, pull her up into my arms, let her wrap her legs around my waist, and balance her with my hands spread under the curve of her ass.

She pops her mouth away from mine and rubs her lips on my neck, drags them along my jaw, and brushes them against my ear, where she whispers, 'Winch.'

Her voice is a plead, a command, an invitation.

I press my forehead to her shoulder and squeeze her tight, about to answer every single one of her needs and all of mine, too, when I hear the one sound I loathe.

'Fuck's sake,' I mutter.

'What is it?' Evan asks, her voice ragged from panting, and so sexy it's a blitzkrieg on my nerves.

The tone plays again. The Animals, 'House of the Rising Sun'. Remington's ringtone.

'It's my brother.' I can hear how flat and harsh my words sound, and I see Evan's eyes widen in surprise.

'You should answer,' she suggests, unhooking her legs from my waist and stepping out of my arms.

I bite my tongue, because fuck my brother. Fuck my phone. Fuck the fact that I have to call him back. She doesn't realize that tonight's over. This is over. She doesn't realize how much I want her, and how impossible it is for me to choose her.

It's been a long time since I contemplated choosing anything over Remington, and there's a bitter taste in my mouth over that fact.

I stare at the phone in my hand until it goes quiet, then grit my teeth and say, 'I'm so fucking sorry. You have no idea how sorry I am. But I have to take you home now.'

She eyes the phone with a frown.

'OK. But maybe you should call him back. Maybe it's no big deal? We're all the way out here.'

She gestures to the house with her hand, and I imagine what it would be like to throw my fucking phone into the waves and take her hand, go into that house, talk her into skipping curfew, peel her clothes off, make her moan and yell my name, stay with her all night, wake up with her in my arms.

Maybe my plan for the night is a long-shot and a pretty bad idea, but now that I know this date is irrevocably over, I let myself imagine the night the way it would have gone in my perfect world.

Except my world is never even close to perfect. Ever.

I run my hands through my hair and try to explain, but there's too much to say. 'It's com—'

'—plicated,' she finishes for me. Her lips curve up in a smile, but her eyes are disappointed. 'Can you drop me at my car?'

'Shit. Your car is all the way back at the site.'

I stare at the phone in my hand. As if it's taunting me, it rings again.

'Sorry. You could drop me at my grandparents' house. It's closer.'

She crosses her arms over her stomach and shifts anxiously from foot to foot.

'It's not that. I just . . . this is our first date, and I'm not even gonna drop you at your door? Sorry. Can't happen. C'mon. Get in. I'll drop you at your car and follow you back.'

She leans her head back and laughs, not an entirely happy sound.

'Winch, are you serious? I've driven home by myself a million times. I appreciate it, but this date has been kind of fucked up. Let's just let it end that way. And, seriously, it's not that big a deal. OK?' Before I can answer, my phone rings again. 'And please answer. You're ruining that song for me forever, and it's a great song.'

She slides into the passenger seat and puts on her big sunglasses, totally unnecessary since the sun is low on the horizon, but it masks whatever is going on behind her eyes.

I take the call, my voice clipped and short on the greeting, and wince at the rushed, slurred words on the other end.

It's worse than I thought, and I have no business pushing my luck in this situation, but I have to see her home, then I'll leave, much as it kills me.

It's going to be a long fucking night.

Evan 5

'And then what?' Brenna's voice screams with total frustration.

And it's just about to get more screamy and frustrated, because the end of my story would make any rational person fly into a throw-down, full-on tantrum.

It's the kind of crazy that makes me want to wrap my arms around her so we can scream together until our voices are hoarse, then split a carton of New York Super Fudge Chunk ice cream and a bottle of something strong and sweet and brain-numbing.

'And then he walked me to the door, gave me this little peck, and his goddamn, piece of shit, idiot-ass, fucking phone rang again, and he told me he had to go.'

I sigh and flop back on my bed. Perfectly made. My closet has been micro-organized. All my homework is done. I reorganized my freaking nail polish drawer. Because I need to keep busy. Because . . .

'So he hasn't called?' Brenna lets out some kind of adorably guttural sound that walks the line between a sigh and a vicious growl. 'It's been a week. Is he insane? Does he think you're just going to sit around in your room waiting for his call?'

'Honey, I *am* sitting in my room waiting for his call.'

I fall into my computer chair, and begin to twirl around, faster and faster, until I'm completely disoriented and woozy.

'Can't you go out? I wish we lived closer.' This particular lament of Brenna's gets repeated at least twice a week, and I would kill for the ability to get into a space–time phone booth and whisk myself to her every time she says it. 'We would have the most amazing girl date and wear our sexiest things and shake our fine asses . . . and we'd put pictures of our hot young selves all over Facebook! Still nothing on that front?'

I stop spinning and pluck a picture off my dressing table of us in Ireland getting ready to go dancing. We look so carefree and fun-loving in our tiny, tight dresses and fuck-me shoes. I had no idea on that sweet summer night so many months ago that I'd leave Brenna and come back to a life that included a prim, stick-up-its-ass school brimming with bitchy girls I would never want to get to know, a criminal record, and a demolished social life.

'He's a ghost. If he even has an account, and I

haven't found one with any combination of his names, I have no clue how else I could possibly connect to him. I have no idea who any of his friends are, where he goes to school. Or college. Is he in college?' If pure humiliation could be expressed in a single sound, that sound would be my groan. 'How do I always manage to get to the sticking-my-tongue-down-their-throat stage without getting basic information first?'

'Because you're more of a romantic than you like to pretend.'

'Or more of a slut,' I sigh.

'Don't call yourself a slut. It's degrading. Also, a slut wouldn't care who the hell she kissed and left. She'd be on to the next guy already. You, my love, are a romantic,' Brenna clucks, her voice marinated in triumph. Brenna is the patron saint of romance, and she holds herself proudly accountable for what she perceives as my conversion. 'So, what's the plan, baby-cakes? Because sulking is totally unacceptable. One thousand percent. Who can you call? Where can you go?'

'No one. Nowhere.' I flick a chip of nail polish off my fingernail and let one tiny, secret tear wobble in a make-up-tinged streak down my cheek. 'This is what I deserve. I drove everyone crazy and got into trouble. I shouldn't be cruising with some hot guy. So hot. So freaking hot.'

Brenna's laugh is the chocolate fudge, whipped cream and double cherry on top to the sad vanilla boringness of my life.

'Stop that right now. You got carried away, but you don't have a mean bone in your gorgeous body, OK? I'm not going to hear you sulk. There must be somewhere you can go. I hate that you're so sad . . . Oh no! You're in your school uniform, aren't you?'

I actually swivel my neck checking to see if Brenna has some sort of video camera set up to spy on me.

'School just got out a few hours ago,' I mumble.

'Get out of that polyester horror! Now!' Brenna's bark is fashion-drill-sergeant strict, and it kicks my ass into disrobing action. When I'm rid of the vile uniform and down to my underthings, I actually do feel better. Brenna's voice dictates through the phone. 'It's like I can hear your mood improving already. OK, you need a bitching outfit. Wear the stiletto boots. You know the ones. Pair them with something soft and sweet. And I don't care what you do or where you go, but you need to get out!'

She sighs, and I can picture her leaning her elbows on her windowsill, gazing dreamily at the road where her sexy boyfriend Jake will roar down in his big truck and take her . . . somewhere terrible like the bowling alley or on a hike. I'm instantly overwhelmed with guilt for crying over my sorry life when Brenna has to live in the backwoods of New Jersey.

'OK, hun. I'm laying an outfit for tonight on the bed right now. And, oh! I just remembered that Granddaddy asked me to go with them to some art gallery opening. I think it will be boring, and I was feeling too depressed to say yes, but I can get all dressed up and be fabulous for a little while, I guess.'

The dress is made of silky panels of bright paisley. I picked it up on a shopping trip in Venice with my mother just before she jetted off to her fabulous Cabo mansion with her new boyfriend.

It stings that she isn't around, but my mother had been perching right on the edge of leaving for good since I was about fourteen. Honestly, it's a shock she lasted as long as she did. She'd emotionally checked out by the time I turned sweet sixteen and wandered around our house with a perpetual pout until just before I turned eighteen. Like she was counting down the seconds until I was a legal adult and she could wash her hands of me without any guilt.

'You make my heart happy! Send me pictures,' Brenna trills ecstatically before letting me go.

I let Granddaddy and Gramma know I'm coming along and try not to feel too pathetic about their joyful, lit-up-like-jack-o'-lantern faces when they realize I actually want to leave the house.

I have time for a bubble bath, so I indulge in a

swimmy expanse of nearly boiling water and wild-flower smelly stuff. I pin my hair up around my head, put on extra-smoky make-up, and when I'm dressed and ready, I know exactly how good I look by the scowl on Granddaddy's face.

'I just don't think it's fair to the paintings, is all. People are supposed to be looking at them, but how could they with Evan looking so damn pretty?' he huffs and his mustache quivers.

I kick one booted foot back and lay a kiss on his cheek. 'Is that your diplomatic way of telling me you think I should wear a turtleneck and khakis?'

'Of course not, darling. It's too hot for a turtleneck. But a nice big T-shirt with a neck up here.' He holds a flat hand under his chin and Gramma rolls her eyes.

'She'll have plenty of time to dress like a matron when she's an old lady,' she fusses, straightening the strap on my dress and holding me at arm's length. 'You will steal the show, love. And there will be plenty of eligible young men, probably college boys. I think you're ready to move away from this high-school set.'

She seethes around the last three words like she's talking about decomposing corpses or imitation hand-bags.

From the backseat on the ride over, I watch my grandparents chat and laugh. My granddaddy puts a hand across the console and takes Gramma's hand. I can see from the rearview mirror that he frisks a few suggestive looks her way, and when she turns, I catch the profile view of her blush-and-smile combo.

It's so different from the tedium of my parents' marriage, and it gives me hope. Maybe it will be like the upright posture or peppery temper I inherited from Gramma, and the true love gene will skip my mama's generation and pierce me through the heart with its arrow.

I can hope. I *do* hope.

By the time Granddaddy hands his keys to the valet and we walk into the cavernous gallery, hope silvers the edges of my dismal mood. Or maybe it's stupidity, because I immediately scan the room, packed with smartly casual, perfume-drenched rich bitches, for Winch, as if he's going to magically appear with his soft blue eyes and the twitch of all our missed-opportunity kisses on his lips.

'Now there's a good-looking fella. That's Marguerite Holinger's grandson. Sweet as pie and so handsome, he'd have to watch out if I were ten years younger,' Gramma purrs in my ear, pressing her hand to my hip to propel me in the direction of a good-looking, overly groomed guy leaned against the wrought-iron railings that circle a mezzanine landing. 'Let me know if you decide to go grab a bite or go out dancing.'

I have community service in the morning, but it wouldn't hurt to go have some fun as long as I don't stay out too late. Gramma and Granddaddy are already pulled into a throng of their noisy, rowdy friends, who all seem way more interested in whispering to each other, stealing crab-cake hors d'oeuvres from harried waiters, and ordering lots of double and neat drinks, than in soaking up the art that surrounds them.

Marguerite Holinger's grandson is hitting on Genevieve Marcusso's grandson, so, though I appreciate Gramma's adorably oblivious suggestion, I'm not about to crash their flirtation. I move instead towards one of the paintings and study it as thoughtfully as I can.

It's dark and messy. I don't get a sense of form. There's no random shock of beauty. I wait, squinting like it's one of those 3D posters I used to love when I was a kid, but the gorgeousness never pops out of the chaotic lines and scribbles. The heady scent of a strong cologne snaps my attention suddenly to the side.

'You're not a fan?'

He's handsome in a tousled, scruffy way: shirt slightly wrinkled, pants too long, blue-green eyes dancing like he's laughing at me.

'Are you the artist?' I gesture to the painting and purse my lips.

'No.' He chuckles softly and clasps his hands behind his back. 'Do I look like an artist?'

'More like a couch-crashing grad student.' I raise one eyebrow at him and he laughs.

'I take it my ironing attempts were unsuccessful?'

He holds his arms out at his sides and the wrinkled patches of fabric do show a haphazard attempt at ironing.

'Half successful,' I concede, and that familiar pull grabs low in my stomach.

I love the chase, the dance, the flirtation. It's not the honest punch of breathless attraction I feel when I see Winch, but that's not going to happen, and this just might.

'Half successful is probably worse than unsuccessful when it comes to ironing. I'm Jace, by the way.' He holds out a hand.

'Evan.'

We shake.

He peers at the uninspired painting and twitches as the liquor-soaked crush presses uncomfortably close.

He turns to me and adds, 'It's getting really crowded here. If you're interested, maybe we could go have some coffee? Get a bite?'

'Let me just tell . . . the people I came with,' I say to him. 'Do you want to get your car from valet?'

His embarrassed smile tells me that if he has a car, he did not opt to valet park.

'Or just wait by the doors,' I amend quickly. 'I'll be right there.'

I find Gramma and she's already crossing over from tipsy into giddy. She gives me a hard hug and shoos me off, assuming I'm with Marguerite Holinger's grandson, but the details don't really matter.

What matters is that I'm out on a Friday night.

Finally.

Jace is at the doors, and his smile is sweet, but his eyes are hungry as they follow me from across the room and out into the humming night air. He leads me down the street to where his car is parked, and we hop in and set off. I make sure to take out my cell and text Brenna, and I mention it, too.

'Just letting my best friend know I left early,' I tell Jace, to make it clear there is electronic proof of me leaving with a time-stamp and location in case he's not as sweet as his pretty eyes make him seem.

He doesn't know Bren is all the way in New Jersey and couldn't save me if she wanted to.

'Cool. Do you want me to swing by and get her?' He quirks an encouraging smile at me, and I shake my head.

'She's with her boyfriend. At the gun range,' I add, and his smile widens slightly.

He clears his throat, I think to keep from laughing. 'If you're game, I got invited to this house party on the beach. A couple of people from the chem program at Southern are going.' He nods to my phone. 'If you want to go, you can text your friend at the gun range the address first. Tonight's the kind of night that makes you want to be by the ocean, right?'

'I don't need to text the address.' I give him a sheepish laugh. 'She really will come, guns blazing, if anything fishy is going on. But a beach party sounds absolutely perfect, and you seem nice. Wrinkled, but nice.'

We share a smile. He has the air conditioning on, but I roll the window down and let the salty air rise and burst through the interior.

'You seem nice, too. Beautiful and nice.' The words spill out and a blush instantly works its way over his face.

I laugh into the night wind, giddy with the promise of a heady evening earmarked for magic, compliments from a cute guy, and the enticing crash of the waves on the beach we're whipping towards.

Winch 5

The moon is perfectly round and hangs low over the ocean like it might crash into the dark waves at any minute. I should be able to see the beauty in it on this perfect night, but lately, everything feels dark and depressing as hell.

'Winchester!'

The yells from the house, overcrowded with dozens of drunk, young, dancing fools, almost drown out my brother's voice. But nothing, not even the world's most insane debauchery, can completely stifle Remington.

He trips across the beach to where I'm sitting, falls next to me in a mini-explosion of sand, and kisses the side of my face, his gnarly beard making me cringe.

'Winchester, brother, what are you doing staring at the . . . ocean? This is . . .' He trails off and burps, his breath beery and sharp with a mix of all the other alcohols he's peppered the beer with. 'This is depressing, my man. There are ladies galore up there. It's a wild rumpus. C'mon.' He pulls at my arm. 'C'mon, brother. What's with you lately?'

'Just not in the mood.' I shrug him off.

I don't need to be on tonight. I don't even need to be here. There's nothing for me to do, officially, but I'm here anyway because it was claustrophobic at home with my mother asking what my problem is and where Lala's been, and at least if I'm right next to Remington, I can take a stab at keeping his crazy ass out of the trouble that always seems to find him.

'Lala is here. Grinding with that professor from Southern, hoping you'll see her.' His laugh is soft and completely amused. 'Used to be, seeing her doing that shit would get your fists up fast, man. Not so much, eh?'

'Not so much.'

Lala could dry hump or full-on screw every professor in every department at Georgia Southern, and it wouldn't make me feel a damn thing. The few days I've had with Evan blow the months I had with Lala out of the water.

'Ma is upset over you two breaking up. She thought she was finally going to get to plan a wedding.' Remington swings his arms in front of his chest, the conductor of his own stupid bullshit. 'Dum, dum, di, dum,' he tones and laughs wildly, pulling a flask from his pocket and taking a long pull that half dribbles down his chin.

I rub a hand over my face and stifle a growl. 'Ma can marry you off if she's so damn ready for a wedding.'

As soon as the words are out, I want to punch myself in the face. Remington can be a dick, but he has the softest heart of anyone I know, and I just squeezed fucking lemon juice all over the one wound that even my happy-go-lucky brother can't scab over.

'I'm sorry, man.' He's already standing. 'Remy! I'm sorry!'

He's staggering back to the house, and I have a feeling my stupid comment is about to unleash a whole wild chain of craziness.

I jump up and kick at the sand, but it's not remotely a good enough release for all the pissed-off shit I have bottled up.

'Fuck!' I scream into the night, loud and long as a wolf's howl.

I stalk back to the house and search all his usual sulking haunts, but my brother isn't anywhere I expect him to be. In the main room, people are sardined shoulder to shoulder, gyrating to the music, guzzling liquor, collapsing in humping pairs on couches, pool-side chairs, and every other flat surface, but I can't find Remington.

Finally I see Lala's long blonde hair and tanned skin, exposed by a total lack of any but the most necessary clothing. She executes her best dirty dancing moves, but she's not dancing with any professor.

My brother droops at her side like he's about to pass out on top of her. She presses a palm to his chest to keep him upright, then turns her back to him so her ass is crammed against his junk, and disgust rips through me.

She catches my eye, and her smile is all triumph.

She thinks I'm jealous. If she wasn't grinding against my brother, if she didn't know full well what he's been through recently, I might actually feel sad for how pathetic she is. But using Remington to punish me is going to get her hot little ass nothing but trouble, and I need to send a clear message tonight, before she does damage I can't undo.

I stalk over and give her a look that sets her mouth into a pout.

'Get lost before I lose my shit, Lala,' I growl, pushing her away from Remington and toward the door.

I pull Remington up, ignoring his slurs and weak-fisted attempts at punches.

'Fuck off, Winch. Seriously, man, I'm sick of you always playing big daddy. Go act your goddamn age, all right? Go chase some tail. Go drink till you puke. Go get the fuck off my back.'

'What are you thinking, asshole?' I shove him against the wall and bang his head back into it a little. 'Lala? You know she's trouble, so what are you doing?'

'You don't want her,' he snarls, bucking against me.

A year ago, I wouldn't have had a chance in hell of holding my brother back. He could have thrown me across the room with one arm. But a lot's happened in a few months, and it rips me the fuck up that I can pin him so easily.

'You don't fucking want her either, so stay away. That girl's got schemes, and we don't need to get tangled in them right now.'

I shove him back one more time, hard. His head droops forward and his shoulders shake up and down unevenly. He's crying, and panic crushes me like an elevator car with a snapped cable.

'Stop. It's OK, Rem. It's OK. You just need to sleep it off. You need to sober up.'

I lead him to the hall of family bedrooms, the ones I keep locked when Remington throws these big, stupid house parties. I yank the key out of my pocket and get his door open. The cleaning ladies get a bonus every month to make up for having to take care of my brother's disgusting room, so it looks all right tonight. But no amount of bleach and scrubbing can take away the dejected, wasted feel that seems to fill every space he's in.

I walk him to the bed, his arm around my shoulders, and let him drop. He moans and his head rolls back and forth. I drag him to the edge of the mattress, tip him on his side, and set up the little garbage can next to the bed.

'Puke now if you need to,' I tell him, my voice low. 'No shame in it, man, and that way you don't choke.'

My brother shakes his head, then heaves once, twice, and finally pukes into the can I hold for him. When it's full of his bitter, sour vomit, I take it to the bathroom and flush it down the toilet, get him a glass of water and a washcloth. I try to hand them over so he can clean up, but he's past that, so I wipe him down, get him to drink a little before I put the rinsed can back by the bed in case he needs it for round two, and turn to leave.

'Winchester?' he croaks as I flip the light off.

In the dark, huddled on the bed, scruffy as hell and slack with sadness, he's unrecognizable from the hero of my childhood. I don't know this guy.

'You need something?' I ask.

'Do you think they'll take her away?' Sobs make his words cracked and wet sounding. 'Tell me the truth.'

'They will if you keep fucking up.'

I tighten my grip on the doorknob, so ready to leave my brother's embarrassing sadness and all the problems that just keep multiplying faster than I can handle them.

'Pop said it would be OK.'

His voice shakes, and he sounds like a much older man and a really little boy at the same time.

'Yeah, well, you asked me for the truth. Night.'

I pull the door shut and turn the lock so no one winds up stumbling in on him.

Lala's waiting down the hall, arms crossed, a scowl on her cute little face. 'He OK?'

The fury I felt for her is already half extinguished. I just don't have the capacity to give a shit where she's concerned any more.

'Blitzed, but he'll sleep it off,' I lie.

If he slept for two weeks he couldn't sleep off all the liquor he has stored up in his body. His liver has to be pickled by now.

'I'm sorry about that, out there. We were just having fun.'

She tosses a strand of blonde hair over her slim shoulder. I lean on the wall across from her.

'You know he's in no place for your games. Between the two of you, I feel like a fucking nanny.'

She takes a step toward me.

'I'm sorry, Winch. Really. I know you've been stressed. And I know I need a lot of attention. But wasn't I good for you, too? Didn't I make the crappy stuff worth it?'

She threads the questions with the hint of sex so hot and fierce, it's tempting. I'd be a liar if I said I wasn't tempted.

'No.' I sidestep her. 'I've got too much on my plate now. And you and I are a train wreck waiting to happen.'

'So, there's a chance?' She rushes me, and before I really know what's happening, her arms slide around my waist and I can smell the sweet musk of her perfume in my nostrils. 'I know I screwed up, baby. But it's always gonna be you and me. We have history. Our families practically arranged our marriage when we were babies. Don't let a few crappy weeks ruin all that.'

I wish I'd stayed on the sand, looking at the moon like a sad old fuck.

'Lala, listen to me.' Her big hazel eyes go wide and her mouth curls up with happy expectation. I shake my head before I shoot her down. 'It's over. We're over. I don't want to hurt you, but you've got to let this go.'

The sweet look cracks and falls right off her face. If I hadn't seen her do this manic emotion-flip a thousand times during the course of our relationship, the complete twist would have shocked me. Since I know her inside out, I'm just tired in advance from the tantrum I know is coming.

'This isn't over by a fucking long shot, Winchester Youngblood! You think you can just use me and toss me aside when you're done? You are so damn wrong, and you're going to regret this!'

She's starting to border on hysterical, so I walk away, leaving her to scream a torrent of nasty curses and threats at my back.

The party is still in full swing and, much as I want to split it all up and go the fuck to bed, I decide not to make a big deal or draw any attention to the fact that anything might be wrong. My family doesn't need any more gossip than it usually has going around.

I crack a beer and manage to keep myself separate from the crowd without standing out. Blending is one of my specialties.

It's the usual group of old friends and cousins, young co-eds, and the odd green business shark here and there. No one interesting enough to spend any time with.

Then I see a girl with her back to me who looks just like Evan. Tall and slim, dark hair all coiled up, dress that hugs every sweet curve, boots that make her legs look long as a smooth, slow high dive. But I know Evan would never be here and, much as it kills me, that fact also gives me a deep relief.

Wherever she is, it's not mixed up with this crap. She shadows my every thought, but I know that distance is what I need to keep her from getting tangled in this mess.

It's not until her laugh rings out that I choke on the sip of beer that was running down my throat.

That's Evan's laugh.

I'd know that sound anywhere.

I'm not entirely sure how I get across the room or what I plan to say or do, but suddenly I'm inches away from her, smelling the soft wildflower scent that can't mask the harsher, sexy, burned-sugar smell of her, and my jaw clenches tight while I wrestle with two warring desires; a huge part of me wants to drag her somewhere private and touch her everywhere without stopping, but the saner part knows the right thing to do would be order her to leave right now, while I still have the sense to follow through.

Some dumbass college boy has his hands all over her. She's crooked against him, his arm snaked around her waist, pulling her close, and my vision goes red.

The guy notices me before Evan does, and he stands straight, letting go of her. I have to rip and kick at the urge to snatch her to my side.

'You must be Remington? Sal told me we should talk. I'm Jace Aldo.' He holds a hand out for me to shake, but I ignore it. I've heard of the guy, but nothing good.

Evan's eyes lock on me, and her complexion fades to ash, then bursts back to a sweet, excited pink.

I want her.

I want her so badly it shakes through me.

'I'm not Remington, and if Sal sent you, you can walk the fuck out the door right now.' The people around the guy go quiet.

'Winch?' Evan's face is going through a crazy stream of emotions, and the one that's clearest is confusion.

I turn my attention to her. 'What are you doing here with him? I thought you were trying to stay the hell out of trouble.'

'I ... we just met. At an art show. He goes to Southern.'

As she trips over her words, her blush gets deeper and her eyes burn bright with a rage that wakes up something in me that used to be sound asleep.

I swing my eyes to Jace and say what it takes to get him to leave before I get my fists on him.

'Hands off. She's in high school. And her grandfather is Lee Early.'

'Winch!' she gasps, and Jace instantly puts five feet between the two of them.

'Leave. I'll get her home.' The music blares, but no

one else is making any noise. I've stopped this party like a speed bump on the autobahn.

Jace looks at Evan and says in a low voice, 'If you want me to take you—'

'I said leave,' I order, and Jace clamps his mouth tight and, with nothing more than a disgusted shake of his head, he stalks out of the nearest door. I look around at the staring guests of Remington's fucked-up party. 'Everyone can leave.'

I flick off the sound system, and it's like popping a balloon. Everyone starts to disperse immediately, and I can't get them out fast enough.

There's a lot of pissed-off murmuring and bitching, but I couldn't give a shit. Evan stalks to the far railing of the deck, texting furiously, but I don't dare approach her until every other person is gone.

Lala is the last to leave. 'Who is she?' she demands, pointing to Evan.

'None of your business. Party's over.' I grab her by the shoulders and turn her to the door.

She twists out of my grip. 'Take your fucking hands off me! This is bullshit, Winch. I don't know what the hell happened to you, but you turned into a real dick.'

'All the more reason to get away from me. Goodbye, Lala.'

I don't touch her again, but I herd her to the door, secretly thanking God that Evan never turned around and gave Lala a good look. Lala has a way of tracking people down and getting revenge when she wants it, and I don't need her targeting Evan.

She tosses her blonde hair and shakes it back from her face, licking her pouty lips and narrowing her eyes. 'This isn't fucking over.'

Her phone is already in her hand, and I'm willing to bet she's texting my sister. Benelli will keep her mouth shut until she talks to me, but she's definitely Team Lala, and I know she'll be curious about Evan. My head pounds with a migraine that's crawling in fast and strong as hell.

I watch as Lala stomps away and keep watching from the deck as her Audi squeals out of the driveway and into the dark night. Finally the only sound is the crash of the waves, over and over, roaring and peaceful all at once.

Evan's back is to me, her long neck bent over her phone. I want to kiss her up and down that neck, make her moan my name the way she did on that stupid date so many days ago. The one I can't stop thinking about even though I know I should put it out of my head.

'Hey.'

I had enough weight to stop a full-blown rave in its tracks, but this girl leaves me feeling like I'm a gangly middle-schooler talking to his first crush.

She whirls around, the tight little dress clingy and perfect against her tanned curves. I imagine how much more perfect it would be peeled off and dropped on the floor.

'What's going on? Why did you kick Jace out? Why did you end the party? That girl who was screaming at you. Is she your girlfriend? Or your ex? This is . . . I feel like . . .' She puts her hands up to her temples and squeezes her eyes shut.

I take a few steps toward her then have to mentally cement myself where I am.

'Who are you texting?'

I am torn between dread and hope that she called for a ride home.

'Brenna. My best friend.'

She stares at the little screen and furrows her brow.

'You told her what happened?'

I kick some cans out of the way and sit a few feet away from her, head leaned back on the chair cushion so I can watch her from my half-closed eyes without looking too obvious. She's fucking gorgeous. I forgot just how gorgeous she is.

'Yes.'

She shakes her head angrily at the phone and tosses it in her purse with a sharp motion of her wrist.

'What did she say?'

Despite the shittiness of the night, something tells

me her friend gave her advice I'm gonna be happy about.

'Brenna, who is a hopeless, insane romantic, told me that I should ask why you kicked Jace out with no explanation. She seems to think you're actually not an antisocial maniac.'

She pulls herself up on the deck railing and the wind blows loose pieces of her hair around her neck and moves the skirt of her dress up her thighs.

'Do you want to ask me?' I close my eyes and wait.

'Is it a good reason?' Her voice is curious. I shrug; she sighs and asks, 'Winch, why did you kick Jace out?'

'Jace cooks meth.' I lift my head up for the satisfaction of seeing her mouth drop. 'That's what he does with his fancy-ass chem degree. My brother Remington is in a bad place. He's had some guys approach him, dealers. I've been working my ass off to keep them away from him.'

'Do your parents know?' Her voice is a bare-bones whisper, almost lost in the screeching wind.

'My parents . . . it's—' I stop before I say 'complicated' again. 'My parents leave these things to me. My brother and I have been close since we were real young, so it makes sense for me to handle all this.'

'Sense?' She chews on the word, shakes her head, puts a hand up, drops it, and sighs. 'Listen, can you just take me home? I would have left with Jace. I didn't know this was your place or anything. Tonight has been so bizarre. This is honestly the weirdest freaking night ever.'

Her eyes drop and her shoulders sag like she's exhausted. I'm half afraid she's going to fall off the railing, so I get up and move next to her.

'I know you didn't realize this was my place. But I'm glad you're here.'

I stand right next to her, close enough to smell her and feel the heat coming off her skin. Her laugh is devoid of happiness. The sound it makes is loud and empty, like a bunch of rocks shaken in a tin can.

'Glad? Really? I didn't hear a word from you all week long, Winch.' I look up at her face when she says my name, and I can see the torn, hurt frustration that I put there. It stabs like a hunting knife in my intestines. 'I hate games, and I feel like I'm getting played by you big time. You're happy now because I walked in here and fell into your lap. But you had your ex or your girlfriend or whatever at your party tonight, and you never would have come to get me, you never would—'

'Lala is not my girlfriend,' I interrupt and run my fingers over her hand. She stares down at my hand on hers. 'She's my ex. Remy invited her, and I was glad to kick her out. I haven't been able to think about anything but you since the last time we talked. I wanted to call you. See you. You have no idea how bad I wanted to.'

'Oh, I have an idea.' Her voice is low and husky. 'I *wish* I could stop thinking about you. I wish I'd never met you, actually. Because all week long, all I thought about was you. And when Jace came up to me, the only reason I was remotely interested was because I hoped he might make me think about anything else for a few minutes.'

This time her laugh is real, and so loud and sweet, it claws with a sharp need low in my gut. 'And he brought me here. Right to you. Define fucking irony.'

She pulls her hand away.

I take it back again.

'Maybe it's fate or something.'

This is an unbelievably bad idea. She hops down off the railing and she's immediately fitted against me, right where she belongs, right where I want her.

Her eyebrows rise up high and her smile is forced. 'You believe in fate? Or something?'

'You make me believe in a lot of things I never thought I would.'

This is crazy talk. This is the result of too many nights thinking about her and not getting any sleep, too many days imagining I see her right around every

129

corner, and too many attempts to deny how much I want her.

Now she's right in my arms for a second time, and I realize I'm not going to get a third chance to make this right. I have to make a decision.

Evan 6

Winchester Youngblood doesn't want me.

He didn't call me all week.

He didn't come by and try to see me.

No Facebook messages, no pigeons with notes tied to their little pink claws, no pebbles clattering against my windowpane.

But when I wind up at his party with another guy, he's suddenly ready to be my gallant defender. It's all cheekbones and soft blue eyes and that accent I still can't place that fills my ears up and blocks out every other sound, like the ocean when you jump in the waves too fast, too deep.

'This isn't a good idea,' says me, Queen of Colossally Stupid Ideas.

I know exactly how bad it is by how incredibly good it feels. When his hands coast just a hair of an inch away from my skin, I arch into them.

And I want more.

'We're not exactly known for our good ideas,' he

says, his voice low, his lips hovering just above my lips, and I want them to commit. Commit to every hot, sweet thing I know we both want, no matter how stupid it is to want it. His mouth hits its target and his lips drag along my neck so slowly, making me shiver with naked desire for him. He opens his mouth, and the press of his tongue makes me jump.

'You weren't even interested in me,' I argue, unclouding my stupid thoughts and pushing him away.

'That's ridiculous.'

He talks like he's some blue-face-painted warrior used to commanding legions. This is the same voice he used when he told a few dozen drunk party-goers to get the hell out of his house, and every single one of them scurried away.

I twirl out of his arms and grab onto the railing, digging my fingernails into the wood to anchor myself.

'It's not ridiculous at all. Actually, it makes total sense. You can't just have me now, because I'm here and available.'

Clouds slipped over the moon while he was turning me into a pool of jelly, so it's dark on the beach, but I search for something to fix my eyes on anyway.

Winch's body mirrors mine, and he wraps one arm around my waist.

'It's getting cold. Come on inside, we can talk. I swear to God, all we'll do is talk.'

He's the path lined with wildflowers, and I'm Red Riding Hood. I've been warned, but I just can't resist the blossom and perfume that calls me over.

The party-silent house creaks and groans in the wind that picks up and rattles the windows, and I nearly trip over a couple of glasses, knocked on their sides, as I follow him through the labyrinth. When I bend to right them, Winch tugs at my hand and shakes his head.

'We have a cleaning staff. You don't need to do that.'

Nothing about Winch screamed 'money' when I first met him, not the way everything about my ex Rabin did. Rabin was all ego and polish and pampered can't-lift-a-finger-to-help-himself syndrome. But Winch doesn't just have money; Winch has control. He's used to being in power.

What does he do?

What does his family do?

He steps quietly along the bleached hardwood floors, past the cathedral-ceilinged living room full of leather chairs, past a granite and stainless steel kitchen, down a long hall lined with brilliant modernist prints, to a series of doors. He slides a key out of his pocket and slips it into a lock, then throws open the door on a room that feels like it's all windows facing the crashing ocean waves – windows and a bed.

A big, soft, inviting bed.

There must be other things in this room, but, despite my mind's very sensible protests, all I can think about is lying down on that bed with Winch and forgetting everything that happened – or didn't happen – this past week.

He leans his long frame in the doorway and his eyes follow me as I walk around the room, his mouth tight. 'You want a drink?'

'Sure.'

My feet manage to move me to the bed, and I sink onto the mattress, suddenly surrounded by the mingling smells of detergent and pure, hot Winch. I hear him put the key in another door, and the low rumble of his voice, then another guy's, I assume his brother's, hits my ears, though I can't make out a single word. I hear him click the door shut, then I hear the sound of glasses clinking, the refrigerator opening, and his returning footsteps.

He comes in, two glasses in hand, and gives me one before he takes a seat in the chair across from me. I'm attempting to position my dress so he doesn't see my underwear and balance the glass he handed me, all the while wishing I'd taken the chair.

And wishing twice as hard that he'd chosen to join me on the bed.

I take a long chug, and my tongue recoils in shock at the crisp lack of bite. This isn't vodka, which I stupidly thought it would be. It's ice water. Winch leans back in his chair and eyes me over the rim of his glass.

'I wasn't going to give you alcohol, Evan. I'm in deep enough shit already with you. We don't really need to mix drinking in with all this.'

I pull my index finger around the edge of the glass, collecting condensation in the whorls of my fingertip.

'What is *all this* exactly?'

I keep my voice tightrope taut, but my eyes hunt his, refusing to let him duck and cover away from my gaze.

He shifts uncomfortably on the chair. 'I don't know.'

'Why?' I bully. I'm not above beating this out of him if that's what it takes.

'Because my life is a clusterfuck, Evan!' His voice bursts out louder than either of us expected. We both jump, then he lowers his voice and explains. 'It's not fair for me to even imagine letting you into it. And it looks like things are going to get a hell of a lot worse before they get any better.'

He puts the glass down with a thump and pushes

up off the chair, moving around the room in a random, edgy circuit. I sit straight on his bed, legs crossed, and watch him.

'I thought I'd be able to just flirt with you when we met. Like that would be enough.' He runs a hand through his hair, then brushes it back down, over and over, his still-fresh tattoo poking from the sleeve of his shirt. 'Then I thought, fuck it, we could just be friends during our shitty community service assignment. I figured I'd get my fill of you and be able to leave. But you know how that worked out.'

'Actually, I thought that was exactly how it worked. You took me on one date, then didn't call for a week. I would have said that was you getting me out of your system.'

I put my glass down and jump up, reaching for his hands because there's no way I can watch him attack his hair like a maniac anymore. He stills instantly but, somehow, it's like he's transferred all the pent-up, pacing momentum of his body to his eyes, so he might as well be climbing up the walls.

I run my fingers over his forehead because I can't convince myself not to touch him. 'Look, if this is so damn hard and so damn confusing, maybe it's not meant to be, right? In the last few months I found out my ex-boyfriend is a sexually harassing shithead, my parents' marriage is probably officially over, and I've had to move in with my grandparents and start a new school I hate, all on top of getting arrested and having to do community service. We're both in a shitty place, and it was fun to flirt, but maybe that's all it needed to be. I'm cool with that.'

His hands break from mine and sweep up and down my arms, replacing his manic hair-mussing with arm-brushing. His words are low, slow, and ringing with solid honesty. 'I'm so not cool with that.'

'We can just be friends.' My voice slaps and smacks, devoid of any real conviction.

His fingers press and draw down my arms 'I haven't stopped thinking about you all week.'

'If it bothered you that much, you would have called.' My voice has moved up several octaves, graduating to a high-pitched squeak.

His voice, on the other hand, is beach-glass smooth.

'I'm crazy good at resisting temptation.' He cups my shoulders and drags the back of his fingers down the skin of my bare back. 'Correction. I *was* crazy good at resisting temptation. But here you are in my room, when I should be on the road taking you home.'

'What do you want?' My voice scratches out of my throat desperately.

'You.' He cups his hand under my chin and rubs the pad of his thumb along my bottom lip.

'This is stupid.'

My voice barely registers at a whisper because his thumb plus my lip equals debilitating brain chaos.

'This is too fast.'

His other hand holds the side of my face, and he traces his thumbs in sweeping crescents over my cheekbones and around the curves of my ears.

'We tried this, and it was worse than a royal fucking mess,' I remind him and myself.

I need a ruler-slap to my brain, because I might be falling way too hard and fast under the wrong guy's spell.

'Try again?'

His mouth closes in on mine, and that second before our lips meet spins out for an eternity. And it makes graphs and flow-charts and PowerPoints underlining all the reasons we should absolutely not be doing this.

But we are.

We so completely are.

Winch walks me back to the bed and lays me down, his entire body pressed long and perfectly weighted over mine. He kisses me with gentle, coaxing pressure for a few minutes, like he's taking my temperature, gauging my heart rate, and determining if I'm in.

I'm all in.

I vice my arms around his ribs, pulling him close, and his kiss deepens, his tongue slides into my mouth and moves sweet and quick over my tongue and the inside of my mouth before he pulls back and sweeps in again. I arch my back and can feel how hard he already is against my thigh.

His thumbs trip under the straps of my dress, and he pulls his mouth away so he can kiss my shoulders. His mouth follows up and down my shoulder and the curve of my clavicle. He presses his mouth to my breastbone and leaves a soft, warm trail of kisses up to my neck and back down until I'm digging my heels into the mattress and straining against him.

His hands reach up to find mine, lock around my wrists, and twist my arms over my head, gently pinning me.

His face is so close, I can see the olive black of his pupils, round and hungry, and the way his mouth is held tight, like he's working hard not to lose control.

'I promised we'd just talk.' He swallows hard and licks his lips. 'This isn't just talking.'

'We can just kiss.'

I want him to press his mouth back on mine. I want his hands under my clothes, I want to peel away everything he's wearing . . . but I know that's sprinting and this is a marathon. I feel a pinch of panic when I realize this could end up a repeat of last week, with Winch turning into a pumpkin with no contact information at midnight.

He lets go of my wrists slowly and bends his head back down until our lips find each other, and this time it's a heart-hammering, blood-pounding, body-shaking tempo.

'Evan,' he moans, pulling his lips away and kissing my temple and the side of my ear.

I stroke one hand through the soft strands of his dark hair, and wedge the other between us so I can open the line of buttons that run down his shirt.

'Evan.' This time his voice is a plea. Or a warning. His eyes flicker down to my hands, flattened on the hard muscles of his chest. 'I want to take this slow. And you're so damn sexy. Seriously, you're beating the shit out of my willpower.'

'You don't have to worry. I'm not a virgin or anything,' I inform him, and his eyes shutter. He pulls back just a fraction, and I sit up on my elbow, surprised at how quickly the sexy got sucked out of the room. 'What's the problem?'

'We just met. We're not having sex yet,' he declares, then shakes his head. 'And, you know what? Here's my other problem. What the fuck is going on with you? You need to give yourself more credit, value yourself more.'

I can't keep the snort back, and he goes into full-blown scold-mode. 'You took a ride out to the middle of nowhere with that scumbag Jace. What were you thinking?' His mouth presses into a long, flat line and his nostrils flare. 'What if he took you to some shithole where they were doing meth? Do you know how violent those assholes get?'

I sit up and yank the straps of my dress back onto my shoulders.

'Jace is harmless,' I huff. I have no clue if I'm accurate, but I do know that I don't need Winch getting all parental on my ass. 'I had my cell phone.'

'You can't be serious.' This time when he grabs my shoulders, it's definitely to full-on lecture me, and I angle my face away, determined not to pay attention to this condescending crap. 'Listen to me. You need to take better care of yourself. Don't trust people so easily.'

I purse my lips and examine his face, so serious and intent, it rubs away some of my moodiness.

'What about you? Do I trust you?'

'Yeah.' He kisses my lips softly, and that brush feels more astoundingly erotic than the full-on make-out session we just had. 'You can trust me because I care about you, and I always watch out for the people I care about.'

My heart leaps into my throat, the way it feels when an elevator drops too fast from too high a floor.

'This is weird. Really weird. I went this whole

entire week thinking that you didn't give a damn what happened to me, and now all this?'

He leans his forehead on mine and runs his hands up and down my back in slow, even swipes.

'This is the beginning. You make me feel crazy, Evan. You make me feel alive for the first time in a long time, and that scared the shit out of me. But I can't risk not having you in my life. I'm so glad that douchebag brought you here tonight.'

I find his lips with mine, and we fall back on the bed. I know it's getting late. We both have community service in the morning. Gramma probably called to check on me. I should be headed home.

But all I can concentrate on is the feel of him: Winch, the guy I haven't been able to shake out of my head for days, kissing me and telling me how much I mean to him, how he wants to hold my hand and plunge off the edge of the highest, scariest cliff I'd ever seen. I'm so ready to take that flying leap with him, and I shouldn't be.

I really shouldn't be.

His hands are warm on my legs, along the waist-band of my barely-there thong and over the skin I'm so glad I shaved extra smooth. His breathing is harsh and sharp, and I love the things he murmurs while he touches me: *gorgeous, beautiful, Evan, mine.*

The entire night is about to implode in a way he

swears we're not going toward but I want, when there's a crash from the room next door.

Winch's hand stops right where it is, his fingers tangled around the lacy waistband of my thong, ready to yank it down. He squeezes the skin at my hip, and when he looks up, his eyes are soft with apology.

'I have to check on Remington.'

'Of course. Go ahead.'

I pull the straps of my dress up again and try not to sigh when he buttons up his shirt, covering the gorgeous expanse of his chest, and walks with quick, decisive steps out of the room.

Then I listen.

I hear what sounds like someone crying, low, keening moans and loud, choked sobs. Those are offset by the tenor of Winch's voice. I don't know what exact words he's saying, but his voice is calm, slow, in command.

Winch watches out for the people he cares about.

The minutes tick by, and when he finally comes back, his face is lined and grim.

'I should get you home. My brother needs me.'

He bites the words off as if he's angry at them.

'It's no problem.' I stand up and attempt to smooth the wrinkles out of my dress with the flats of my hands. 'I need to get back anyway. My grandparents will be waiting.'

For a split second, life tilts back, and I don't know where to put my hands or how to hold myself in front of him.

Then he closes the gap between us and pulls me into his arms. His mouth relays a trail of kisses down my hairline.

'I wish I could stay with you tonight, Evan. I feel like I might fuck this up again if I don't hold onto you.'

'You won't.'

I let the words slide out with a lazy cool I don't feel at all.

'Can I call you?' He runs his hands over my arms and squeezes at random intervals, like he's checking to be sure I'm really in front of him. 'Feel free to tell me no. It'll probably be really late.'

'Oh, trust me, I have no problem at all telling you no.' His smile makes my heart buzz like a hive full of bees. 'But I don't want to tell you "no" tonight. I'll sleep with my phone under my pillow, like some sappy lovesick girl.'

His smile widens and sweetens his entire face, a spoonful of honey in a tall glass of iced tea.

'I can't lie. I'm loving the idea of you getting all sappy and lovesick over me.'

His arms twine around my waist and hold me tight. My face is tilted to his, lips ready, tongue ready, all ready for him when another low, long moan rips through the house like a ghost in a horror movie.

'You should check on your brother, and then we can go.'

I give him one last kiss before I watch him walk down the hall and to the darkened bedroom, his face grim as a reaper's.

Winch 6

Evan was so cool about Remington, I actually started to think I could pull this whole thing off.

We both went to our community service tired as hell, but the dark circles under her eyes only made her more gorgeous to me. They were there because she had spent time with me. In my bed, in my arms, on the phone for a good three hours talking about a thousand things, and the funniest part is, by the time I was so zombified the phone was slipping from my hand, it still felt like there were so many more things we needed to say to each other.

But I had to leave her after community service for family time, and I could tell she wasn't happy about it. Which made me so damn happy on one hand, and made me consider fratricide on the other.

Fratricide with my bare fucking hands.

As the endless afternoon wears on, my mother won't leave me alone about my 'mood'.

'What's wrong with you? You've had that face on

this whole time.' She sloshes some of my beer when she hands me the bottle.

'Nothing's wrong.' I take a long pull. 'Seriously, Mama. Same face as always.'

'Not the same as always.' She hands beers to my brother, who's already half in the bag, my father, my uncles, my grandfather, all leaned forward, practically falling off the edge of their seats as they scream at the UFC fight on TV. 'You haven't smiled in I don't know how long. I can't remember the last time. Tobar, do you remember the last time Winchester smiled?'

My father looks up from the fight and pinches my mom on the ass. She squeals and he smiles at her, then frowns in my general direction.

'Sure. Just the other day. He was wearing that pink bonnet with all the bows on it, and he smiled so pretty, I wanted to take a picture. Look, the boy says he's fine, Jazmin. I'm sure he's fine. Leave him the hell alone.'

He pats her backside and refocuses on the game.

My mother clucks her tongue and scratches my head with her long, sparkly silver fingernails. Pissed off as I am, I love when my mom scratches my head like I'm a kid again.

'It's not like you. You're usually happier.'

'I think you're thinking of Remy,' I gripe, eyeing my brother, who's sitting on the couch with a boozy, oblivious smile on his face while our cousin shows him some stupid card trick he just learned.

Remy looks up at the sound of his name, and his happy smile skids a little. 'What's that?'

'Your brother!' Mama's voice rises to compete with the yells of the guys as the pummeling on the screen gets more intense. 'He doesn't look happy.'

Remy squints at me. 'Same ugly face as always.' He shrugs and adds, 'I think he's just lovesick.'

I grit my teeth. This is payback for the other night. Undeserved on my fucking part, since I mopped up his puke until his guts were empty, but that's another thing with my brother. When he gets blitzed, he conveniently forgets all the stupid shit he does.

Though his memory for my fuck-ups is totally sharp.

Mama leans closer, her dark hair falling over my shoulder.

'You could have asked Lala. I know this is a guys' thing, but she would have been so welcome to stay with me and the girls.'

One unintentional dickhead comment, and this is my punishment? I glare at Remy, who blinks with slow, unconcerned triumph.

'Mama, c'mon. Lala and I are done. How many times do I have to tell you that? Remy's just being a jackass.'

The slap on the back of my head is swift and brutal

as always, despite how soft and small her hands look.

'I'll wash your mouth out in that sink. I don't care how big you think you are. Don't use that language about your brother.'

My cousins snigger and I rub the lump already forming on the back of my head.

'Sorry, Mama,' I growl.

Thank God, she moves back to the kitchen, where I can hear all my aunts and sisters and female cousins laughing and screeching. Lala always fit in perfectly. She was usually the one who brought me my game beers, and sometimes she even perched on the edge of my chair and watched the fight, commenting coolly now and then so she could soak up the approving smiles of the other guys.

I have no idea if Evan would fit in, and I don't really want to find out. I want her to be separate from this part of my life. I want Evan to be all mine. And I don't want my family passing judgment or making comparisons.

I count down until the fight is over, then all through dinner. It's so loud and chaotic at the table, nobody notices how quiet I am. Except Benelli. She parks herself at my side, all ninety-eight intimidating pounds of relentless sister, and, just like I thought, Lala had called and outed me, which puts Benelli in high gear.

'Lala was pretty upset last night.' Her voice is low, her eyes on her pecsenye, the traditional pork dish every girl in my family learns how to make when she's in, like, kindergarten.

I wonder if Evan cooks.

'Winch?' My sister's voice interrupts my thoughts. 'She said you were with some girl from town.'

I scoop up a big mouthful of food so I can get my anger under control before I answer. My sister's long eyelashes bat fast, making those blue eyes of hers look all wide and innocent, and I want to tell her that she can save herself the trouble of attempting to use them on me. We've been close since we were kids, and I know every damn trick in her book. None of them work on me any more.

'I have no idea how Lala noticed anything. She spent the night dry-humping some professor.'

This time when Benelli's eyes go wide, it's because I shocked her, not because she's trying to manipulate me.

But Lala and my sister have some kind of girl treaty going. She brushes her hair back behind her ears and dives in for another round.

'She misses you, Winch. She knows she messed up, and she wants to make things right. I don't understand how a few weeks ago you could have been so in love with her, and now, over nothing, she's just cut out of your life?' Benelli grabs my hand and squeezes it hard, all her sharp little glittery rings biting into my skin. 'You guys are meant for each other. Don't give up on what you had.'

I shove my plate away, my appetite gone.

'You have no idea what the hell Lala and I had. And what we had is over anyway. No questions.'

I'd excuse myself, but there are too many damn people here for me to make a scene, so I sit it out while Benelli alternates between scowling at me and texting under the table.

Good. Maybe she's telling Lala I'm an asshole and she should keep her distance.

As soon as I can, I grab my keys and start to head out. My dad stops me with one strong hand on my shoulder.

'You headed by the shop? I need something out of the safe.'

'I can go if you need.'

That's what I'm officially around for.

Whatever anyone needs.

I move to the driveway and my dad follows, I know so he can sneak a cigarette while my mother's busy cleaning up after dinner.

My father was always a giant in my eyes. Now I have two inches on him and his sagging stomach slows him down a little. It's not as bad as the feeling

I get when I'm around my brother, but I hate that the giants of my youth are shrinking.

He squints at me. 'Look, I don't want to nag at you. Your mother does enough of that, God bless her. But is everything all right?'

I nod. 'Everything's fine,' I lie.

'If you were thinking about getting a ring for Lala, use my guy on Bleak. He's got a hard nose, but he owes me a favor.' My father rubs his hand over his chin in thought. 'If you need a raise—'

I hold a hand up. 'No, it's fine. Lala and I aren't together.'

I've said it so many times, everyone should be pretty clear on it, but, for some reason, no one seems to hear what I say.

'You aren't together *today*.' My dad chuckles, the crow's-feet next to his blue eyes deeper than I remember them. 'Young love, boy, it's a funny thing. Your mother is the single best thing that ever happened to me. I hope . . .'

His voice goes low, and he leans so close I can smell the smoky cling of the Marlboro he snuck in before dinner. 'Just, look what not having a woman's touch has done to Remington. Boys will be boys for so long, but men need women to make a full life. Lala is a good girl, she's got her priorities straight, she fits in, she's loyal to you. She'll make you happy in the long run, and that's what really matters. Don't wait too long, or someone else will scoop her up.'

There's no point in arguing. I nod along, ask my dad what he needs me to get, and head out. Now that I'm on an errand, I can take my sweet time and no one will bug me.

I text Evan, but don't get a reply. I'm in and out of my father's shop in a few minutes, and I'm only a few streets over from her, so I circle her block.

The lights in her house are all out except one of the upstairs windows. I wonder if she's out, since I told her that I didn't know if I'd be able to get away tonight. I don't expect her to sit around waiting for me. I might secretly want her to, but I don't expect it.

I pull down a side street by her house, park, and walk as nonchalantly as I can so I don't arouse any suspicion. Not that I have to worry, since my talent for blending in is so good, it's almost like I have the ability to become invisible. I keep my eyes on my phone and don't get a second glance from the couple walking their dog and the old lady watering her plants.

Which is good, because I'm about to jump the wall that rings the garden outside Evan's grandparents' house like a shady burglar.

I know from talking to her last night that her room has a balcony and overlooks the garden.

It's a match for the lit window.

I hop the fence and walk quietly through the flowers and shrubs, scale the wall, gripping the brick and finding footholds while trying to keep quiet. I jump to the first low roof right under her balcony. The French doors are open, and the curtains flutter in and out in the light breeze.

I check my phone again, but there's nothing from her. Just when I'm sure I made a mistake and she isn't home after all, I see her silhouette in the room.

'Evan!' I call, keeping my voice low. 'Evan! Are you there?'

The curtain whips to the side, and Evan is there, so beautiful, it kicks the breath out of my lungs.

Her long, dark hair is damp and kind of curls at the bottom. She's wearing a tiny tank top and even tinier shorts, so she's all never-ending tanned legs and smooth arms. And her face is scrubbed clean, no make-up.

She doesn't need any. The way her eyes are so blue, with those soft black lashes, her lips and cheeks stained pink, she's too damn beautiful to cover it with anything at all. She leans down and all her hair tumbles over her shoulders.

'Winch!'

The way she says my name, like she's excited to see me, like I'm the one person she's been waiting for, burns away every stray shred of irritation I had stored up after the long day with my family.

'Hey, beautiful. You have a minute for me?'

'Why didn't you call? I would have gotten dressed if you wanted to go out somewhere.'

She tucks her hair back behind her ears and it makes them stick out just a little bit.

'I texted. You must have been in the shower. But it's cool. I like having you here, all to myself.'

Being out in the night, looking up at her, all clean and sexy and mine, turns me a little romantic.

'Are you sure it's not just because you're being super cheap?' she teases.

I take a few steps back, give myself a decent head start and jump at her balcony.

Evan lets out this little yelp, but doesn't miss a beat. She grabs me by the wrists while I swing my feet up and get enough traction to scale the side. I fall over the edge and into her arms, and she's laughing so hard, she can barely breathe.

'Are you insane?' she gasps, wiping hysterical tears from her eyes with the back of her hand.

I pull her face close and kiss her, soft at first, then hungrier.

'Nah,' I say when I pull back, liking the way her eyes stare at me all big and bright. 'Not cheap either. But I am damn excited to be spending time with you.

Put some clothes on, and I'll take you somewhere swanky to eat. Wherever you want.'

She traces her fingers down my cheek.

'I'm not hungry. For food.'

'Where are your grandparents?'

I look through the curtains billowing in and out, to her open bedroom door and the hallway past it.

'They are at a golf tournament and dinner in South Carolina. They'll probably get a room for the night.' She bites the edge of her bottom lip, and my body goes rigid. 'We could hang out.'

'I'd love to.' I thread my fingers through hers and try to steady myself. I've got time, no need to rush things. 'You have a pretty sweet view from here. It looks like a jungle down there.'

She peeks down, and I let go of her hand and watch while she paces along the edge of the balcony.

'It does, right? I love it. This was always my room in the summer, when I stayed with my grandparents while my parents went out and wandered all over the world.'

She leans her elbows on the ledge and arches her back, giving me heart palpitations. I sit in one of the little wrought-iron chairs set up on the balcony and enjoy the view.

'Every summer?'

Who would leave this girl anywhere for any

amount of time? I'm already pissed off that my chances of being able to stay all night with her are slim to none with Remy currently riding the fucking crazy train.

'Every summer,' she echoes, her words dry.

I hold my hand out to her, and when she takes it, I thread her delicate fingers with mine and pull her, all coltish legs and wild hair and fresh-smelling skin, down onto my lap.

'Did you like staying here?' I can smell the shampoo on her damp hair, sweet and flowery.

'Yes.' She snuggles against my chest, and I wrap my arms around her, memorizing all the lines and curves of her body. 'My parents are high maintenance. High drama. It was so nice to be here and just not have to deal with their shit for a while.'

I kiss her right along her hairline, loving having her in my arms and listening to the smoky, honeyed sound of her voice in the hot night. 'When did you last see your parents?'

Her sigh loosens all the tightness out of her muscles, and she sags against me at the final exhale.

'Mom went to Cabo in May, so the end of my junior year. Daddy hung around until July, but I was in Ireland at this writing workshop, so I came straight back to my grandparents', like I do every year, but this summer I never left. It's no big deal anyway. Next year is college.'

I bet she can hear how hard my heart is beating,

and I wonder if she realizes it's all because I'm here with her.

'Where are you going to college?'

I mentally calculate the number of months I'll have with her before she leaves and, probably, starts a new life that I won't be part of.

I can't be part of.

It's been hard enough to be with her just the last few weeks when we live ten minutes away from each other. How the hell would I manage years and possibly hundreds of miles?

'My grades are pretty bad.' She cranes her neck to look up at me. 'I'm not dumb.'

I tug on a piece of her hair and narrow my eyes her way. 'I know. I don't date dumb girls.'

She twists in my arms so we're face to face, the tip of her nose brushing my cheek, her big blue eyes staring into mine.

'Are we?'

'Are we what?' I struggle to keep an even handle on my breathing as she wraps her legs around my back and twines her arms around my neck.

'Dating?' She brushes her lips over mine while she asks, and my brain feels like it's been in an industrial explosion.

'Yeah.' I manage to keep my voice calm. 'We're dating.'

'You didn't even ask me.' She pops her bottom lip out, I kiss it, she smiles.

'I'm not asking. Asking means you might be crazy enough to say "no", and I'm not taking "no" for an answer.'

I kiss her hard, pulling at her until she's firmly on my lap and caged in my arms. I kiss her until I feel the breaths rasp out of her mouth and taste her sweet little moans. I run my hands over her body, hot and smooth under the practically nonexistent shirt and shorts she's wearing.

When she drops back, her swollen lips part and her eyes, slammed wide open, look almost black with too much pupil.

'I think you may have made some really good points about you and me being in any kind of a relationship. I don't really remember them, though.'

She sucks the corner of her bottom lip in and bites down just enough to make all kinds of insane, sexy images run through my head.

I tug her hips closer, and she nudges her lips onto mine. This time I make sure that I slow down and keep things steady until she's imprinted against me without an inch of space. And then her hand goes down to my fly, and I hit the brakes.

Not yet. Not before she's totally mine, and it means what I want it to mean to her.

'You never answered my college question.' I grab at her wrists like we're just playing, but hold her hands back with real intent.

Her scowl looks like it may turn into a bite. 'I don't want to talk right now.'

I slide my hands down so I'm holding hers and run my thumbs over the skin of her wrists, where I can feel the excited drum of her pulse. It's hard for my pulse to resist getting infected by that beat.

'I *do* wanna talk. I wanna know about you. So get talking.'

'You're pretty damn bossy, and I don't know if I like it.'

She softens that gorgeous mouth, bats those pretty eyes, and leans that curved body close.

I give her one quick kiss and say, 'Bossy is how I am, take it or leave it. Now quit trying to seduce me, and tell me about college.'

She sighs, rolls her shoulders, crosses her arms, glares, but I'm stone. I bounce her on my legs, because it's damn hard to look tough when you're getting shaken all over the place. I give her major credit; that stubborn little ass tries like hell to keep a pissy face, but she finally laughs and swats at my arms.

'Fine! Stop! I give up, and you're shaking my brains.' She presses her hands on either side of her head. 'OK, college is weird right now. I applied to Trinity—'

'In Ireland?' I ask, and love the way surprise widens her eyes.

For a delinquent, I'm surprisingly well-informed about world topics.

'Yes, in Ireland. Because I wrote this essay in a program they hosted over the summer, and I guess it impressed the big shots there—'

'Can I read it?' I interrupt.

'Stop interrupting. Yes. Not now, though. So I applied to Trinity, in Ireland. And I applied to Rutgers in New Jersey, because my best friend lives there and it's one of her safety schools, so even if we don't get into our top schools, at least we'll have a decent chance of being together. Plus it's huge and close to New York City, which I feel, weirdly, might become like a second home for me. Plus it's a state school, so it's not as grade-crazy as some of the private schools.'

She takes a hair thingy off her wrist and puts her hair into a sloppy ponytail. 'I applied to SCAD for dance, but I don't know if I want to do that. I've fallen behind in the last year, and I don't know if I'm as passionate about it anymore.'

'What about Armstrong or Georgia Southern?'

I run my fingers up and down her arms for the pure joy of seeing all the dots of goosebumps on her skin, while I pray she decides to stay local next year.

She wrinkles her nose. 'SCAD is bad enough. I

want to get out of here. I figured art school will at least keep me away from all the preppy silver-spooners I've been around all my life.'

She makes her two fingers walk up my arm and do a little jig on my bicep.

My laugh feels like an old shirt shaken out of a suitcase, wrinkled but still wearable. I nod at her fingers, still doing a vicious little jig.

'Is this the kind of dancing you do? That Irish stuff where they have all that bouncy hair?'

'How do you know about step-dancing, Mr Youngblood?'

She scoots off my lap with a grin, and I shrug.

'My kid sister Ithaca found this crazy movie about some Irish kid who does all that dancing, and she made mom drag her to all these classes. Winds up, she was only interested in that fake bouncy hair, so my parents got her some and she quit the dancing.'

I never talk about either of the twins with anyone outside the family. They've been pretty damn protected from everything since we were young. They even go by mom's maiden name, Wharton, so they could get a clean slate at their stuck-up private school.

'I'll have to meet this Ithaca and show her there's so much more to it than bouncy hair. Though the hair is pretty damn cool.'

I stiffen at her words.

Ithaca never got along with Lala, which makes sense, since my baby sister is the outspoken rebel of the family, and Lala's all about a woman's place and shit like that.

But Ithaca'd probably love Evan.

The problem is, anyone or anything my baby sister loves would almost definitely be shunned by everyone else in my family.

Evan brushes the curtain aside and moves into her bedroom. She stands up straight on the shiny wood floor, leaves her arms relaxed but straight at her sides, and starts this complicated dance where her legs and feet move fast and precisely with all these high, quick kicks and twists. She's a natural; totally graceful, totally comfortable with her body, and I can't take my eyes off of her while she dances.

When she finishes and takes a bow, I clap and call out, 'Bravo! Bravo! Encore! Encore!'

Her cheeks glow bright pink, and her ponytail fell out when she was dancing, so her hair is all tangled around her neck. She shakes her head and comes back to me, sitting on the ledge of the balcony.

'Nope. You gave me the third degree and got some of my deepest, darkest secrets out. Now I want some of yours. Who are you, Winchester Youngblood? Why aren't you in college? Will I ever get to meet these intriguing siblings named after guns? What are your plans for the future?'

Each question is a spear stab to my gut.

I get up, hook my arms around her, nestle between her legs, and lean in to kiss her. She kisses me once, short and sweet and pushes me back.

'No way. You can't use my own tricks on me.' Her hands link lazily around my neck. 'You know, the fact that you don't want to answer any of my questions just makes me more curious. What are you hiding from me?'

This is the logical next jump for us. It makes sense that if I care about Evan, I'll open up and let her see what I keep closed tight. I'm afraid to blow this night wide open, make her question whether or not she should be with me.

Because the answers to her questions aren't going to make her happy, and I know that for a fact.

Because it's been a long time since the answers to any questions about my life made *me* happy.

Which is a whole different problem, all its own.

Evan 7

Pushing forward physically equals pulling away emotionally for Winchester.

I feel like such a girl to put it in those terms, but that is the God's honest truth. If the following fact makes the truth any more palatable, here it is: I so desperately want Winch to get tangled up with me physically, I'm almost willing to put our emotional connection on the sacrificial altar and carve it up with a big, bad knife.

Almost willing.

Winch has pestered me about the sexy way I see myself, which never bothered me one tiny bit until he started doing that thing where he clenches his jaw and shakes his head really quickly.

It's kind of hot, getting him riled.

Mmm, so very hot.

But not what I want.

I want Winch to respect me.

So, I pull away physically, and push him towards sharing and stories about himself. I do it because

Winch is becoming more real by the nanosecond, and I want all that. I want to connect with this mysterious boy on a deeper level and not have it be just a wild romp.

No matter how deliciously perfect a wild romp would be.

'Tell me,' I coax. 'I can see in your eyes that you're about sixty percent of the way to spilling your guts.'

His cheekbones get this red tinge, like he might be blushing, and I have no clue why, but I figure it means I'm punching big ole dents in his armor. 'Let's start with simple stuff. Where did you graduate high school?'

'I got my GED.' He throws his chiseled chin out and looks at me from the comfort of narrowed eyes.

'You've got nothing to prove to me.' I keep my voice lazy as a fat cat on a warm lap. 'I'm barely passing the basics at my fancy li'l prep school. I think it's harder to get your GED. No teacher holding your hand and making sure you finish your work. It's all on you to pass the test. Did you think about college?'

I put my arms over my head and run my hands through the tangles in my hair to keep everything light and easy, but also because I thoroughly enjoy the way his mouth drops open when he notices my breasts straining against the front of my shirt.

'No.' He snaps his mouth shut, and I like it. I love

it, actually, the effect I have on him. 'College isn't for me.'

'How would you know if you didn't try?' I challenge, raising my arms higher over my head and smoothing my hair into the world's slowest, most perfect ponytail.

His swallow is so loud it's practically in surround sound.

'Because my family owns a business, so I came out of high school with a job lined up. That's the whole point of college, right? To line up a good job. But I had one, so I figured I was way ahead of all those over-educated jerks paying out the ass for a piece of paper most of 'em would never use.'

I pat my hair and practice my best round-eyed, admiring look on him. 'Oh. So, what kind of work do you do?'

He doesn't even twitch. It's like watching a rabbit hop into a snare.

'My family owns a few businesses. I make runs for them. Settle accounts. Practice diplomacy when it's needed.'

He inches closer, and I hop off the balcony ledge and move into my room, toward my desk, bending over to pick up imaginary scraps of paper so I can keep his attention and get him to talk more.

I don't even take a second to truly process what

he's telling me or unjumble exactly what I think about it. I need to shake the information out of the tree like so much ripe fruit and grab every piece before it goes rotten. I'll be able to paw through it all with my full attention later. He follows me in and leans against the frame of the French doors.

Winchester's eyes are very firmly planted on my backside, so I ease out the next question, trickier than the last two.

'And what about Remington? What happened the other night?'

I have a nice, round backside, plenty of cushion, but shapely and proportionate. More than one guy has declared my backside the finest he's ever seen, but it's not enough to keep Winch on track.

Like he's snapping out of a spell, he gives a groggy shake of his head and runs a hand over his hair.

'Nothing. It's nothing. I told you, my brother's in a little bit of a bad place right now, but he's coming through fine. Just fine.'

I stop shaking my rump, stand up and look at him.

I really look.

His eyes are shifty. His mouth is drawn tight to one side. He cracks every knuckle on one hand. Because he's worried. He's upset. And he can't trust me enough to tell me why.

I stop all the stupid crap, all the pouting and booty

shows and just go and sit by his side. I reach one hand over and knit his fingers with mine, then take an extra deep breath.

For a few quiet beats, neither one of us moves or talks or does a single thing except settle into the art of being together.

'My daddy is a stupid, stupid man,' I start, embarrassed that my voice is only a whisper, but that's the loudest I can manage. 'He bets on things—' I shake my head so hard my own ponytail whips my face. 'He bets on things that lose. Always. It's like reverse luck. You can always count on my daddy to pick the loser.'

I try to pull my hand away, and I tell myself it's just to wave a stray piece of hair out of my eyes, but I know, deep inside, that I need to not be physically connected to Winch while I tell this. His eyes snap at me, like your loyal dog trying to warn you there's danger ahead, willing to bite to make you listen. He squeezes my hand, and I hold tight because he gives me no choice, and the words keep pouring out.

'I can always pick the winners, though.' I eye him to see if this lucky titbit interests him in the 'let's go bet on the horses' sense, but he just watches my eyes and leans forward, anticipating my next words. 'Seriously, always. Like magic. I could be rich, picking horses. I'm that good, no joke. Daddy figured it out when I was tiny, of course. And, at first, I helped him.'

'Hamburger days?' Winch finally breaks in, remembering the story I told him earlier.

'Yes. Well, they came later.' I squirm, but there's no turning back. 'For a while we were swimming in money. There was no losing. We had it all, and it seemed so damn easy. Then ... eventually we lost everything . The house I grew up in. My school tuition. My mama. She left because Daddy was such an embarrassment, losing all the time. Losing can make you really ... distant. And mean. And weak. And he just kept losing.'

I can't bring myself to tie it all together. I look sideways, begging Winch with every worry line to figure this whole damn story out and not ask me to say the obvious.

The rabbit and the snare? It was never Winch walking into the trap. He hopped close and wiggled his nose in disdain.

I'm the idiot with one furry foot in the noose, about to be slit and skinned for the pot with my unlucky foot on someone's keychain, an ironic good fortune trinket.

He brings my hand to his lips and kisses my knuckles with a ticklish brush. 'You don't have to tell me.'

I take my furry foot back out of the trap and get ready to hop into some clover.

But the relief in his eyes stops me in my tracks.

So this is where we are?

I say nothing, he says nothing, we lose nothing, we gain nothing.

It's cowardice.

I put my foot right back in that noose, the pot be damned. I need to get caught by Winch. I need to trust that he wants me for more than my lucky foot.

'I could have stopped it.' My voice is firm and heavy with leaden shackles of shame.

He shakes his head, and pulls me closer.

'Listen to me. You couldn't, OK? What your old man wanted to do, that was his business and you—'

'Could have stopped it.' I slice into his excuse for me and shred it with a single, gentle slash.

'Don't do this to yourself,' he warns, his voice frantic for both of us.

I'm about to drag us into danger, out of the natural orbit of our day-to-day. We're two cowards. We ignore the fact that life slips by while we're busy hiding out, unwilling to risk living if it means we might fall into a trap along the way. We're supreme cowards.

But I want to change that. I can do it. I can start the change.

'I could have saved my parents' marriage.' I let the words march out and trample our delicate field of lies, spoken and unspoken. 'I could have gotten him money. I could have picked the right damn horse every single time, Winch. Every time. It would have taken me less than a few hours a week. And we would have been living together, rich as thieves.'

My voice shakes around this one version of a fairy-tale ending that exists, bright and clear, in the depths of my imagination.

He moves his lips in several shapes that look like they'll disagree, then his mouth snaps into a frustrated scowl.

'So why not?' His words lash out. 'Why not make it easy, Evan? What did you gain? Daddy and Mommy split. You got pushed out of your house, out of your life. The money is wasted. Your father is probably ashamed. Why do that?'

I let the trap engage and feel gravity release its hold on me as I'm jerked through the air.

There are four tears on my face, and I have to coat every nerve in steel to keep any more from falling.

'I did it because . . . it got out of control way too fast.' I gasp. I am swinging way out of my comfort zone, kicking for ground that's way out of reach. 'He was using me. He was losing himself. She was a shell. We were in trouble. And it was the only shot . . . it was the one and only shot to make things right. Attempting to save my family was absolutely worth that gamble to me. But in the end—'

One sob wrenches from my throat, like the

bugle-loud cry of a wounded animal. 'In the end, neither one of my parents was strong enough to gamble on us. So it all fell apart.'

I wipe my eyes with the back of my free hand, moving it with quick, vicious strokes. 'My lucky eye doesn't work for me and the people I love. I couldn't see who would win when it came to my own family's fate, you know? It wasn't simple, like the horses. And I wound up getting slapped with what my dad must have felt.' A long, shuddery breath cycles in and out. 'Total and complete humiliation. I lost everything. I took a gamble on them and . . . stupid, so stupid, they let me down. They completely let me down in every way imaginable.'

I haven't even told this to Brenna. She would never, ever get it. Her family is so amazing and close. She'd do anything, anything at all to help them, and they'd do the same and more for her. And I'm genuinely happy that she has that. I would never want her to be in my shoes.

I thought Winch might get it, but now that it's splattered out between us and he's sitting like a boulder, it's clear I exploded something that he'll never understand and I can't put back now.

I never should have tried to pull us closer. I'm good at pushing. It's my specialty. I can push anything, anyone, far away with no hope of bringing back what I've torn asunder.

I push away from Winch, ready to joke about what a pansy I am, how stupid my pathetic life is, how right he would be to detest me and my disloyalty to my own damn parents. I'm swinging high above the ground, and I give up the fight and wait for the knife to slit my throat.

Only it doesn't.

'What you did . . .' Winch's voice trembles until I'm positive it's about to fracture. 'What you did is so fucking brave. You know that? Not many people would have the guts to do what you did.'

'My parents divorced. My life was ruined.'

I shove those bitter counter-arguments out under the glare of his judgment, only because I want him to strike them down.

And he does. 'Yeah. So they did. So it was. But you took a chance. You saw that things were wrong and you were brave enough to try to fix them. It's especially hard when it's your blood – your parents.' He pulls me closer, until I'm pressed against him. 'Trust me, your parents wish they were half as brave as you.'

He's cut the noose and let me hop free, unharmed.

'Why?' I press, giddy at my own freedom, the lightness confession has brought me, and the sweet relief of Winch's admiration.

'Because they live with all their own fears and

weaknesses every minute of every day, Evan. You set yourself free. That's . . . that's crazy. I've never heard of anything like that.' His voice pools around me, and it's like sinking into a bubble bath. 'I admire how brave you are. It's a pretty big turn on.'

'Oh yeah?'

I stare into his eyes, hunting me, and I'm happy to be his prey.

I should be ashamed, considering I just spilled my deepest, darkest secrets. But I'm just plain old horny.

Winchester Youngblood is in my room, a few feet from my big queen bed. My eyes go to the plush piece of furniture that dominates the space, calling to us, demanding us to roll around in the sheets. I want to. I want to so badly.

'My grandparents won't be home until morning. Why don't you work up the courage to ask me to fool around with you?'

For a split second, I expect him to pull back, tell me no, keep things clearly delineated between us. But then his arms snap around me, and he scoops me off the floor, walks me the few feet across the room, and plops me onto the bed.

I giggle for a minute, caught in the crazy jump of the bouncing mattress, then my giggle gets lost in the dark of Winch's stare.

Winch 7

She's lying under me on the bed, and I have my arms steepled over her, a human bridge over the river of her body. I should be doing more than staring down at her. My mouth, my hands, my body should be acting out every crazy hot scenario that's been torturing me and keeping me awake every night for these last few weeks.

But something is driving a wedge between me and the girl I haven't been able to stop thinking about since the day I met her.

Her hands slide under my shirt and press in a long, smooth glide up the skin of my back.

'Winch? Seriously, they're hours away. Even if they don't stay the night, they always call before they leave. We're so cool.'

I push myself over and move to sit next to her, on the edge of her bed, and out of her immediate vicinity.

'No, I know it. I'm not worried about that.'

I stroke one hand over her forehead, trying to press

away all those little worry lines that pop up whenever we spend too much time together.

'So, what is it?' The lines furrow deeper.

'I feel like a liar, I guess.' Her eyebrows knot, and I explain, 'You told me things I know were hard for you to put out there. And I gave nothing.'

Her lips purse into a perfect, sexy kissable shape.

'What does that have to do with you coming here' – she smoothes her hand over the spot next to her on the bed – 'and kissing me until I agree to all kinds of other bad things?'

'First of all, you know it's not going down like that.' I run a thumb over her lips and she sticks her tongue out and swipes my skin. I groan and try to keep a handle on my stupid, crazy urges. 'Secondly,' I manage to get out, 'I feel like a fraud. And I hate that. I always try to be honest with the people I care about.'

She gives me a long, patient look, batting her eyelashes at me every now and then until I'm having a hard time swallowing, then finally says, 'So be honest with me.'

'It's compl—' I cut myself off before I use my crutch of an excuse, but her groan interrupts me anyway.

'Just say it!' she cries. She sits up on the bed, knocking me back, and hugs her pillow to her chest with ferocious intent, her eyes humming with anger and frustration. 'Just say "complicated", OK? Don't lie to me, because *that* I can't deal with. But don't be afraid if you can't tell me the whole truth yet. That doesn't make you a fraud. It means you have issues, just like everyone else. I didn't tell you my secrets to get you to tell me anything you aren't ready to share. This isn't Truth or Dare. This is you and me. We can go at our own pace. All right?'

She's so beautifully honest.

And what she said? It's freeing. It makes me brave. It makes me want to be better, do better for her.

'OK.' I lie down next to her and hook our hands together. 'I need to tell you some things.'

She pushes her face closer, and her eyes are such a glassy blue, I feel like I can see through them.

'Remington, my brother, has some fucked-up shit going on in his life right now. He's got this girlfriend . . . I don't know if they're still a thing or not, you know? She loved him. She's a real cool girl, but Remy? Jesus Christ, he could tempt a saint. They have a kid. Remy's been . . . unstable. Mom and Benelli watch Alayah when he's got her, you know, so there's nothing to worry about. But he's a mess. A fucking mess.'

It feels like all of that was pressurized inside me, like shaken soda in a can, and I just popped the tab and let the whole damn mess explode out.

Evan trails her fingers down the sleeve of my shirt and pushes it up to my elbow. She lets the pads of her fingertips glide over the slightly raised skin and the black ink.

'It's beautiful.' Her eyes flick to mine, changing the subject, giving me an out if I want to take it.

I don't. I can't. I need to tell her. Everything.

'I got it for Remy.' I study the midnight details of that ferocious black horse on my skin. 'It's called a pooka. It's this animal, this creature that steals people and takes them on wild rides over the moors in Ireland. My brother has this thing for mythical crap, so he got a tattoo.'

The rest is hard to come out and say.

Evan nods, and the motion of her head on the pillow messes her hair up, so I reach up and pull the hairband out of her ponytail. Her hair spreads over her shoulders and makes little dark waves on the blankets. She leans in to kiss me, her mouth hot and urgent against mine, a distraction from talking about the tattoo and what it means.

If I have to choose between confessions about my brother's stupidity or Evan's irresistible sexiness, the choice is obvious. My hands pull and press all over her, first with the safety net of her tank and tiny shorts. Her tongue flicks in my mouth, and my brain backfires.

I lose the safety net and run my hands under her clothes and along the soft, hot skin of her stomach, up along her ribs, to the lacy edge of her bra, and before I put my hands under the cups, I pull them back down her stomach. She whimpers in protest, but it turns to a moan when I get to the waistband of her shorts. The whimper comes back in full force when I stop again.

She rocks her hips up in an effort to move my hand lower, but I'm locked where I am, in no man's land, my palm just over the dip of her bellybutton.

'Winch?'

Her fingers are at the back of my neck, kneading a place that, for some reason, makes me crazy.

'Yeah?'

I choke the word out.

'I know you didn't think it was funny when I joked about the guys I'd been with. But it wasn't *that* many. And I was always safe. Always. So if that's what's stop—'

'Shh.' I kiss her so she cuts her crazy confession short. 'Stop it! Now!' I look down at her. She's keeping her jaw tight and strong to offset her shaky, embarrassed words. 'I don't care if you've been with a thousand guys before me, all right? We're together now. That's all that matters. It's not you, nothing to do with you. There's nothing—'

I break off and look her up and down, letting it show on my face how sexy I find every single thing about her. 'There's *nothing* at all about you that's stopping me. Trust me, it's like an opposite problem. I feel like I gotta finish telling you some stuff. It's not fair to let you get involved with me if I don't. All right?'

Her smile is supposed to make me feel all good, like nothing could split us apart and everything is A-OK, but she has no clue. Not many girls outside my family's circle would want anything to do with the life I lead, which is why everyone in my life is pro-Lala. And would be anti-Evan on principle.

You have to be raised our way to understand how we do things and why.

Even I don't always understand. But it's my code. So I have to make it work. Now that I'm involved with Evan, I have to at least explain it to her. Even if it means I'll probably get an invitation to back the hell off her balcony in a few minutes.

I give her one last hard kiss, trying not to regret all the things I'm going to miss when she tells me to leave. I thought I'd be able to keep her separate from the rest of my life. I didn't count on feeling this impossible-to-ignore need to tell her everything.

I sit up again and rub my hands over my face, trying to talk myself back into a few more minutes with her curled in my arms, but I can't do it. It's all or nothing with this girl.

I say a quick prayer that I might get another swing after I tell her everything anyway and just dive in.

'This tattoo isn't really my thing.' I push my sleeve up and hold my arm out while I'm talking, like it's evidence in my criminal case, and I'm making one final appeal to Evan, asking her to save me from myself. 'I got it to protect Remy.'

She folds those gorgeous long tanned legs so she's sitting cross-legged.

Focus, I tell myself.

'This tattoo was something I had to get.' I flex my arm and the pooka jumps. Evan wants to ask: I can see her working to keep her mouth shut, but she definitely wants to know.

'Remy'd been fucking up and causing shit everywhere he went. He's always been . . .' I need to tell her more, but my inner loyalty sucker-punches me. This is my brother I'm about to talk shit about. I have no business revealing his secrets to someone outside the family.

I look over at her, her eyes right on my face, totally trusting, and I realize that I trust her, too. Blood or not, this girl belongs to me in a way I can't deny, and she deserves to know the truth.

I take a deep breath. 'Remy's always been a fucking

loose cannon. But nothing too serious. Then he met his ex, or whatever they are, and things got good for a while. He got her pregnant, and then . . . he just wasn't ready, I guess. He just didn't get that he needed to grow the hell up. It was like he was thinking he'd get to be an even bigger kid now that he was having one or something. And his girl got tired of all his stupid shit, and she left him.'

I rub the heels of my hands into my eyes, wishing brain bleach were a real thing, because I'd love to sanitize some of the crazy, awful despair I watched my brother go through from my memory for ever.

'I'm sorry for him,' Evan says, laying her hands loosely in mine. 'I know how that can be. To have someone in your life, and when they leave, it's like they were holding all the water back, and your ship just starts sinking without them. Even if the two of you weren't right together.'

I try to picture her that night in the orchard, the flames licking the grass and the bark of those big old trees, and I bet I know exactly what she was feeling: this weird mix of panic and adrenaline, like the slate is finally clean.

The problem is, it never lasts. Destruction never solves the situation in the long run. Remington crushes things, smashes them, rips them apart, and feels that surge of satisfied power for about an hour or two.

When it all falls apart, when I come in to act as his personal cleanup crew, all he's left with is an emptiness that he can't ever beat his way out of.

'I'm sorry for him, too.' I kiss her palms, one, then the other. 'But he's a black hole right now. He sucks everything in and destroys it. He's dangerous. To himself and to the people around him.'

'To you?' Her voice is just-above-a-whisper hushed.

I stare at the pooka. 'I got this tattoo because Remington went on a bender. He did a shitload of stupid crap in a few hours, and the tattoo kept getting brought up in descriptions.'

I look up at her face, but she hasn't recognized the ugly constellation because of all the dull stars I've thrown into her sky.

'You got a matching tattoo?' Her fingers drum on her thigh. 'Why?'

'After his night of fucking mayhem, Remington went too far, and there were witnesses who made statements. The tattoo was in a few of them. So I needed one that was the same when I showed up in court.'

The missile of my insane confession just hissed from the sky to the ground and is about to detonate.

'You were with him that night? You did some stupid stuff, too?'

The desperate sadness in her eyes tells me she knows my answer before I have to say it.

'No.'

I can see the moment it explodes in full force for Evan.

Her head tilts to the side and she squints at me, like she's seeing a different version of me, one she isn't sure she likes.

Her words come out slow and low. 'You look enough like him. Jace thought you were him, close up. You took the blame.'

A half-dozen emotions ricochet over her face, none of them good.

'You *take* the blame!' she accuses, her eyes flashing, her head shaking back and forth. '"House of the Rising Sun" is Remington's ringtone. You know you have to leave when you hear it because you have to go get your brother out of trouble.'

She unfolds her legs and paces the room. I watch her walk back and forth, back and forth on those amazing legs, those legs that I wish were wrapped around me right now.

She turns to me and asks, 'Is this just a recent thing? Just since he broke up with his girlfriend?'

I give serious consideration to lying, before I settle on a soft variation of the truth.

'It's gotten more extreme in the last few months.'

She turns on her heel and stomps back toward me. If she wasn't so damn beautiful, I'd say she looked like a bull I just waved a bigass red cape at. She catches my wrist and twists my arm around so my tattoo is level with my eye.

'You marked your body. Permanently,' she accuses, her voice ice cold. 'You have a criminal record. Permanently.'

Her manicured fingers pack a bite I'm not expecting.

'You're being melodramatic, Evan. His blood runs through me. What's a little ink? And I had a record before.'

'*You* had a record for *your* crimes? Or you carried your brother's record?' Her chest rises and falls with an intense, mounting fury.

'He's my family. You don't understand. His crimes are my crimes. His record is mine. The Youngblood name isn't a one member thing. It's all of us, together, against everyone else.'

I lose my trademark calm and my voice picks up.

'Against everyone else?' The question punctures the quiet left by my declaration of loyalty. 'Or against each other? Because what he's doing seems to be hurting you pretty exclusively unless I'm missing something serious.'

Her blue eyes hold wide and fierce, like some kind of battle leader's.

What she's saying is obvious; it's not like I haven't been thinking this for years.

I've been thinking the same thing since the first whipping I took for Remy, and then after every detention and suspension, four stints in juvenile detention, six in community service, and three years on probation, but I've never had to do any hard time. Yet. My luck has held all these years, but the rope is getting shorter and my time is running out fast.

Soon people like Judge Schwenzer will work their asses off to rip this whole thing open, and I might go to jail, or get shipped to the family compound in no-name backwoods Hungary. That's the inevitable end to this road unless Remy makes some huge changes soon.

And I'm not enough of an idiot to hold my breath waiting for my dipshit brother to change his stripes.

But there's something about hearing someone gorgeous and funny and brilliant say this truth to me.

There's also the fact that, as obvious as this might be, it's also way more complicated and only partially true.

I can't tell her that, though. Mainly because I'd be using one of her least favorite words: 'complicated'. There's a sick, sinking feeling right in the center of my gut. This isn't jail or probation, but it's the beginning of the end of the first thing I've really wanted in longer than I can remember.

'I hear you. Really I do.' I stand up and check my pocket for my keys.

They've fallen out and are lost in the bright mass of blankets and sheets on her bed. I pick through all the bedding I was just rolling around with her in to grab them. She's looking at the floor. 'And I know, it's fucked up, especially if you're outside looking in. But it's the way we do things, all of us, every lowdown stupid Youngblood. It's my way. And not everyone is OK with it. I can't blame you for not being able to accept that.'

I'm so close I can smell the wildflower burned-sugar mix coming off her skin, and I want to bury my damn face in it and breathe it all night. But she's just one more thing on an increasingly long list of amazing things that aren't meant to be part of my life.

'Evan? I'm gonna get lost, all right?'

I run my finger along the smooth curve of her shoulder one last time, for luck.

'You're leaving?' Her blue eyes are perfectly still and focused on mine. Fury makes them look hot and clear. 'I get that you might not like hearing the truth, but that's it? That's all you can take?'

'Wait. I thought . . . you said . . . the whole thing

with Remy? The tattoo? Wasn't that, like, an invitation for me to fuck off?'

A dangerous edge of hope runs through me. One word pulses through my mind: maybe.

'I said your stupid brother seemed to be messing things up for you. If I wanted you to fuck off, I would have said, "Fuck off, Winch".'

Her smile is probably a little forced, but mine sure as hell isn't. Here's the chance I was praying for. I held my breath and rolled the dice, and my luck stayed; I came up with an eleven on the first go.

'What are you smiling about?' she asks.

I tuck her into my arms and rub my face in the soft mass of her hair. 'You. Me. That big old bed and your grandparents all the way in South Carolina.'

She sits back on the mattress, and I sit with her. She leans back and I follow. We've said enough sour truths for one day; we give ourselves a break and put our mouths to much better use. Her lips are quick and eager, and I'm so tempted a dozen different times to follow her lead like some poor sailor chasing a siren's call right into the jagged ocean rocks.

But I can't.

This deserves taking our time, so tonight, it's all about her.

She's attempting to wiggle out of her clothes for the third time when my phone rings: 'House of the Rising

Sun'. I crush my teeth together so tight my jaw aches.

She catches her sigh and staples it back.

'Go ahead. It's been the ruin of many a fantastic make-out session,' she mutters, bitterly changing a line from the song. She thumps a pillow over her face, muffling a furious line of obscenities.

I zip my pants back up and walk to the balcony, figuring I can go back in for my shirt and shoes if I need to leave. I really hope to hell I don't need to leave.

'This is Winchester.'

The bugs make a wild buzz in the dark garden below and the moon is low and almost full with a yellow tinge. I want to go back in, switch off Evan's light, and not face whatever it is that needs my attention on the other end of the line.

'Wi'shester,' Remy slurs.

'Where are you?'

I should be putting my shirt back on. I should have my feet in my shoes and be jumping down the balcony to find him, now, before he breaks more unfixable shit.

A low, keening whine breaks over the phone line, leaving me half deaf.

'Phine!' he screams. 'Phine, I know you're there!'

I hear what sounds like my idiot-fucking-brother stumbling over garbage cans, doors opening and slamming shut, and yelling.

I click the phone off and grab my shirt and shoes. Evan is shaking her head. I have no time, but I stop anyway.

'I'm so sorry. You have no idea how sorry I am. He's at his ex's house right now. I don't want her and my niece to get caught in this.' I take her hands and she nods at me.

'Can I come?'

I shake my head. 'You don't need to see this. It's gonna get ugly.'

'Sometime can I come with you when the phone rings?' She chews on her bottom lip. 'Or is the phone like your personal Bat Signal? Do you fight this fight alone?' She pulls her voice low and throaty.

It's not a time for jokes, but that doesn't stop me from laughing.

'Your Dark Knight impression is damn sexy.' I kiss her, and the minute our lips brush, I want more. 'Wow. This fucking blows. Can I make it up to you?'

'Breakfast tomorrow?' She raises her eyebrows eagerly.

Shit. 'Can't.' I finish tying my shoes and kiss her again. She's intoxicating. 'I have mass.'

'I'll come,' she offers, and I immediately imagine her in the old church where my entire family and Lala's goes for hours every Sunday, and I panic.

'No! I mean, it's so boring. And the service is in

Hungarian. I do it for my mom, you know?' I can see she's trying to hide how my rejection is crushing her. 'Can I get you for a late breakfast? Just you and me.'

'And the phone?' She crosses her arms.

I hesitate. 'I can't really turn it off, but—'

'Promise you'll take me if it rings,' she cuts in.

Her blue eyes narrow when I open my mouth to turn her down one more time.

I can't.

I'm swimming with a laceration in shark-infested waters.

No reason to panic. I've managed way bigger shit than this. I'll just have to make sure my goddamn phone doesn't ring.

'OK. It's a deal.'

I lean in and kiss her one more time, trying to trap the sweet, hot smell and feel of her that's already getting addictive, and I have to go. I rip myself away, run to the balcony, and jump down the way I came, landing hard on my feet. I slide down the wall fast, and take one second to glance back in the yellow-mooned night.

She's standing on the balcony, leaning on her elbows, long, dark hair falling over her shoulders, her skin bright in the moonlight, and my pang of regret is knee-weakening.

Maybe I really won't have to worry about my fucking phone tomorrow. Because there's a damn good chance I'll wind up beating Remy to a bloody, unconscious pulp tonight.

Evan 8

'And then?' Brenna's like a little kid drooling over her favorite candy in the bright store window.

I'm like the dentist, showing up with a drill to remind her she has a mouthful of cavities.

'And then his phone rang.'

'No!' And just like a sugar-deprived kiddo, I wonder if she's going to tantrum over this devastating development. 'Was it "House of the Rising Sun"? Did he leave? Are you seeing him again?'

Her questions pummel my tired brain.

'Yes,' I sigh. 'And yes. And yes.'

I try to make the last one sound as reluctant as the first two, but there's no sneaking anything past my best friend when it comes to feelings and romance. She's the Sherlock Holmes *and* Watson of love.

'What are the rules? You can't just let him show up after he leaves and waltz right back out with him.' She gives me time to answer.

'I . . . I just want to be with him, Bren.'

'Evan!' she wails, only she takes the two syllables of my name and pulls them into twenty-two. 'You can't do this to yourself again. You got so wrapped around Rabin and his games, and look where that wound up, sweetie.'

I prop the phone on my dressing table and plop down in front of the mirror to begin my long, involved make-up routine.

'Winch is nothing like Rabin. Nothing. Seriously, there are no games. It's just who he is, what he has to do. And I have to compromise a little because of that. But he's definitely not another Rabin.'

I want to list all the differences between the two of them, but that smacks of desperation. Instead I focus on blending my foundation.

I can hear Brenna deep-breathing before she pours her warning out.

'Listen to me, because I'm going to tell you what you need to hear, all right? Here we go. Rabin and Winch. Similarities? Both rich. Both in trouble with the law. Both have a shady past with girls. Both come in and out of your life without explaining why they keep disappearing. Both have you waiting in your room for them to show up. Both lack commitment, work ethic—'

'He's nothing like that,' I interrupt in a blaze of fury that shocks me into gulped silence.

This is *Brenna*, my best friend, the person who I trust to be honest with me. If she won't tell me the bald truth, who will? So why am I on the defensive? I wait a few beats, but the line is so quiet, I'm nervous she hung up on my stupid ass.

'Bren?'

'I'm here.' Her words are clipped and strained with hurt.

'Didn't mean to snap.' I keep my voice tiny in an attempt to control the emotion welling up in the back of my throat.

I can feel her sigh practically move my curtains through the phone.

'I love you. So much. And I want you to be careful with yourself sweetie, because, can we face it? You're not. You're so not! You let guys in before you should. And I don't know anything about this guy, but what I do know, I really don't like. I could be wrong.'

Her last four words come out with so little conviction, I know she's not even trying to trick me into believing she means them.

'I know.' I pick up my mascara and begin my neat, precise eighteen-coat application for luck. 'I know you love me, and I love you right back. But loosen the strings, Mama. I promise, this guy is different. I know what he seems like, but it's just that he's—'

I bite the word back.

'Evan? I think the connection dropped.' Brenna's voice trembles with anxious worry.

'No, I'm here. I was just saying that Winch is a little . . . complicated. But I promise you, I'll keep my eyes open this time.'

I suck my cheeks in and sweep blusher over my apples and tell myself to keep calm.

Keep calm.

Brenna's little snort is fueled by the sting of my earlier jab, and in the mirror I see my cheeks go pink under my blusher.

'There's nothing like thinking you're in love to glue your eyes shut.' She clears her throat. 'Well, have fun, but be careful.' Her strict mom-voice wavers. 'Seriously, take care of yourself. It was super-hard to watch you go through all that pain with Rabin. You're doing so much better. Just look out for yourself, OK?'

We both have huge lumps in our throats.

'OK,' I croak, batting back tears. 'Love you!'

'Love you more,' she warbles before she clicks off.

I know Bren loves me. I know she said what she did because it matters to her that I'm happy, safe and sane. No guy has ever made me snap at her before. But there's something about Winch. Something that makes me feel protective of him. And protected. And sure.

So I keep her warning in my head, but I decide to

dress like I don't have a doubt in the world when it comes to love and Winch.

I pull out a gorgeous white poplin strapless sun-dress and gold sandals that lace up my calves. The outfit makes me feel very Greek goddess, and when I hear Winch's car pull up, I have to force my knees to lock under me and wait. It feels like hours before the doorbell chimes.

I put both feet on each stair as I descend, convince myself to check my reflection in the hallway mirror, and leave my hand on the cool glass doorknob for a few extra beats, but it's all just stupid games. My heart is driving me to whip the door open quickly so I can see him again.

It's exactly like the feeling I get every single time I see the ocean; no matter how many times I take that sprint over the dunes, the first sight of the crashing waves always knocks my heart back in my chest. No one ever made me feel that way before I met Winch.

He's holding an armful of pink tulips and wearing a hungry, focused expression. His blue eyes travel up and down over my body, and I feel almost shy under his gaze.

'You're a goddess.'

He says it like a normal person would say, 'Your dress is white.'

A lazy-afternoon-sunshine glow unfurls low down

between my hips and blooms up my spine, climbing fast and high as a magic beanstalk to my heart.

'That's exactly what I was thinking,' I toss out so he won't sense how pathetically giggly I am, and I reach for the flowers, leaving his arms tulip-empty, pressing my face to the petals possessively. 'For me?'

'Of course.' His smile is sweet, but tired.

He stays outside the door while I find a vase in the hall cabinet and fill it with water from the powder room. 'You can come in if you want,' I tell him, but he just leans one shoulder on the doorframe and watches me set the pink blossoms out. 'How was last night?'

'Long and aggravating.'

He must have shaved this morning, and I catch sight of a tiny nick on his jaw from the razor. His white shirt is pressed but rolled up to the elbows, allowing the tattoo he shares with Remington to show. His grey pants are also pressed and neat.

'You look dapper today.' I primp the tulips up one last time and make my way to him. The clover-clean, sharp smell of his skin makes my senses reel.

I want to touch him, to reconnect, but it's like what we had last night is a powerline that's been severed. All the electricity is still spitting and crackling, but I don't dare attempt to touch that kind of raw power.

He holds his hands out at his sides.

'Church duds. I ditched the tie and jacket, but I was

in full dapper-mode this morning. My grandmother would pass out if we didn't wear suits every Sunday, heat be damned. And that old-as-all-hell chapel has a busted air conditioner. I was sweating my ass off.'

I'm about to say something about church or grand-mothers or the lack of air con when he crosses right over the threshold and grabs me around the waist. One hand takes the small pair of pruning shears I'm still holding lightly in my fingers and sets them on the table, then his lips seal over mine, hot, fast, and famished.

The first moan rips out from low in his throat, and a hand curls behind the back of my head and presses my lips closer, giving his mouth the leverage to edge mine open and allowing the sweet heat of his tongue to swirl against mine. I knock into the small table the tulips sit on, splashing water everywhere.

Winch's kisses are sweet and quick, with a desperate edge that makes me forget every detail of where we are and who might catch us because all I can think is *more, him, need, yes.*

As if he can read my mind, he has his arm wrapped around my waist and hoists me onto the table with no effort at all. I lean back, and he follows me forward, never breaking the contact of our mouths.

His hands fall flat to my knees and rest for one second, palms down, before they begin a slow and steady incline up along my thighs, up until his finger-tips brush my hips and his thumbs rub over the tiny piece of silky fabric that makes up my sexy-date underwear. His thumbs stroke once, three times, six or seven times before I'm squared in heaven and ready to let him do whatever he might possibly want to right in my grandparents' fancy hall.

Maybe he really can read my mind, because the instant 'grandparents' hall' jolts through my brain, his hands withdraw back to my knees, and his lips brush over mine in softer and softer sweeps until he's one inch too many away from me.

It takes us both a minute to catch our breath. His laugh is warm and low.

'So, that's pretty much what I've been thinking about since the minute I left your bed last night. You?'

I laugh back, breathless and high. 'That, yeah. And more. Do you want to . . .'

He shakes his head and the decisiveness of the gesture halts my question. 'Let me take you out some-where. Away from here. Because I can't slow down if I start.'

'I'm not looking for slow,' I offer, but he holds a hand out and, gallantly, politely, helps me off the table where he was building me up to a perfect orgasm a few seconds before.

'Not in a rush. Not like this.' His voice is at once

sure and full of command, and apologetically pleading.

'So, if you're not planning to rock my world, what are we doing?'

He waits as I lock the door and holds my hand as we rush down the white stone stops. I love the hint of a smile he attempts to hide when we're face-to-face, feet balanced on the curb.

'Breakfast. And it *will* rock your world.'

He holds my door open and helps me in, perfect gentleman style, and this date has all the unexpected newness and excitement our actual first date was lacking.

He pulls out and looks over at me, his hands curling over the steering wheel in a way that makes me think he's doing his best to keep them off of me. I roll the window down and Winch cuts the air con, delivering a satisfied smile my way.

'What's that about?' I ask.

'What's what about?' He smiles again, and there are a million secret thoughts I'm dying to unwind and reveal.

'The look you gave me just now.' I point at him and close one eye, shaping my fingers like a gun. 'I notice everything, mister.'

'Or, like my mom, you think you see something when there's nothing there. My look was just a look.'

He's still teasing me, but his voice drops from light-hearted to serious faster than pennies out of a hole in a pocket.

'Hmm. Maybe your mom and I need to have a talk.'

This time the look is a real look, a panicked, terrified, furious mix. It lasts a single instant, but it was there, and he's trying to hide it behind a neutral, calm, phony look, so I call him on it again.

'You can't deny *that* look! It meant something; I just have no idea what. C'mon, I'm not an idiot, Winch. There's no way you can deny that something notable went through your head when you gave me that look. So tell me.'

He shrugs, and I can read that I'm wearing him down.

'Tell?' I request nicely, and when he holds firm, I spread on the guilt. 'Tell because you left me all alone last night and I didn't even whine about it all that much.'

He winds down a side street, which pops out in a place that's both long-ago foreign and memory-filled familiar.

He parks the car and announces, 'I'll tell you after we eat, because I'm starving. What's the matter?'

I shake my head and swallow hard, the ghosts of my mama and daddy in happier days shaking their chains just outside Clary's. I get out of the car and he's instantly around the front end, at my side.

'I used to come here as a kid.'

His hand is cupped under my elbow for support, for comfort, for something to lean on if I need it.

'Say the word and we'll leave.'

'Nah.' I shake my head and look right into those blue eyes, like faded denim flapping on the line in the summer sun. 'If I'm going to come back here and enjoy a peanut butter and banana sandwich, I want it to be with you.'

He locks eyes with mine, and I can read this expression perfectly. It's pleased possession, and it makes my skin go hot.

'You eat the Elvis?' His lips tickle close to my ears.

'No,' I admit. 'But my daddy always did.'

This time he loosens his hold on my elbow, and his arm is, instead, strong and sure around my waist as he leads me to a table in the back. A waitress hurries over and calls Winch 'Mr Youngblood'. He's cool but polite, ordering two orange juices without asking if it's what I want.

It is, but still.

'You sure you're OK here? I'll have us somewhere else in three minutes if you want.'

He taps the menu absently on the wood table and looks at me like he's attempting to read my mind.

'I told you, it's fine. Really.'

I look around at the mismatched interior with the black-and-white tiles and the stained glass behind the counter, and it feels comfy, homely. If I block all the times my daddy came here so full of disappointment he couldn't walk straight, it's actually a very charming place.

The waitress hurries back and Winch orders the sourdough French toast, and I order the eggs Benedict Florentine.

'Good choice.' He rearranges the little black box of sugar packets with quick fingers. 'I think breakfast choices say a lot about people.'

'Funny. I think people's *looks* do. Since you already know what my breakfast choice is, let's analyze that weird look you gave me.'

I blow the wrapper from my straw at him and he blocks it with the palm of his hand like a ninja.

'You're relentless.'

He looks around, like he's praying the waitress will come back and interrupt this uncomfortable confession time.

'I'm shamelessly relentless. A watched breakfast order never cooks. Attention here.' I cup him under the chin and turn his face toward mine. 'Now, spill. Why the weird look before?'

'I barely remember what we were talking about,' he evades with a lazy shrug.

'You and your mysterious looks. And your mom.'

At the word, his shoulders go stiff and he drops all the sugar packets haphazardly back into the container.

He leans back in the chair, spreads his legs, and clasps his hands behind his head. Anyone who didn't know Winch would think he was comfortable as could be, but I notice the twitch in his jaw and the incessant nervous tap of his toe. I notice, but I don't let them stop me from peeling back, layer by layer, the enigma that is Winchester Youngblood. I stare at him, eyebrows raised, mouth set, eyes fierce, just to let him know I'm not backing down.

He lets out a dramatic sigh and feigns confusion again.

'OK, what are we talking about again? Oh, right. You and my mom and my looks.' I nod for him to go on. 'OK. All right. So you are a gorgeous, sexy, brilliant woman.'

He leans across the table and takes one of my hands. I try to yank it back, but he tucks it in his and kisses the knuckles.

'Flattery will get you nowhere. Spilling your guts? That's the key to unlocking all kinds of interesting doors.' I let my voice purr out with my best sexy feline persuasion technique.

Winch blinks. 'OK. Spilling my guts and those interesting doors.' He pinches the bridge of his nose.

'My mother,' he says finally, 'is not an easy woman to get along with.'

'You'd be shocked how much parents like me. I'm not kidding. I've never met a mother yet who didn't immediately think I was great.'

Well, that's a partial lie. I'm pretty sure Brenna's mom thinks I'm an obnoxious, pushy brat. I say it takes one to know one. Other than that, my record is fairly squeaky clean. I give off a good-girl vibe mamas just eat up.

'But my mother is nothing at all like normal mothers. Nothing. At all. OK?' It's like he's desperate for me to take his warning seriously. 'She has really old-fashioned ideas. And she's so stubborn.'

'OK.'

This actually doesn't bode well. My grandparents aren't very old-fashioned at all. They're very laid back, very open to suggestion. I'm not exactly sure they'd eat Winch up knowing his background and shady present, but they'd hear me out if I wanted them to meet him.

'So, am I some kind of secret girlfriend?'

The look on his face makes me feel like he suddenly popped me into the freezer and pushed the door shut; I feel the creep of a bitter chill. Where the hell can we go if I can never even meet his family when they obviously mean so much to him?

He opens his mouth to answer, but the waitress is bustling over to us, putting our plates down and warning us they are hot. I murmur a thank you. I feel the fork and knife in my hands and make cutting motions. I love eggs Benedict, but I have no clue if it's good or not, because it's like I'm suddenly ice-coated, unable to feel or taste.

Winch doesn't pretend to enjoy his breakfast and keep up polite, respectable appearances. He reaches across the table and takes my wrist, leaving my forkful of egg and buttery, delicious Hollandaise suspended in midair.

'You are *not* a secret girlfriend. I'm proud to be with you.'

'So I'm just your girlfriend no one knows about?'

I try and yank my wrist away and a few drips of yellowy sauce splatter on his white shirt. He doesn't even notice.

'No one knows about you because the problem is them, not you.' His grip tightens for one harsh second, then relaxes. I look up at him, a little shocked, and he releases my wrist. 'I've never been happier than I am with you, Evan. But my family doesn't think you should be with people because they make you happy. Like I said, they're old-fashioned. They'd judge you before they even got to know you, just because you're . . . not like us.'

'What does that even mean?'

I continue to cut and eat my food. Since I burned down a very influential family's orchard, I don't like to bring negative attention to myself and my family while I'm out. Even if I'm choking with undignified rage and upset, I try hard to put a high-sheen polish on any situation and always bust out my best company manners.

'What makes your family so different? Are you in the mob or something?'

I expect him to laugh, not because it's such a witty or original joke, but because not laughing implies there could be some possible crumb of truth.

'Winch?'

It's becoming nearly impossible to cut neat squares of food and eat them politely, with the desperate need to know his answer tugging at my guts.

He's sent his plate cruising to the middle of the table and is rubbing his temples, eyes screwed shut. When he finally sits straight and looks at me, there are a thousand shades of regret in his eyes and my bite of buttery, egg-soaked bread turns to an unswallowable lump in my throat.

'Not the mob,' he clarifies, but that only makes panic bob closer to the surface for me. 'Not exactly one hundred percent above the law.' He leans close and his voice drops. 'We handle a lot of business. We make a lot of deals, and we have a lot of secrets that can't get leaked, you know? So we tend to not trust anyone outside our circle.'

Most of what's going through my head involves the bloodiest, Scorsese-directed, monstrous gangster violence and mayhem imaginable. I want to get up and go to the bathroom, splash some cold water on my face, grip the sink and take deep, controlled breaths. But I just keep cutting my food and eating calmly.

'Say something,' Winch instructs.

I look at him with one raised eyebrow and go right on eating, the only sign of my irritation the aggressive scrape of my knife on the plate.

'Eat. Your breakfast is getting cold.'

My words come out frost-coated because Brenna was right and I was wrong. I like him so much. He just told me his family is seriously bad news, and I'm trying to think of reasons why that might not be such a big deal.

He eats, looking up at me with nervously shifting eyes between bites. 'You have a right to be freaked out. It's a lot.'

My plate is almost empty. I lay the fork and knife across the top edge and wipe my hands on the napkin.

'I need to use the restroom.'

He gets up to follow, but I rush by too fast, my sandal heels clipping on the checkerboard floor. By the time I'm in the cold, shiny bathroom, I have to bite my bottom lip hard to hold the swell of tears back. I knock my forehead into the stall door over and over.

'Why did you have to prove me wrong, Winch?' I whisper into the echoing tiles.

Winch 8

Fuck this breakfast. Fuck this date, fuck this already shitty day following the shittiest night I've ever had. Fuck the truth. Fuck believing in some fairytale happy ending. Fuck my responsibilities and fuck, fuck, fuck the fact that I just, no questions asked, lost my shot at being with Evan Lennox.

My appetite is shot to shit. I pay the bill and wait at the far end of the counter, my face one big fucking moody-ass glower that confuses the shit out of Lisa, the waitress who always chats with me.

Because I'm always in a damn genial mood. Because I know how important it is to keep up appearances, show off my best side, keep my emotions off my damn face.

But all the rules get tossed and shredded when Evan's in the picture.

I wait forever. I wait so long, I get worried and, even though I know I'm the last person she wants to see, I crack open the ladies' room door and rap it with my knuckles.

'Evan?'

I listen for sobs or the silence of an empty bathroom, but she answers.

'I'll be out in a minute.'

Her voice is ice-rimmed and flat.

Five minutes go by. Ten. The place starts to fill up with people for lunch. Women and little kids go in and out of the restroom, but Evan doesn't make an appearance. I keep tabs on the frazzled moms and elderly ladies entering and exiting, and when the bathroom finally empties of extra people, I slip in and make my way down the row of stalls until I see those crazy sexy sandals with the tie thingies under a stall.

'Evan?' I keep my voice low.

She gasps. 'Winch! Get the hell out of this bathroom.'

'Not without you.' I run my finger along the crack in the door. 'C'mon. You asked, I told. I knew you wouldn't like what you heard, but that's my truth. If it makes you feel better, I was picturing this exact moment in my head every time I wanted to pick the phone up and call you last week, so that's why I didn't.'

Her sigh stops short. 'You predicted this?'

'Not all the details. But you hearing all about me, and wanting me gone? I knew that was coming. Because being with you? I thought being with you would probably be amazing, but I had no idea, you have no idea, how hard I've fallen for you already.'

I wait, but there's no sound except the cautious movement of her feet, edging closer to the stall door. I think I hear someone swing the outer door open, but it's a false alarm. Someone will come in soon, though, and I'd love to get out of the bathroom with her before I cause a ruckus.

'Every time I think I've heard the worst version of your story, it gets even worse.' One eye peers through the crack at me. I can hear her voice, clear and summer-creek sweet. 'I get that you're keeping me in the dark to protect me. But you have to stop. I have to know everything. All of it. No matter how bad you think it is.'

I can see her fingers toying with the stall bolt. I want her to slide it open.

'All right. Full disclosure. I swear. But you gotta come out of there. I can't talk to you about this in the girls' bathroom. I don't need to get arrested for this.'

It's meant to be a joke, to break some of the deep ice that's surrounded us, but she slides the lock over and steps out, her eyes flashing.

'You don't need to get arrested for *this*. But you'll

get arrested again, right? If Remy needs it, you will, and that's OK with you?'

I look down at my spit-shined shoes and think about the night before, Remy's crazed behavior, the neighbors I had to pay off, the family I had to reassure. He's running wild and wounded as hell, and it's only a matter of time before he gets his ass caught in a bear trap so big and sharp, no amount of money or apologies will manage to smooth it over for him.

'I might.'

Her frown is the last thing I want to see, and I wonder how frequently that look will be on her face when she's with me.

'You wanted honesty.' I take her hand in mine, pull her to the door and brace it open a crack. 'C'mon. I'll let you play Twenty Questions with me, all right?'

The faintest glimmer of a smile breaks over her face.

'What if it takes more than Twenty Questions to figure you out, Winch?'

Her dark hair brushes my arm as she leans out with me to check up and down the corridor.

'Twenty-thousand Questions then. You happy with that?'

It's all clear, so I pull her through, past the tables with mismatched, half-pulled-out chairs, and out of the restaurant into the baking sun.

'Twenty thousand?' She rubs her slightly pointed chin. 'Will *that* be enough?'

I shrug and twine my fingers through hers. 'I think I'm pretty simple. But we can find out. Wanna walk and talk?'

I'm edgy, nervous and a little excited to try and pull this off. I want her. I've never wanted anything so much, and I like a fight, a challenge. Maybe I can do this, keep her, let her know everything and still manage to win her over.

'Sure.' She nestles close to me despite how damn hot it is, and I think about the long litany of 'fucks' I listed when she was in the bathroom. Maybe they were all premature. She clears her throat.

'First question: when do you plan to stop taking care of Remy so you can start your own life?'

And maybe those 'fucks' were as warranted as I initially thought.

I watch the cracks in the sidewalk. It was shitty of her to start with a trick question, but I still need to answer and do it honestly.

'I'm gonna have a life *and* take care of Remy until he's back on his feet.'

I wish I had my cigs, but I've been cutting back since Mama found a pack in my bedroom and went on a screaming tirade about lung cancer and my Great-Uncle Pepe and his voicebox.

'I do work, Evan. It's for my family, but I don't just get handed a pile of money for sharing my dad's last name. I work long, crazy hours, and I get fair money for what I do.'

'If you didn't do what you do for your family, what would you want to do?'

A little bit of a breeze comes rushing down the street and lifts the hair off the back of her neck, exposing skin that's glistening with sweat.

I help her around another uneven break in the concrete, using any excuse to drag her closer and keep my hands on the warmth of her skin.

'If I didn't work for my family?'

I watch two guys jog down the street in matching lime-green spandex outfits. A group of college girls in flowery skirts and big sunglasses walk by and giggle. The breeze whips through again and flags clang on their poles. I'm trying to answer these questions like I'm playing a game of chess, but my head is buzzing with all the distractions.

'I don't know. I like to work with my hands. Maybe masonry?'

Evan tilts her head and swishes all her hair over one shoulder, leaving the long, perfect line of her neck exposed.

'Masonry?'

'You making fun of my dreams?'

I rub my thumb over the ridges of her knuckles, optimistic. This girl likes me. I can do this.

She squeezes my hand. 'Nope. It just sounds really . . .'

She trails off and chews on her bottom lip to keep from laughing.

'What?' I bump my shoulder into hers gently. 'Come on. I know you're laughing at me. My feelings are already hurt. You might as well tell me the joke.'

'Masonry is, like, a really stereotypical mafia job.' She tenses and relaxes her hand in mine.

'Well, since I'm not in the mafia, I guess that little detail never occurred to me.'

I drop her hand and wrap my arm around her shoulders instead, loving the way she fits against my body like she was custom designed for me.

'Are you going to tell me why masonry?'

She leads me off the curb without even checking for traffic, and we run to the nearest square opposite, where we flop on a bench.

I pull her tight to me, gather her legs over my lap and glare at the old couple who click their tongues at us as they dodder by. I lay my hands on the skin right above her knee, where they started this morning, in her grandparents' damn foyer. This time I keep them put and explain what I've never uttered out loud to anyone in my life.

'The job I do now? For my family?' She sits a little straighter, out of my hold, but I fold her back near me. She looks down at the glossy blue polish on her nails and waits. 'The job I do is keeping the peace. It's lots of talking, arguing, finessing. I talk all day. I talk until I'm sick to death of the sound of my own voice. And I talk so much bullshit, I hardly ever go to bed without a couple aspirin and a shot of Jack.'

She tips her dark, cat-eye sunglasses down and purses her lips. 'That doesn't sound good.'

I can tell that she's biting her tongue in her mouth, not saying more about it, even though she really wants to. Instead she tumbles to the next question.

'What's the worst thing you've done?'

I take a breath so deep, it feels like it starts at the soles of my feet and works its way up to my addled brain. My fingers drum on her tanned skin.

'Can I ask you a question about your question?'

She wiggles her toes in her sandals. 'Sure.' Her knees rock back and forth slowly, a totally opposite rhythm from my rapidly tapping fingers.

'Do you want to know the worst thing I've ever done from a legal standpoint? Like the worst thing I've done if all the stick-up-their-ass do-gooders had a vote? Or the thing I think is the worst, according to my conscience?'

I watch her eyes stretch wide and her mouth work into a perfect O-shape.

'Both.' Her answer is greedy, but her face looks nervous, like she knows she's going to regret having asked once I tell her.

The sun is high up, but the only light hitting us is the speckled, diffused stuff breaking through the dense, dark greenery of the trees in the square. Even in the shade, the heat sticks to us, making our clothes damp with sweat. I want to ask her to come some-place else with me, but there's nowhere to go right now.

The apartment I rented for myself got com-mandeered by some second cousin who just moved over from Hungary with a heavily pregnant wife, two little kids, no money, and fewer skills. He needed it more than I did, so I went back to my old set of rooms at my parents' house, and they're out of the question for me and Evan.

'Worst thing from society's viewpoint,' I begin, and her attention is rapt. She even leans forward a little. 'I broke a guy's femur.'

She pulls her hands back and curls them into each other.

'On purpose,' I add. Then I take it a step further, 'And I wish . . . I really wish I'd broken his other femur while I was at it.'

Her hands fly up to her mouth, and she gasps the question from behind her fingers. 'What did he do?'

'Distributed child porn.' The horror in her eyes settles my conscience, not that even Evan's disapproval would make me feel bad about what I'd done. 'I found out because I do sweeps of the company computers for security breach stuff. My father brought him in for some, uh, accounting things.'

Since I was mid-story about breaking a guy's fucking femur, it occurred to me that adding in the detail that my family hired the guy to cook the books probably wouldn't matter. Still.

'He was damn good at his job. Damn smart with computers. It took months before anything came up. Then I saw a bunch of it, and I swear to God right now, Evan, that asshole is lucky all I broke was his femur, because I have never felt more justified about beating the shit out of anyone before.'

She takes one hand down from her mouth and puts it back in mine. 'OK. That actually makes perfect sense to me. What is your personal worst?'

I squeeze her knee and avoid her eyes for a minute, because here's another story buried in the Shut the Fuck Up Winchester Vault.

'I shot a horse.'

'You shot a horse?' The tone of voice she uses is

more confused than accusatory, which makes it easier to go ahead and get it out.

'I had to hang out with these assholes my father was doing business with, and they were always out in the wild, hunting and fishing. One day we were tracking deer. I didn't love being around a bunch of jackholes I barely knew anyway, and every one of them was armed to the teeth with every weapon you could imagine. Anyway, they wanted me to bag a deer, and I was scared shitless. Just wanted the day to be over with. I saw this brown shape running, and, I swear to you, I was trying to miss. I'm not really into the whole hunter thing. But I guess I was a better shot than I thought. Or worse. Anyway, I hit it. But it wasn't a deer.'

She grips the back of the bench so hard little flecks of old paint flake off.

'You killed a horse?'

The memory of it is a bitter bite at the back of my throat.

'Everybody thought it was hilarious. The guy who owned the horse, he said he bought it for his little girl because she begged for it, then said something about wanting to put it down anyway 'cause it was old and crazy, but he never did because he didn't want his daughter to have a nervous breakdown. So there I was, knowing this kid was going to break down and go crazy when she found out I killed her pet, and I felt like shit. I had to laugh along, because that's my job. That's who I am. But I killed a fucking horse, and, I don't know, I wanted to feel shitty about it.'

She bites her lower lip and something in her eyes drives my next point home.

'I realized how sick I was of hanging out with people who didn't think it was fucked up that a horse got killed and that we should maybe – I don't know . . . Maybe . . . be sad. Just be sad that something running and alive the minute before was suddenly gone.'

Evan stops peeling chipping paint and puts her hand on my cheek, her fingers so damn soft on my face. 'That's sad. To always have to put on a show. To always have to pretend. Don't you get really sick of it? Like sick enough to just want out?'

'Yeah. I do. But everyone gets sick of what they have to do sometimes. That's life, right?'

I close my eyes and focus on the feel of her hand. I feel good. I feel like I don't have to put on a show with her.

The sun is intensely hot. I undo the top button of my shirt and think about the beach. I haven't gone to the beach with a couple beers and the whole day spread in front of me in so long, I can't even remember the last time.

And then I think about Evan in a bikini. She's

always got these cute-ass outfits, so I'm willing to bet her bikini is tiny and hot as hell.

'You wanna go to the beach today?' I ask, and Evan's whole face brightens to the point where it would be easy to forget about the sun, no matter how hot it blazes.

'Do you have bathing trunks with you?' She reaches up and unbuttons the next button on my shirt, then one more.

'I don't even know if I still own any.' I slide a finger along the golden tan of her shoulder and down to the point of her elbow. 'I bet you have a couple of cute bikinis.'

'Of course.' She bats those sexy long eyelashes. 'All of them itsy bitsy.'

'So.' I don't want to ruin where this is going, but we've been going back and forth since this morning and I want to know which direction we're taking now. 'You were pissed off about what I do and about my family, and I get that. But is it just that you seriously love the beach, or are you going on this date because you and me make sense somehow?'

She straightens up and takes a deep breath, squints her eyes at me, wrinkles her nose, and shakes her head, slowly, side to side.

'You . . .' She pulls her shoulders up. 'You make me crazy, OK? And I think what we're doing might be stupid. Correction: what we're doing *is* stupid. I don't want to get in a relationship with someone who's going to break my heart. But I can't stay away from you, Winch. I want you. So much.'

I lean my forehead on hers and curl my hands around her shoulders, resisting the urge to jump up and scream to every random person walking by, 'Hey! This girl is mine! This girl wants to be with me!'

I hug her tight and smell her hair, sweet with the scent of wildflowers.

'I will never break your heart. I will never hurt you. I might fuck up, I might not be perfect, but I'll never deliberately hurt you, Evan. You have my word.'

No man in my family gives his word lightly, so, whether or not Evan trusts what I just said, I've made a vow as a Youngblood, and that's not something I can just go back on.

'So, we can just be a normal couple on a date going to the beach today?' Evan asks.

I nod and kiss her neck, lick the salty warm place where her pulse is beating hard.

'Yeah.' I say, running my hands up and down her back.

'And you'll be in half a suit, and I'll be in a tiny bikini?'

She rubs her nose on mine, some cute little Eskimo-kiss thing. It's so adorable, I never would have expected it from someone as sexy as Evan.

'Yeah.' This time it's hard for me to get the word out.

She hops off the bench and grabs my hand, pulling me up and dancing a quick little jig like the one she did for me in her room. We head back through the square, into my car, and drive back to her house. She runs inside while I wait, my hands gripped on the steering wheel, and my heart pounding like I'm about to have a coronary.

I see her rush back down the stairs, and the only hint I get about what that bikini looks like is the two tiny red strings that go over her collarbones.

And as if my heart isn't already pounding out of my chest, my brain fast-forwards to the beach and slow-motions through Evan peeling off that tiny black cover-up, running down the sand, jumping in the water, tanned skin wet and shiny, tiny bikini barely covering her curves, and my mouth dries out.

I get out and open the passenger door for her, catching her against my body just before she slips in. 'You're torturing me, you know that?'

'The beach is not torture.' She reaches up on her toes and presses her lips to the side of my mouth. 'It's fun.'

'Sand whipping everywhere. No escape from the sun. Sharks. Sounds like torture to me.' I smile as her lips move across my jaw and to my ear.

'All that terrible stuff. Then me. In a bikini.' Her words whisper right against my ear.

'More torture.' I pick her up by the waist and my fingers pluck at the knot holding her bikini top on. 'But I'm a glutton for punishment.'

She presses her body to mine, and I'm enveloped by everything that's her, ready to free-fall into whatever we're about to do, however we're about to do it, excited about a freedom I never imagined.

Until the noose that's always around my neck gets tugged.

My phone rings.

Evan startles and pulls back, her face relieved. 'It's OK, right? It isn't "House of the Rising Sun".'

I pull the phone out of my pocket and stare, willing the call to go the fuck away. Evan's fingers suddenly half cover the screen. When I look up, her brow is furrowed.

'Winch? It's OK, right? You can ignore it? We can go to the beach?'

'It's not "House of the Rising Sun",' I agree, but I tug the phone away from her hand. 'It's my . . . it's someone I used to know.'

The call goes to voicemail, and I make the decision to finally put it all on the backburner when a text beeps through.

I open it and stifle a groan.

Yr brother and 2 Murrays on 4th and Little. Jimlo is taking bets.

I have a serious urge to hurl this fucking phone onto the street and run it over a few dozen times.

I told her I wouldn't deliberately break her heart, and I won't. But I have to break our date, and that feels like the first step on the long road that will eventually lead to Evan's broken heart.

Evan 9

This morning has been like every other tangled, crazy, hot time Winch and I collide. It's strange how it's possible for me to go from thinking he's the only guy I'll ever want to be with to considering slicing him out of my life completely and possibly punching him in the nuts as a send-off.

But there's something about him that keeps me right in the eye of the storm, no matter how nasty it gets.

And it's just gotten rip-off-the-roof, flood-that-will-float-your-car-away nasty.

I am snuggling in his arms, enjoying the clover and spice tang of his skin, my tiny bikini burning to have his eyes all over it (and his hands all under it), when his damn phone plays 'She's Like the Wind'.

My first thought is, *Who the hell would he use that ringtone for?*

My second thought, tripping right on its heels, is, *It's not 'House of the Rising Sun'!*

My second thought is so overwhelmingly ecstatic, it blots out my first entirely, and I don't even have the urge to vomit over that cheese-tastic ringtone or grill him about who would have inspired it.

Until his mouth opens and he starts to say words I'm not ready to hear.

'It's about Remy, Evan. I'm so sorry—'

'No, no, no, no, no,' I interrupt, pressing my fingers against his mouth urgently 'No! I've got a bikini on. A scandalous bikini! I picked it up in Paris. No one in America has a bikini this sexy.' I push close to him, the phone locked in his hand between our bodies. 'Winch, you *promised* me, ten minutes ago, you promised me things would be different. You promised—'

Winch closes his eyes and groans. 'Oh, baby. Please. Hear me out.'

It's the first time he's called me 'baby'. A pleasant tingle thrills through me, up my arms and down my spine, in direct contrast with the molten anger that's volcanoing through my blood.

'Explain, then,' I demand.

His eyes fly open, and I take two big steps back before I cross my arms in the international girl-sign that states 'Watch what you're going to say very closely.'

He clears his throat, runs a hand over his hair, double checks the message on his phone, moves toward me, groans when I move back, and finally opens his mouth to talk.

'Remy's about to fight.'

He stops. I glare.

'Really? Behind the baseball dugout at three sharp? What is he, in middle school? If your brother wants to fight, let him fight.'

Winch grips the roof of the car and grimaces.

'OK, listen. You're gonna hate this, but listen. My family . . . where I come from, a fight is more than a fight, OK? When the families fight, there's a lot at stake, and Remy just picked a really, really powerful family to throw down with. Pissing them off isn't a good idea, and it will mean a lot of shit for all of us if he loses. So I gotta go have his back and make sure it all works out in our favor. It will take half an hour, an hour tops, then I come back, get you, and you let me see that sexy-ass bathing suit that's already making me crazy.'

He holds his hands out in front of his body hopefully and gives me his best charming, begging smile.

'You know that saying, *A picture's worth a thousand words*?' I ask. Winch nods slowly. 'Well, a live fight is probably worth twenty-thousand questions. So I'm in.'

I pull on the passenger door handle and attempt to swing the door open, but Winch already has his hand on the frame and is shutting it before I can slide in.

'Out of the question.' He takes me by the shoulders and moves me two steps back toward my grandparents' house. 'A fight is no place for you. It's dangerous. I'll be out there in the mix. I won't be able to help you if anyone messes with you, and—' He pulls back and lets this long, low whistle escape his mouth. 'You're gonna get messed with. Look at you.' He shakes his head. 'Anything else you want, you got it. Anything. Just not this.'

Every internal alarm bell is sounding off like crazy, and I decide to give Winch a final trial by fire.

'What if I asked to be invited to dinner at your family's place? And to go to mass with you? Next week?'

The color leaks out of his face and leaves it looking drawn and ashen. His mouth pulls tight and his eyes blink fast. Then he looks at me levelly and nods.

'OK. Done.'

'Really? You'd do that for me?' My heart does this little slide, shuffle, slide before it leaps up and kicks its heels together.

He delivers the sweetest half-smile, all sexy curve of the lip and gorgeous eyes.

'Of course. You're my girl. You gotta meet them all sometime anyway. Might as well be sooner than later. I'm warning you, though – they are crazy as hell.'

The fear and worry on his face is so blatant, it's dizzyingly hilarious. I slide my hands down his arms and pull on his elbows.

'I don't want that until you're positive you're ready.' He sags with visible relief. 'But I do want to come with you to this fight. Now. No more arguing. And I can take care of myself.'

He tenses back up.

'No way. Dinner every night with my family for the rest of the month if you want. By the way, I'm positive you're gonna regret asking for that. My family is not the party you might think they are.' I purse my lips and he rushes to add, 'Dates. Weekly dates. Phone call check-ins, love letters, that sonnet I promised you. Anything, Evan, but not this.' He comes toward me and takes my hands in his. 'I'm begging you, not this.'

It's romance. Every word out of his mouth is like the first time I wrapped my arms around a boy's gangly neck and slow-danced in eighth grade; thrilling, exquisite, exciting romance. But I've let him direct enough of this relationship, and I know I have the leverage to make this happen.

'I. Want. To. Go.'

I set my feet apart in a determined stance and radiate a pure refusal to back down. Winch's guilt, lust and lack of time conspire and work a miracle for me.

I watch it play out in slow motion: fierce pissed-off refusal, agitated uncertainty, desperate resignation, and complete shock that sets those sexy blue eyes wide.

'I can't fucking believe I'm saying this, but c'mon.' He opens my door, his mouth flattened in an angry line. 'But I don't like this.'

My door slams shut, and I watch him stalk in front of the car, his mouth moving a hundred miles an hour, like he's having a heated argument with himself. When he opens the driver's side, I get the gist.

'. . . stupid, insane ideas. This isn't some little boxing match in a ring with refs and rules. This is nasty stuff, and no one there is gonna be watching his manners or behaving. How the hell am I gonna take down two Murrays when I'm worried about making sure no one puts a hand on you? How am I supposed to manage this?'

At first, the whole complicated argument is only with himself, but he suddenly turns his scowls and howls on me.

I look him dead in the eye and ask, 'Who is "She's Like the Wind"?'

Silence fills the car. I'm just glad he stopped raving like a lunatic, and I don't honestly expect a response, but he surprises me.

One of the things I love best about Winch is that he

always manages to surprise me, just when I've written him off as bad news.

'That song isn't a song that means anything to me,' he says, his voice even and low. 'It means something to a girl I dated. The last girl I dated. She programmed it in my phone, and I just never erased her from my contacts.'

'No?'

I'd deleted pictures, updated my FB status, burned collected couples memorabilia, smudged out all contact information, and drunk myself into oblivion the very night Rabin and I split up. I thought that was common behavior.

'No. The end, with me and my ex, it was a long time coming. And I stopped hating her a long time before things self-destructed. I just started feeling bad for her. Lost a lot of respect for her, and that translated into not really giving a shit. So I didn't delete her out of my phone or change that stupid ringtone, but it doesn't mean anything.' He reaches over and takes my hand, locking his fingers with mine. 'Unless it means something to you. Because then I'll delete it so fast, it'll be unreal. I hate that damn song anyway.'

I pull his hand, linked with mine, up to my mouth and kiss his knuckles. 'Doesn't matter to me.'

A strange, sweet heat bubbles up inside me and makes my head feel light on my neck, like I'm floating on a million bubbles in a champagne bottle.

We go the rest of the way in a gentle quiet, the first sweet, trusting quiet in our entire relationship. And it just happens to fall right before we drive up to a nasty, jeering mob, trigger-ready for a massive fight.

When Winch looks over at me, his blue eyes are hot and serious.

'*Do not* leave this car. Sit on the hood, the roof, inside, but don't you dare leave this car. Understood?'

I glance through the crowd, undulating as groups of people jab back and forth, throwing themselves into the fray, and backing up away from the heat just as quickly. Winch's hands grip mine, and I jump, meeting his intense gaze.

'I get it,' I promise him.

He leans over and cups my face, runs his thumb over my cheekbone, brushes his lips over mine, eyes shut tight, brow furrowed.

'You gotta forgive me for this, ahead of time, OK? It's what I have to do, like it or not. Forgive me, Evan?'

His voice is so desperate, there's nothing else to say. 'Of course. Be safe. Promise me, Winch?'

'As safe as I can be.'

His lips are hot and hard on mine, and I want more, want him, all of him, with me, all alone.

The crowd rushes the car when they recognize it's

his, and I lose him in a throng of cheering, drunk guys who pull at him and draw him toward some cleared center, where the lineup is denser and, I'm sure, more vicious.

I grab the keys Winch left on the seat, slide out the door, depress the locks, and try to make it out of the space between the car and the opened door as I elbow against the wave of people crushing me on all sides. I get pushed back into the interior twice by the groups of people coming from nowhere and everywhere to see what, I don't know yet.

Their enthusiasm is unsettling. This is Roman Colosseum excitement, and I stand on my tiptoes to catch Winch's back, the muscles of his shoulders strained through the thin fabric of his shirt. Worry needles at the edge of my throat, but I try to tell myself it will be OK. Winch is strong and smart. He's used to this kind of violence. This is his world, and he knows how to navigate it.

But I don't believe my own comforting words. I scramble onto the gunmetal grey hood, careful not to make a dent, but I still can't see, so I pull up onto the roof. It's not much better. Not only is there a thick congregation of stark raving lunatics screaming in the middle of all this, there are more bodies heaving and shoving every second.

I see a huge guy, big as a black bear on its hind legs,

with thick ropes of dreadlocked hair and a scruffy, coarse beard, batting people away with the flats of his enormous hands.

'Move outta the way, fuckups! Anyone touches these girls, you have me to answer to!'

People repel away from him, giving him a clear circle amid the chaos.

Half a dozen made-up, dressed-up teenage girls cluster and disperse a few feet from him, always in his orbit, but never too close to their hulk of a bodyguard. Seeing my chance, I slide off the car and fall into the guy's shadow, quietly melding with the group of girls. I don't stand close enough that I'd be considered one of them, but I don't stray so far away that anyone would bother me.

The air is hot and sticky, and there's the sour smell of beer everywhere. At this point the only kind of violence going on is one red-faced, sweaty guy with his shirt half off yelling at another growling, teeth-bared idiot with his fists up. All around, small groups of divided alliances hurl insults at other small groups. It's total cacophony, but bearable, because there's no real violence.

But it feels like it's simmering right under the lid of this pot of boiling emotions, ready to explode at any second. That would make sense. Violence in books and movies is always like a powder keg and a spark, and this jostling, yelling, inarticulate, drunk crowd is crawling a clear path to open-season chaos.

I keep one eye on my bear-like protector and move closer to the center of the crowd where the main action seems to be happening. I guess I was waiting for this to work like a boxing match, with a referee making the fighters knock gloves and a little bell to ding before things get too awful, but I suddenly realize the brawl has already started and it's anything but a civil, fair fight.

The people in the tightest inner ring seem to be taking bets and keeping score, but I don't know how it all works.

I peer through the press of people. Two guys are circling each other in the center of the inner ring. There's no doubt the thinner one is Remy because he looks so much like Winch. His dark hair is falling into his blue eyes and he's got a slight beer gut which gives him an older, sloppy look. He hops from foot to foot, bobbing and weaving back and forth, fists up, blood already leaking in small streams from his nose and mouth. He takes a bare knuckle hit to his eye, and the ferocious smack of skin and bone makes my stomach churn.

Remy shakes his head a few times, snorts, and runs at the guy who hit him, a brawny blond with a ruddy face. He knocks headfirst into the guy's stomach, knocking him to the ground with such intensity, he smashes the wind right out of him.

Half the crowd erupts into eardrum-shattering cheers, and half hisses and snarls with jeers and threats.

'One more, Youngblood! Take that Murray-fucker down!' Remy's fans roar.

There are tons of them, and they all gasp in horror when the blond guy catches his breath and comes up swinging, packing a blow on each side of Remy's head. Remy falls back into the arms of a guy who calls out some numbers, drags him back, and pushes Winch into the middle.

The entire crowd suddenly loses its volume and focus and my vision blurs at the edges.

He's stripped off the white shirt, and he's all flat-packed muscles and smooth tanned skin, with more tattoos then I had a chance to see in the dark of my bedroom the night before.

'Youngblood' is scrawled in swirling letters in an arc across his abs. There's a huge cross between his shoulder blades, a rifle on his ribs, and two diving swallows on his pecs.

There are more than a few girls in the crowd, and every one of them starts whispering with pleasure when he comes into the center.

I don't want him to know I broke his only rule about leaving the car, but I'd like him to see me, know

I'm here for him. And, much as I despise that whole piss-on-your-territory vibe some girls give off, I'm feeling a bit like a dog by a hydrant when I see all the shiny hair flips and mascara-laden eyelash bats Winch is getting from every single direction.

But Winch doesn't see me or anyone else. His expression is grim and determined. He shakes off well-wishers who pat him on the back as he takes his place, feet apart in a relaxed stance, fists up and ready.

My heart is punching in my chest, holding onto the bars of my ribs and banging itself against them. My mouth is parched, my palms are slick with sweat, and my entire body gives little jerks and jumps based on the swirling mix of worry and anticipation.

The guy who fought Remy is pulled back, and an identical-looking replacement falls into the center of the ring, already snarling and lunging. Winch holds back, taking a graze on the side of the head and another weak jab to the ribs.

Seeing him get hit in any capacity make me crazed with worry, but I trust him to know how to manipulate this whole situation. This is how he's gauging the fight, how he's going to calculate his moves for an ultimate win. I have to trust that he can handle himself.

He takes a harder hit to his shoulder, ducks down and weaves back. The crowd around him starts to hiss and boo, thirsty for more blood from this show.

I don't know if I've ever hated a crowd of people more than I hate these people right now. I honestly wish the earth would open under them and suck them into the bowels of hell. I choke back a gag when the first face punch lands.

A fountain of blood erupts from Winch's nose, crimson red and so horrifyingly alive and gruesome, pinpricks of silver spot in front of my eyes and I feel like I'm looking down a long, black tunnel. I stagger a little and bump into a guy who gives me a callous shoulder push-back. I swallow hard, but my saliva tastes acrid in my mouth. I take a few deep breaths and steady myself back on my feet, ready to see this to the finish.

Winch simply wipes the blood in a long, wild, red streak across his cheek. There's still a trickle leaking from his nose, but it seems to interest his opponent more than it does him.

The blond takes one more swing, and this time we all know it's over before he follows through. With that massive an amount of force, aimed right at Winch's temple, I know full well I'm going to be in the ER with him, getting an MRI to make sure his brain still operates.

The silver pricks of light are back, and I pitch forward, hands braced on my knees, and will my legs not to give out, not yet, and close my eyes when two solid thuds burst through the air and bring gasps and cheers from a portion of the crowd.

I open my eyes and Winch is rolling his neck from side to side, the other guy is doubled over, and the crowd is getting louder. The blond guy attempts to stand up straight, but he falls back over, and his brother bursts forward, fists poised, and delivers a vicious punch to Winch's back that rips a scream from my throat before I can hold it back.

Winch twists and punches back with quick, knuckle-heavy jabs on the guy's lower back and rib area, and he manages to take the huge hulk, writhing in pain, down to the ground, the two of them throwing hard punches as they fall.

The crowd is jostling hard now. I have no idea where the bear of a guy I thought I'd stay close to is, and I can only see snippets of the fight through the moving bodies stepping closer for a more direct view of the gore and at the same time nudging me farther back. The last thing I see is a smear of red glistening on the concrete.

Winch's blood or the other guy's? My stomach recoils, and I swallow back the urge to vomit right on the stomping boots of this crowd. I press past, getting pushed one step backward for every two forward I manage to take, but by the time I hit the outside edges of the inner circle again, I manage to catch Winch's eye.

His head jerks up, and he glares through an already bruised, purpling socket, putting a strangle-hold on the other guy and punching him in the ear with a menacing fist. Just when I'm sure he's going to drop the guy's head onto the cement, a police siren screams in the near distance.

The congealed crowd of raging, yelling lunatics suddenly disperses into every imaginable direction, stampeding into waiting cars, slipping down shady alleys, ducking into suddenly opened doors which close just as quickly.

I try to run toward Winch, but he yells to me, 'Remy's in the back!'

'I'll bring the car around!'

He locks eyes with me, and for one long second, he debates giving me the OK. I don't wait for his permission. If I want to get out of here and have a chance in hell of getting Winch and Remy away from this craziness without another arrest, we have to move.

I use my elbows, knees, head, whatever I can to break through the insane, crazed stampede and finally get back to Winch's car. I tug the keys out of my pocket and slide in, then back down the nearest sidestreet as quickly as I can while checking for darting, panicked spectators on the run, praying the cops are coming from the other direction and that no one is coming up the one-way street I'm illegally driving down like a lunatic. Part of me is scared shitless, and another huge part of me feels like a badass cowgirl living on the edge.

I whip the car around and bump the back fender into a cement planter full of tiger lilies. The bump makes me grimace with the realization that I almost definitely dented Winch's car.

I make a more careful circuit to the back of the ring of buildings where they were fighting, and Winch runs over, dragging Remy under the shoulders.

I reach across the car and push the passenger doors open, and the guys fall in. I'm pulling out before Winch has both legs in, and he slams the door shut as we negotiate our way down a quiet street that borders the back-alley fight clubs, apparently, but doesn't attract much police attention. I keep to a decent speed, don't rack up any traffic violations, and glance over at Winch.

'Where do you need to go?' I ask, trying not to let my eyes linger too long over his sweat-soaked muscles.

This is perversely sexy. Like Googling 'sexy, sexy, sexy man' and gazing at pics for hours. My hormones are officially out of fucking control.

'Why the hell didn't you stay in the car?' Winch demands, his nostrils flared in fury.

And it's like he just ignited a spark against the propane tank of my temper. 'This isn't a game, Evan. This is exactly what I was afraid would happen. Girls show up at this stuff, and it's like porn for them. They can't resist it.' He squirms in the passenger seat, obviously uncomfortable not being the one driving.

I grip the steering wheel and try very hard to come up with something not entirely vulgar to say to him, especially considering I was just ogling his muscles a second ago. I'm not about to acknowledge that, though.

'Porn? Are you kidding me? You think I wrestled through that big-ass, scary-ass crowd so I could see you with your shirt off? If you think your muscles are worth all that trouble, your ego needs some major taming.'

Remy, head leaned on the backseat, lets out a scratchy chuckle. 'I like this girl.' He lifts his battered face and squints. 'This the one that made you all antsy at dinner? I get it now. I so get it now.'

'Shut up, Remy,' Winch growls.

'Make me, Muhammad Fucking Ali.' Before they can get into a spat, Remy's phone plays the Storm-trooper March from *Star Wars*.

'Hey, Mama,' he answers, and I have an instant

fit of the giggles. Winch doesn't drop his glare for a single second. 'Fight? Not at all. I mean, we were there, but we didn't *fight*. Well, you know those guys can get a little rough, so we had to defend some girls – Uh-huh. OK. Yeah. Twenty minutes.'

He slides his phone back in his pocket and winks in the rearview mirror at me. 'Guess who's coming to dinner? Take the next left and make a U-turn. We're off East Taylor.'

Winch massages his temples, and I look at Remy in the mirror in frantic panic, especially because their house is off East Taylor, one of the oldest, richest streets in Savannah. Which means that I will be judged based on how I look and talk and carry myself from the moment I walk through the doors.

'I'm not dressed for dinner!'

I have on my black 'have your way with me on the beach' sexy cover-up with my scandalous red bikini under it. I glance in the mirror and see that my make-up is a smudged wreck and my hair needs more than a brush; it needs a fresh wash, deep condition, and style.

And Winch, bloodied, bruised, exhausted and in-furiated, looks up at me and meets my eyes for a brief second. When he speaks, his voice is solid with an unquestioning conviction.

'You look perfect, Evan. You look completely

fucking perfect, you *are* completely fucking perfect, so stop worrying. Now.'

And I listen to him and drive to East Taylor with a blush and a smile on my face.

Winch 9

Evan is coming to my house.

I've never been so fucking pissed off at my brother in my life. My adrenaline is pumping like a drug, and punching him a few times in his fat head definitely occurs to me. The only thing that stops me is the look in Evan's eyes when we pull up to my family's monstrous house. Like she's scared. Like she shouldn't even bother. Like she's not ready for all this.

Remy rolls out of the back. 'I'll go in and let them know you two will be in in a minute, OK?'

I glare at him and he stuffs both hands in the pockets of his pants, flecked with blood, and whistles like a fucking clown while he walks to the house.

'You can take me home, right?' Evan's voice has this wavery quality I never imagined coming from her before. 'Because I know I asked for this, but the joke's on me. Hardy har har. I'm ready for you to tell me what an ass I am and drop me back home now.' She taps her fingers in a quick, vicious beat on the steering wheel.

'You look unbelievably beautiful.'

I mean it when I say it, but I know she's seeing herself the way my mother will see her. And I know my mother will disagree with me one hundred percent.

'I can't go in there with them, Winch. This whole day has been a mess. I want ... I want it to work between us, and that isn't possible if I screw this all up.'

She checks the mirror and her mouth flattens. She lets out a strangled gasp and wipes at the smeared make-up under her eyes. I put a hand out and touch the delicate bone at her wrist, slide my fingers against her skin, and rub slow circles I hope help calm her down.

'I can help. Trust me?' It's a lot to ask her, after everything I dragged her through.

'I do,' she says, her voice soft.

We get out of the car and I take her by the hand and lead her around the back of the house to the French doors outside a patio with a fountain, and little stone benches. I rap my knuckles on the glass and Benelli's face peeks through. She yanks the door open, brow furrowed.

'Winch? What happened? Lala said there was a fight. Are you OK? Is Remy—?' My sister's blue eyes flick over Evan and she frowns, but doesn't ask a single question about her.

'Remy got in deep with the Murrays.'

'Holy Mother of God, what is he thinking?' Benelli makes a fist and shakes it, her lips pulled back in a snarl. 'He's going too far. We have to tell Pop . . .' Her voice trails off and she clears her throat gently, making a point to not look at Evan. 'Winchester, I need to speak with you in private.'

'Not now.' I narrow my eyes and shake my head at my sister's attempt to argue. '*Not. Now*. Mama is setting up for dinner and Evan is coming. But she was at the fight and she's not exactly dinner ready.'

Benelli crosses her slim arms and tosses her shiny hair over her shoulder. 'Wait a minute. You' – she pauses and jabs a finger at my chest – 'took *her* to a fight? A fight with the Murrays? Have you lost your damn mind?'

'We were on a date when he got the call—' Evan begins to explain, but my sister throws a palm in her face and shushes her.

Rage burns dangerously hot through me, and I do what I never do. I snap at Benelli.

'Don't you dare disrespect her!' Benelli was all wound up to deliver some tough-girl, shoulder-swaying, hip-shaking speech, but her mouth falls open and she's standing totally still, perfectly mute. 'Evan is our guest.' I look over and Evan is breathing hard through her nostrils, fists balled at her sides. 'And my girlfriend. I need your help, Bene. Do this for me, please.'

At the word 'girlfriend', Evan's fingers unfurled.

At the same word, my sister growled in indignation. 'Girlfriend?'

Before she can say anything else, Evan cuts in. 'It's time for me to leave.'

'No offense, Winchester, but you should listen to your *girlfriend*. Dinner with Mama? After a big fight? This is going to be crazy enough.' She runs her eyes over Evan like she's not sure what she thinks.

Evan nods and grabs my arm. 'Listen to her, Winch. I don't want to make anything harder for you right now. And I want your family to like me. Since, let's face it, the odds are stacked against me, just listen to Benelli and take me home.'

Her eyes are swimming with tears I know she's not about to shed in front of my sister. They're begging me for mercy, to release her from this catastrophic situation, and I'm ready to do what she needs. I've been beat down in too many ways to count today.

Benelli's voice cuts through our wordless conversation. 'Evan?' She huffs a little, but her eyes are lowered with something that looks an awful lot like shame. 'We may be a little . . . eccentric. But we're not monsters. There's no point in your going home. Mama always cooks enough for the whole town. And I have

a dress – if you want to wear it. I'll completely understand if you want to run away from all of us, but
seriously, you have the coloring to pull this dress off
and I so don't, so I'd be happy for you to have it.'

My sister still sounds half pissy and rude as hell,
but it only takes Evan a few seconds to make up her
mind. I can tell by the way she squares her shoulders
that she isn't going to go down without a fight, and I
have a sudden, weird thought: I'm glad Evan wasn't
born a guy and a Murray, because I wouldn't have
had a chance in hell in the ring today if she had
been.

'Thank you. I would appreciate it if you could also
lend me a brush and a little make-up.'

Evan and my sister stare at each other like two
queens from warring nations, ready to make a tenta-
tive peace.

'Shoo, Winch.' Benelli flicks her fingers my way,
and I give Evan a look to let her know she can back
out if she wants to.

But she pushes a straggly piece of hair out of her
face and says, 'You heard her. Shoo. We have an
emergency make-over, and I'm going to need all the
help your sister can offer me.'

I feel a relieved clutch in my chest, but before I can
kiss her or whisper anything sexy and secret against
her ear, Benelli yanks Evan into the pink-and-gold

girlie sanctuary of her room and slams the French doors closed on me.

I head to my rooms and wash, change into clothes that aren't covered in blood and grime, and bandage the worst of my injuries. The good news is that I won't need to visit the ER. The bad news is that I may have broken my nose, but it's still too soon to tell. Remy pops in.

'Dinner in twenty.' He reads my confused face – dinner is never late – and grins. 'Benelli came to the rescue, and Mom suspended the rules for once.'

'She ask about your bashed-up melon?'

Unlike me, Remy hadn't yet bothered to change his clothes or wash off the blood, and I'm not sure he would bother at all except for the fact that my father insists you come neat, dressed, and on your best behavior to dinner in his house.

'I gave her a song and dance. No reason to get her all worried. We were the knights in shining armor, in case she asks.'

He leaves me hanging on purpose, the same smug face he always wore when we were kids and he was dangling a toy he knew I wanted in front of me.

'Did you tell her about Evan? What did she say?' I'm surprised to see the gleeful look wipe off his face.

'I thought you'd ask what got me in the ring with

the Murray brothers today.' He leans a shoulder against the wall and zeros in on me.

Why didn't I ask him? I'm usually running like a fool, trying to figure out what makes Remy tick and why, so I can try to predict his next move. Which was always a pretty useless plan. You can't predict anarchy.

'I figured it out already. It's because you're a fucking idiot. What did Mama say about Evan?'

Remy's silent for two beats, enough time for me to see the confusion and disappointment roll across his face.

'She said, "Not Lala?" Then she said, "Twenty minutes." I think she's making *szüz tekercsek*. You know how into it she gets when she's making that.' He backs out, smacking the edge of my door with the palm of his hand. 'See you at the table.'

His voice is ringed with an anticipation that makes my stomach queasy.

It's a long, anxious twenty minutes, and I know Benelli must have worked some kind of strong voodoo on our mother, because dinner waits for no man at her table. It's after six. I never in my life remember dinner starting after six. It's six straight up, and most nights every one of us is expected around the table, plus usually a handful or three of our closest relatives and family friends.

We're all seated when Benelli comes in, followed by Evan.

I almost knock my chair back when they walk in, and I feel like someone sucker-punched me in the throat.

My sister is a schemer, and the dress she put Evan in is this innocent soft yellow, light and sweet enough for our grandmother, never mind our mother, to approve of. But it's also made of some kind of fabric so lightweight, it clings to every curve and makes her skin look even more touchably soft than it usually does.

I'm dying to skip this whole migraine-inducing dinner and take her to the beach, to my room, to my bed, to do whatever we want for however long we want, while my brother and all his bullshit rots in hell for all I care.

I pull the chair next to me out for her and let my hands furtively graze the sweet curves of her body as I push it in.

'You look amazing,' I murmur for her ears alone. I watch the pink deepen around her cheekbones and the roots of her hair. When she's settled, I turn to the table. 'Mama, Pop, this is Evan Lennox. My girlfriend.'

Mama clanks the serving spoon she was holding into the dish with a little more force than necessary.

Evan looks each of my parents in the eye. 'It's so

nice to meet you both. Thank you for having me over on such short notice. I hope it wasn't an inconvenience.'

She smoothes her napkin on her lap and graces everyone with a cool, collected smile.

I want to fist-pump with satisfaction. Evan knows exactly how to fight this battle, and she'll mutilate everyone in my family with her awesome manners.

Mama rushes to tell her that it was no trouble at all, and the tense first minutes get replaced by the usual food distribution flurry. I pour Evan some white wine, shipped over from my great-uncle's vineyard in Hungary. She takes a sip and smiles, and I feel a twinge of worry. She's so deep in character at this table, I have no idea if I can read anything she says or does accurately.

Does she like the wine, the food, my family, or is this all an act worthy of one of my own performances?

My mouth goes dry.

It's like I'm living my worst nightmare. The passionate girl I'm so damn in love with is all of a sudden moved by the same marionette strings that dictate my every waking moment. She's playing a role as much as I always am, and it's because I brought her to a place where everyone is expected to play along.

'So, where did you meet my brother? I didn't think Winch had any friends.' My little sister Ithaca, the light-haired, green-eyed rebel misfit of my little clan, pipes up with an outrageously rude question that has my sister and my mother simultaneously shushing her.

Evan wipes her mouth and smiles, and, this time, I'm sure it's real. Or she's an even more amazing actor than I initially imagined.

'It's OK. Ithaca?' My sister nods like she's conducting a government interview. 'I met your brother at community service. I'm a senior at St Anne's School for Girls. I also live in Savannah, off of Ardsley Park, with my grandparents.'

Ithaca raises an eyebrow. 'You don't live with your parents?'

My baby sister is old enough to know how to act, but being the spoiled youngest, she gets away with pretty much anything.

'Ithaca,' I warn, reaching for Evan's hand under the table. She laces her fingers with mine and squeezes, but her eyes stay locked on my sister's.

'No. My mother moved to Mexico and my father has a gambling problem. So I live with my grandparents because they're the best people for me to be with right now.' Evan keeps her eyes trained on Ithaca, which is probably a good thing.

My mother's face is openly disapproving, my father looks annoyed, Benelli is texting like crazy under the table. My guess is she's filling Lala in on everything that's going down. Remy is pouring himself an extra glass of wine and not bothering to try and hide his chuckles, and Colt looks like he wants to get back to practicing football as soon as humanly possible.

'Why Mexico?' Ithaca demands.

'I think she loves being on the beach. And the real estate market is decent,' Evan muses. 'Also, my mom loves vacationing. And this is kind of like a permanent vacation.' Her hand has a vice grip on mine.

'I hear that. My mother constantly says she needs a vacation after she takes a vacation with us.' Ithaca jabs at her dinner with her fork.

Evan's laugh bubbles out politely, but her words rip at me. 'Maybe that's why my mother didn't take me along.'

'Ithaca.' My mother finally swoops in with laser eyes and a hard-set mouth. 'That's the end of your little question-and-answer session. Evan is a guest of your brother's, and we don't put our guests on the spot like that.' She turns to Evan. 'I apologize. Ithaca is . . .' She glances at my sister and grits out, 'A free spirit.'

'She means a pain in the ass,' I whisper. Evan bites back a smile.

'So, Benelli, speaking of vacations, you mentioned

Lala might be coming with us on our trip to the Cayman Islands this fall?' my mother asks, taking a delicate bite of her pumpernickel bread.

I grimace and shoot a look at my plate I don't dare direct at my mother, no matter how much I want to. Evan sits a little straighter at my side.

Even Benelli looks a tiny bit shocked that my mom would play her hand so obviously. I guess she's more threatened by Evan than I initially thought.

'Yeah. Her family was thinking of doing Bermuda right around the same time, but we thought it would be more fun if we had each other for company.' Benelli lays her phone aside for a minute and throws me a pleading glance, I guess hoping that I'm not pissed about her and Lala taking their schemes to another level.

Mama purposefully keeps her eyes off of Evan, as if she's not sitting next to me. 'Well, that's just silly. We've all been friends for so long, it's like our families are married in. I'll give her mother a call and see if we can't all arrange something. What do you think, Tobar? Maybe we could rent a villa for the adults, and keep the kids in another one. They could have some privacy, we could have some privacy.' She nudges his arm, and he gives her a distracted look.

'Whatever you think, love. I have some big ship- ments coming in right around then, so I may need to fly down later.' He rubs the back of his neck and up through his thinning, graying hair.

My mother never disagrees openly with my father, but she offers a quiet, 'It's our one vacation together all year, Tobar. I understand that work is important, but family always needs to come first.'

The words are directed to my father, but her dark-blue eyes bore into me when she says it.

'Family vacations are wonderful, Jazmin, but we need money to afford them, and that's where the boys and I come in.' He takes her hand and rubs it.

She looks at him, her face twisted with shock. 'You and the boys? Tobar! The children have never missed a vacation.'

My father tucks a huge, scarred hand on the side of her face, rubbing his thumb on her cheekbone, his fingers loosening little pieces of her dark hair from her bun.

'The *children* are grown men, love. When I was Remy's age, we already had two kids and Benelli on the way. I was working on getting us a second mortgage and opening the Florida branch of our demolition company. It's time you stopped treating them like children.'

It's a gentle scold, but I'm shocked my father brought it up with Evan at the table. My mother's blue eyes flash at him.

'My sons will always be their mother's children.'

My father is a wise guy. He knows better than to push any more buttons. 'Let's save this conversation for when it's closer to our vacation time. You make the reservations, and the guys and I will work hard to see that it all goes according to your plan, OK?'

Mama nods, but takes an extra-long gulp of her wine. Colt finally can't stand another second of this tense, stomach-curling dinner.

'Mama, Pop, may I please be excused?' he pleads. 'Coach went through a few new plays he wants me to practice.'

'Dinner is dinner,' Mama objects. 'You spend too much time with football. By the time your brothers were your age, they were working for your father.'

Colt nods to his plate, working hard to keep the aggravated scowl off his face.

'Yes, ma'am,' he murmurs.

Luckily, Colt doesn't have to wait too long before we run out of awkward, stupid, griping things to talk about and dinner is over. Evan attempts to help clear the table, but Mama and Benelli shoo her away in a move that's less 'you're our guest' and more 'you don't belong in our kitchen'.

I seethe on Evan's behalf. I love my family, would lay down my life for them, but they're doing their best to cold-shoulder Evan right out of our world.

Which is good. I should be glad. She doesn't belong with all this insanity anyway.

So why am I feeling so panicked that this dinner, which I knew would be a disaster, wound up being catastrophic beyond even my expectations?

Evan 10

I feel like an imposter. Wearing this sweet dress that isn't mine and isn't me, sitting at the big cherry table and keeping my mouth shut while Winchester's mom does her damnedest to make me feel like an intruder. She goes on and on about Lala, who I assume from the look of pure horror on Winch's face is his ex. She talks about family and how everyone has to work together and be together and eat together and give up their dreams together.

Ugh!

Not only did she warp every fairy-tale image I had of big families – their camaraderie and abundance of love – she made it clear to me why Winchester Young-blood has been so reluctant to take even a baby step forward in our relationship.

And, for the first time since I met him, I feel a sinking sense that maybe he and I really aren't meant to be. Maybe our relationship is being blocked by obstacles we have no hope of overcoming. And maybe, for the first time in my entire life, I see all the distinct warning signs and can get out of this before I get myself into a mess I can't bounce back from.

For the first time, I cannot say I didn't see it coming, because this is clearly a train-wreck just waiting to happen, and even I'm not that blind.

I'm sitting on the wide, open front porch of the Youngbloods' palatial house wondering if I will be able to deal with walking away from Winch and leaving him here, without me, for good. Defeat buckles me. I have never felt so sapped of strength or will.

'Would you mind if I tossed a few passes with Colt?' Winch asks, rubbing my hand in his. He's all apology tonight, and it makes me feel miserable. I feel miserable for everything that's happened on this foul mess of an evening. 'You could go in the kitchen with Mama and Benelli,' he offers.

I stifle a sigh and give him a sensible glare. 'Really, Winch? I'm just as willing as you to pretend tonight wasn't as horrific as it actually was, but sit in the kitchen alone with them? I don't have a death wish, thank you very much.'

He puts an arm around my shoulders and leans his head on mine. I turn my face so my nose brushes his cheek, and I can smell the clean clover smell that always seems to cling to his skin. 'I knew we should have waited to do dinner.'

I pull back and raise my eyebrows. 'Waited for what exactly? It was inevitable that your family would hate me.'

'They don't hate you,' he insists, but his words are so unsteady, he can't even convince himself he means them.

'No, you're right.' His eyes snap to attention, bright with hope. 'If I thought they hated me, I'd be implying that they are worried I pose some kind of threat. I'm something nasty they stepped in on the way to better things. They're just going to wipe me off the bottom of their shoe and never give me a second thought.'

His eyes go brighter, but it's not hope this time. Not at all. This time, they're wild with rage.

'Don't you dare say that about yourself,' he snarls, his hands digging into my shoulders. 'You hear me?' I know my eyes have gone wide with shock, and that may be what makes him loosen his hold, and what extinguishes the raging look in his eyes, replacing it with something so promising, it makes my entire body tremble. 'You are the most goddamn amazing person I've ever met. And my family is just gonna have to learn to love you as much as I do, because I'm not letting you go. Ever. No matter what anyone thinks. You're worth fighting for. OK?'

He looks so sweetly sure, his battered, purple-bruised face still heart-stoppingly handsome. I trace my fingers very gently around the damaged skin of his eye and the slight swell of his nose.

'I don't like the idea of you fighting about anything anymore.' He starts to protest, but I put a finger over his lips, gently, because they're broken up, too. 'Winch, I almost threw up watching that today. I've never seen anything so horrifying and brutal in my life. And it tore me up that it was you. That you were hurting. And then tonight . . .' I drop my voice and look over my shoulder, just to be sure no one from his family is nearby. 'Tonight it was like no one cared. No one even asked about what happened. That whole awkward dinner where everyone got lectured about how amazing family is, but no one thought to ask how you got your face bashed in or if you need medical attention.' My voice goes thick and I take a few long, deep breaths.

Winch wraps his arms around me and smoothes my hair with his hands.

'It's OK. It's all over. And I promise I'm getting away from all that. I am. I'm sorry you had to see what you did today. That's why I didn't want to take you. That's why I told you to stay by the car.'

I throw my hands up.

'Seriously? Just stop and *listen* to yourself. My being there saved your ass. You could have been arrested or trampled by the crowd. And my not being there wouldn't mean it never happened. I'm glad I witnessed it, because now I know how horrible it is, and I'm hell-bent on making sure that never, ever happens to you again. OK? And I may be the only person in your life who can give you some perspective. What happened to you was scary and terrible. I am *freaked out* about it, and I'm even more freaked out that no one else is freaking out with me. This isn't normal, Winch.'

I snap my mouth closed when I realize how loud my last words were. I have no idea who heard, and right now, I just don't care. Someone has to stand up to all this strange denial before Winch winds up beaten into a coma, or worse.

'Listen, we can talk about this all later, I promise. Let's go. I'll spend a few minutes with Colt like I promised, and then you and I can get the hell out of here, OK? Forget this whole day ever happened.'

He presses my hair back on either side of my face with both hands and kisses me, full and soft and sweet on the lips. I move my hands up and hold him around the neck for an extra-long second.

I don't want to get sucked into this. I don't want every day we spend together to end with his plea for a redo. I hate Winch's constant insistence that we forget things happened. Maybe that's why crazy shit keeps happening to him. Maybe it's because he's always charging ahead into the next disaster, never learning from what happened before.

He leans down and offers me his hand, but I shake my head. 'Go ahead. I don't want Colt to feel rushed. I'll be right here when you get back.'

Winch's eyebrows press together. 'You sure?'

'Positive. Go.'

I watch him walk away, throwing an odd look at me over his shoulder now and then, and try to figure out what I'm supposed to do now that things have gone so wrong in a way I can't possibly fix.

'He's a good guy.'

The words surprise me so much I almost fall off the step. Winch's father stands behind me, an unlit cigarette in his mouth, and a lighter in his hands.

'Mr Youngblood.' I get up and press down on the skirt of my dress with nervous, clammy hands. *Shitshitshitshitshit*. Did he hear anything? Should I say anything? Parents don't usually rattle me like this. 'I was just going to, uh—'

'Sit,' he interrupts, squinting as he holds the cigarette tight in his lips and lights it with a few clicks of his lighter.

I sit and instantly wish I hadn't, because he's still standing, leaned against the porch railing, and I feel diminutive and young with him towering over me like this.

'My son is a good man,' he repeats, inhaling a long, slow drag and letting it course out of his mouth in a lazy stream of bluish smoke. 'Don't tell anyone' – he looks down at me and smiles a conspiratorial smile – 'but I sometimes wish Winchester was my firstborn.' He shakes a finger at me. 'Don't misunderstand. I love Remington from the bottom of my heart. He's exactly like my own brother, Becse.' He laughs around his cigarette and plumes of smoke billow out through his slightly crooked teeth. 'Funny as hell. Clowns, almost. But sensitive. Remington feels everything deeply. He isn't strong like Winchester. He can't put his feelings on hold or let things go. When he's angry, he feels it from the bottom of his soul, you know? He's like a human hurricane.'

'Do you think if he wasn't firstborn, he'd listen to Winch more?' I ask, tucking the fabric of the thin yellow dress under my knees more securely.

Mr Youngblood has been nothing but polite since I came to their home. He didn't display any of the underlying menace his wife directed my way. But there was something quietly and dangerously power-ful about him. It's a trait Winch shares, but with Winch there's so much more ease and good humor. I just have the distinct feeling that Mr Youngblood is one hundred percent charming and gentlemanly . . . as long as everything is going his way.

'If he wasn't firstborn, he wouldn't have our company to worry over. He'd have the kinds of freedom Winch has.' He shrugs his broad, powerful shoulders. 'But that wasn't his lot. Remington is firstborn, so he'll take my place when it's time for me to retire.' The cigarette nestles between his lips as he looks into the distance musingly, sucking smoke in and out in gentle puffs.

'So Remington will run your company even if he's not the best person for the job?' I've noticed how secretive the Youngbloods are, and I half expect something negative: a glare, a harsh word, a shake of the head. But Mr Youngblood's smile is cruelly polite.

'In our family, we have old-fashioned ideas.' He shrugs as if he's half apologizing, though he clearly doesn't feel remotely apologetic for the uncompromising way he runs his family. 'But those ideas have kept the Youngbloods prosperous and successful for generations. It's a tough economy out there. It will be twice as hard for my sons to gain half of what I had at their age.' His eyes, grayer and starker than Winch's, focus on me for a long minute. 'This family protects one another. Supports one another. If one of us suffers, we all do. One of us celebrates, we all do. That takes a certain kind of sacrifice. You understand?'

He smiles again, this time slightly kinder, as if he's trying to tell me, *I know you don't and can't understand,*

and here's your cue to leave well enough alone, little girl.

I know that smile. I've been an outsider in a crystal bauble my entire life, looking into worlds where I just couldn't fit or didn't make sense. Sometimes it was because of the taint of my notorious father and his crazy gambling habits. Or my flighty mother and her string of revolving-door younger men. Or my form- idably rich and eccentric grandparents whose circle was peppered with other old, rich people like them. I never had a solid social circle in school, my best friend is half a country away, and most of my boyfriends were users and cheaters.

And now I have Winch, and he's all I ever wanted.

Why, just when I truly let myself begin to fall in love with someone, does the situation prove too impossible to overcome?

My pounding heart and churning stomach make it difficult to answer Winch's father, but I'm saved by Winch's return with Colt, both of them slightly sweaty, with huge, matching smiles on their faces.

'Pop, have you seen this kid's spiral? Unbeliev- able.' Winch shakes his head, his dark eyes bright with pride, his arm draped over his little brother's shoulders with easy grace. 'He'll have the college scouts fighting over him like a pack of hyenas.'

Colt shrugs his wide shoulders, but he is still lean and lanky. If he keeps playing football in college he'll bulk up, but right now he looks more like a javelin thrower or a fencer.

Their father stubs his cigarette in a bronze urn and frowns. 'Still football, Colt? Soccer isn't good enough?' His smile has morphed, no longer condescendingly polite, but indulgently disappointed. Colt's face falls and Winch's eyes flash hard, then neutralize.

'Soccer's not really my thing, Pop,' Colt says, tossing the football back and forth in his enormous, long-fingered hands, and it's like that ball is a part of him. The gray in his father's eyes darkens as he drinks in every minute detail.

'Soccer was good enough for generations of Youngbloods. I don't know if you gave it a fair chance. Maybe a few weeks back on the homestead with your cousins this summer—'

'But I'm captain of the football team, so I'll be in for extra training, Pop.' Colt presses his lips together as his father goes very still and quiet. 'Sorry to interrupt, sir.'

Immediately Mr Youngblood's charming smile radiates again. 'Don't be ridiculous. We'll talk about Hungary and soccer in a few weeks, when you've had time to think about how good it would be for you. Now come on in and we'll watch that movie about the UFC fighter Remington keeps going on about. Winch, you coming?'

Winch looks at me, and I try hard to keep my nerves under control. I feel trapped. I feel trapped inside a maze that's in a sealed box that's been thrown down a deep, dark hole and I'm crashing to the bottom.

'You OK?' he asks, his voice low.

'Fine.' I say the word, but I look right into his eyes and he takes half a second to read my every obvious thought.

'I won't be able to watch tonight, Pop. Evan and I have plans.' He threads his fingers through mine and the pressure is slow and deliberate, like he's willing the calm strength of his hold to transfer through to me.

'Go out later. Evan's welcome to stay with your mother and the girls. You come join me and your brothers. Your grandpa and uncle are coming around later.' Mr Youngblood's voice has all the confident exuberance of a circus ringmaster, and there's so much charm, anyone not listening closely would fail to detect the sharp edge of unequivocal demand in his words.

Winch only hesitates for a second. 'Sorry, Pop.' His father's shoulders tense, and Colt jerks his head in Winch's direction, his mouth quickening up and down with a nervous twitch. 'I have some things to do at the shop later tonight.'

but it makes vicious goosebumps prickle stiffly up my legs.

I wonder if they called him. If he'll go. If he'll come back and say goodbye first. If he does come back, will he tell me he loves me again? He doesn't have to. This weirdness, this badness is all my fault. I'm to blame. For every stupid turn the night took, I'm to blame.

I never expected him to be so honest, so fearless. I didn't think he'd strip down and make me blush and have sex with me like he was born knowing exactly how to make my body race, then jump headfirst into the pool and my games, professing his love.

I never, ever expected him to put me in the 'always' category.

Even if it is only a game.

Even if it isn't real.

But isn't every game real on some level?

I hold my head in my hands and feel miserable, chilled, lonely and used; a million and one empty, clanking adjectives that don't quite put a finger on my loss and sadness.

The sliding door opens, and I grip the pool edge, waiting. His footsteps come close, and a towel covers my shoulders. 'Come in. You look cold.'

'No one called?' I clutch the towel to my chest and crane my neck to look at him.

'I have no idea. I didn't check.' He's dressed, but

barefoot, his hair still wet and shiny from the pool water, but lying neatly on his head. 'Come in. We can watch TV.'

'I don't want to watch TV,' I say, the petulance in my voice immature but unstoppable.

He's silent. I can see his shadow, cast from the porch light. I can see he's stuck his hands in his pockets.

'What do you want to do?'

His voice is calm and even, Winch all buttoned-up again. I had him loose and free, and now I've pushed him back to buttoned-up and unattainable.

I kick my feet under the water and hold my legs out, stiff and hip-high in front of my body.

'I think it was that water, that cold water. I think it froze my heart a little. I think that's why I was such a raging bitch.'

'You weren't a bitch.'

Winch always says the right thing, the polite thing. Like a diplomat or something. I wish he'd argue, growl, grab me and kiss me hard, because I messed up so badly, but he loves me. He does. He said it.

I let the towel slide down off my shoulders and hear the intake of his breath. I know it's just Winch appreciating my skin, but it makes me feel better. I close my eyes and wish he'd yell at me for being so awful before. But I know that when Winch is really hurt, he goes cold.

And it's feeling pretty frosty out here.

'I was a bitch. And I'm sorry. And I'm sad.' I tilt my head back and look up at him.

He looks down at me, and his smile is indulgent, but guarded. He steps forward so his feet are on either side of my body. 'Why are you sad?'

'Because you're dressed.' When his smile turns into a chuckle, I push my luck. 'But if you got undressed and got in the hot-tub, I'd be warm, so less bitchy, and happy, since naked is kind of a requirement for hot-tubbing.'

'You're that desperate to see me naked?' He moves closer to my side, then sits next to me on the damp cement.

I walk my fingers to his hand and squeeze. 'I may have played down just how spectacular you look. Naked. And otherwise.'

'You freak me out a little when you're being nice, you know that?' He leans forward, and I half pucker, sure I'm about to be kissed, but he swipes a fingertip gently under my eye and holds it up for my examination. 'Eyelash.'

I nod and choke back my raging disappointment. My fault, my fault, my fault. I asked him to open up, he did, and I smashed him where he was most delicate.

'Or, you know, TV would be OK.'

'Blow it.' I raise both eyebrows into my hair, and his

puzzled look twists into a chuckle. 'Uh, not that. The eyelash.'

It's a little embarrassing that I'm half disappointed.

'Blow it?' I repeat.

He holds his finger closer. 'Off the tip of my finger. And make a wish.'

I level that little poke of black hair a dubious glance. 'You want me to wish on a fallen eyelash? I never would have pegged you for such a romantic.'

'You should stop trying to peg me at all.' He gestures with his finger again. 'And it's more superstition than romance. Blow and wish.'

My dirty interpretation of his suggestion makes the blood run hot and fast all through me. I clutch the towel tighter to my chest, lean forward and pucker for the second time in these last few minutes. I close my eyes and wish, with everything in me, that this night will weave some kind of lasting magic. That we'll wake up with everything figured out, and we'll survive as a couple. That our relationship won't be a tug-of-war or bumper cars or a roller-coaster. I blow, but before I can open my eyes, Winch's hand is covering them and his voice softly instructs me to blow again.

The second time, I blow harder, and when he uncovers my eyes, his smile is just over the line of bashful.

'I can't walk under ladders, either. I avoid black cats like the fucking plague. And I never put new shoes on the table.'

'What?' That one makes me giggle. 'New shoes? Where else would you put them? I always put them on the table.'

'If you have any feelings for me whatsoever, you won't freak me out by doing that. Ever. Even if you and I . . .' His words trail off and his eyes dart over to the softly lapping waves of the pool.

'You and I won't.'

I don't go any further with my statement, because imagining life devoid of Winch is a specifically breathtaking kind of pain, and I don't have the courage to speak that possibility out loud.

'Shall we?' He puts a hand out and I stare at his inviting gesture while I untangle what he's asking.

'Go in the house?' I ask. He shakes his head. 'Watch TV?' He pulls his hand back and takes his shirt off in one slow tug, gripping behind his neck and letting the cloth slide over his bruised skin and tight muscles. 'Hot-tub?'

I pull myself to my feet without waiting for his assistance.

Everything with Winch and me seems to be the double side of a coin flipping through the air, with no one sure which side it's going to land on. When we're on heads, it seems like life is going in the right direction; it's all stolen kisses and that kind of deep and complete understanding that you only ever get with a few people who truly know and . . . love you. But when it's tails, it's all freezing, shut-down, hopeless resignation.

Winch walks to the hot-tub, his shorts hanging half off his hips, and pries the cover off. I turn it on and he helps me climb into the bubbling, warm water before shedding his shorts and following.

In the cozy, warm rush of this soothing water, I wonder what the answer to our flipping-coin relationship conundrum might be. Hope the coin always lands on heads? Stop flipping it? Melt it down and make a whole new coin, smooth on both sides?

'What are you thinking about?' he asks.

In the shadows, it's hard to make out his features, but my legs float slightly, and one foot lands on his thigh. He moves closer to me.

'Us. Coins. Us.' I smile at his frown.

'I'm trying to make this work, Evan. You have to know how hard I'm trying.'

His body goes from mirroring mine to paralleling it, and the heat of his skin on mine is identical to the heat of the water. We're all hot, warmed up, that frigid distance between us melting like I hoped it would.

'I feel like I'm balancing too much. More than I can hold all at once,' he explains.

'I get it.' I lean forward and kiss the side of his mouth. 'I don't want to make things harder for you.'

He kisses back, his tongue pressing into my mouth in a slow, steady slide.

'I know that. But you do.' I stiffen and try to pull back, but he pulls me forward. 'Maybe that's exactly what I've needed all this time. Things have been . . . my life has been on the same course since I was too young to remember. And my parents and family dictated a lot of it. I'm not very good at questioning the way they want things to be. But I've known I wasn't happy for a long time. It used to be just this pull . . . like this misery I got dragged along with. When I met you . . . things changed when I met you. Good changes. But things also got harder.'

'So what do we do?'

We're side by side, and it feels good. But I'm not satisfied with just good, so I half float, half slide onto his lap, looking over at his dark-blue eyes, squinted in serious thought, bordered by the wet spread of inky lashes.

I wish one was loose under his eye, so I could offer him the chance to put his faith in a wish. 'How do we balance all this?'

His hand moves over my face, pushing the wet hair back. And when it's all pushed away, he just keeps rubbing my skin. 'I don't know if there *is* a balance.'

I weave my arms around his neck and press against his chest, all the soft, needy places on me matched to his hard, bruised body. 'Why?'

His hands grasp either side of my face. 'Because you're young enough that you haven't fucked things up with your life. And I'm old enough that I should have started to think about these things a while ago.'

I laugh softly. 'Winch, we're four years apart. You act like you're in a nursing home and I'm graduating eighth grade.'

I rub my nose along the bristly stubble on the side of his face.

'Four years can make a hell of a difference if you use your time wisely.' He's so serious, it's almost funny. I kiss his frown. I kiss his jaw. I kiss his chin before I lay my head on his chest and listen to the jumping pace of his heart. 'I'm willing to let you go if it means you get a chance to avoid everything I did wrong. I want better for you.'

'The best I can possibly have is all right here.' I lay both hands over his heart. 'With you.'

He sits up and pulls me closer, sloshing water over the sides of the tub.

'How did I get so damn lucky?' he asks, his mouth blanketing mine.

We kiss and touch and tangle until things are back where they were before the pool and the games and his question. And when my head is pillowed on his shoulder and all I can think about is him, forever, and never going back to real life, whatever that means, I say to him, 'You're the best I've ever had. I don't like talking about the guys before you. Because, honestly, there were a lot. A whole lot. But it's never been like this, Winch. And I guess that messed me up.'

I'm looking right at his hand twined with mine, half under the water, when I tell him this. Because I don't want him to see me blush and wince while I confess.

He strokes down from the crown of my head to between my shoulder blades with his free hand. 'Shh. That was stupid of me to ask. It's none of my business.'

'Well, it is.' I would never, ever have said this to any guy I dated or had sex with before. That was the thing, the thing that kept everything else in line. My secrets, my feelings, my interests, were all mine. All mine. No sharing whatsoever. But because I know Winch would never take from me without giving back, I want to share. 'I want to be your business.'

He doesn't say anything, but he crushes me close and we sit still and listen to the steady hum of the hot-tub, bubbling and insulating us from the clear, cool sounds of the night.

'Winch?'

'Mmm?'

I love how relaxed he feels and sounds. But I have to ask, no matter how it might tense up all those lax muscles.

'Is it really only going to be tonight?'

He gathers me tighter.

'I'm willing to do whatever it takes for this. For us.'

I know he means it. I know he does. And, nervous as I was, I never really doubted that he'd say anything else.

But life has a funny way of conspiring to keep us from doing what we mean to do, despite our best intentions. And I never want to hold the attempt to do the right thing against him. Even if it blows up in our faces.

'What are you thinking?' he asks, his lips at my ear.

'I'm thinking about you and me,' I whisper back.

He nuzzles my neck. 'All good stuff, right?'

'Of course. What could be bad?'

We lose ourselves in the slow, sweet tumble of a kiss that ignites our passion, but also runs away from the question I just asked, which neither one of us wants to answer.

Winch 12

The phone rings. I let it. The moon rises. Evan sleeps soundly in my arms, and the weight of her in them marks the first time I've held my responsibility close and didn't feel crushed by it. The weight of taking care of her is the kind of weight that will make me stronger. I know it.

Remy's ringtone only breaks the silence once, in the dead of the night. I watch the screen glow bright while the song plays out, and wait for a second or third or twentieth call, but no more come through, which means one of two things; Remy is dead or he was calling because he knows I said not to and wanted to find some way to tell me to fuck off.

I would bet everything I own on the latter.

Douchebag.

In the early, breaking dawn, my phone rings again, and this time, I'm surprised the ringtone is Ithaca's. I almost don't recognize the soulful croon of some emo or goth or whatever the hell she's listening to nowadays. It's crazy how quickly she's growing up. Seems like she was just toddling around the other day, her tiny fist clamped hard around my finger for support.

I manage to slide Evan onto the pillow without waking her and grab the phone, pulling my pants on with one hand while I answer.

'What's up, kid?'

'Winch?' Ithaca's voice is trembly and upset. Dread coats my stomach like thick ice. 'Um, where are you?'

'Wherever you need me to be. Tell me where to go and you can explain while I'm on the way.'

I plug one ear so I can hear her over the crash of the waves. The sliding door opens, and Evan steps out, rumpled and so damn gorgeous, it takes my breath away. She's wearing my T-shirt and a tiny pair of panties, and even in the midst of Ithaca's crisis, I feel a pull for her so strong it floors me.

Remy? she mouths in my direction, her face controlled and neutral, but I shake my head and mouth back, *Ithaca*.

She holds up one finger, her blue eyes wide, and whirls back into the house. I'm trying to listen to Ithaca's jittery, broken story, told through a few rounds of disjointed sobs, but all I really care about is the address and getting there as fast as possible. My little sister never cries; her tears are a swift kick to the back of my knees.

Evan runs back out with my wallet and her purse, her dress thrown on and my shirt shoved at me. She drops my shoes at my feet, and we run to the car. I feel a relief like I've never known.

Truth to be told, even though I've faced down huge guys and beaten the piss out of them, every single time my family gets into shit, I'm gripped with a fear I'm embarrassed to fess up to. I have no clue what's going to happen when I get to Ithaca's fancy-ass private school. The thought that I might find her hurt or helpless fills my heart with dread.

But, for the first time, I don't have to face all this on my own. I have Evan, cool as a fucking cucumber, setting up the GPS and asking if she needs to make any calls for me.

'I don't know.' I do a quick scan for early-bird cops, and decide to take my chances and floor it. She doesn't bat a gorgeous eyelash. 'Ithaca is at her school, but it's early. I don't think there are any teachers or anything. I have no fucking idea what's going on. All I know is that she's panicked and she needs me.'

Evan's nod is quick and tight. 'We'll be there in no time. She's gonna be OK.'

It may be a load of horseshit, but it's all I need to hear. I focus on driving. Evan is silent, but when I glance over, her face is determined, and I love that. I love the fight in her.

I'm barely stopped in the private, live-oak-lined parking lot when Evan leaps out and we both run to the area behind the sports fields, where it's slightly wooded and overgrown. The sound of fists pounding into faces is familiar enough to close my throat down. I leap through the brush and find a small group of young, preppy guys beating the piss out of each other. My idiot sister keeps jumping into the fray, only to get pushed back out by one of the cursing, bruised fighters.

Evan immediately grabs Ithaca, hooks her arms around her elbows and drags her, crying and screaming, away from the fight.

I rip two of the guys apart and hold them at arm's length. I could bench-press the two of them together, but they're full of raging testosterone and adrenaline, so I get punched in the shoulder and kicked in the shin pretty damn hard before I manage to calm either one down.

'What the hell is going on?' I yell.

Three guys back up to the side. The other fighter, quieter, his face badly bruised, not wearing a pretty, private-school uniform, wipes a long trickle of blood from under his nose.

The private-school boy starts mouthing off immediately. 'This fucking punk—'

I shake the little jerk by the scruff of his neck. 'Watch your damn mouth. Start over, and this time put that fancy education to work and use real words.'

His dark eyes drop, some of the bravado gone from his whole act.

'Sorry, uh, sir.' It must occur to him that he could be in deep shit, because he starts to wise up and use his manners real quick. 'This, eh, he . . . I caught this guy prowling around my house the other night. There's been a bunch of thefts in our neighborhood, then I saw him here. I confronted him, and he went nuts.'

'Liar!' Ithaca lunges out of Evan's arms, her light skin splotchy and pink, her blonde hair knotted and stuck to her cheeks. 'You are a liar, Rick! You accused him and threatened him when he never did a single thing! And then you all attacked him!' Her chest rises and falls and she points a shaking finger at them, her lips trembling with rage. 'All of you. Like a pack of wild dogs.'

She spits the last words out, then her shoulders sag.

The quiet guy makes a motion toward her, but I grip his shoulder hard and shake my head. He nods, but I can tell by the look on his face that seeing my sister upset is killing him.

It may be biased, but my allegiance falls immediately with this guy.

'Rick Wong?' I squint at the kid who gave me the

phony story. A red flush creeps up his face, like he's been caught with his pants down. 'Your family lives across the street from us.' He nods, but avoids eye contact. 'Your dad has three pit-bulls and a security system. I wouldn't worry about your precious shit getting stolen. Trust me, it's all insured anyway.' I toss him back to his friends, and he gives a hard stare to the ground.

I turn to the quiet kid, his dark eyes glued on my sister and wild with worry.

'What's your name?'

'Andre. Sir.' He shifts a look at the Wong kid and scowls, not about to be outdone.

I can't help it. I immediately like this Andre kid.

'This guy, Andre, he's none of your concern, you got that?' I shake Wong by the shoulder. 'Hey! Look at me when I talk to you.' He lifts his eyes and nods. 'And next time you think someone is doing something shady, handle it like a man and leave your little brute squad behind. There's no reason for four of you to jump a guy just because he's hanging around near your damn house.'

'Yes, sir.'

Rick, my dickhead neighbor, squirms under my look, and I'm sure there're a thousand things he wants to tell me to stick in a thousand places. But he doesn't.

'You mess with my man Andre again, I'll beat the

hell out of you. And your gang. And I don't give a shit who your daddy is. Now get the hell out of my sight, and I better not hear a word about you being a little asshole again.'

I dismiss him with a shove, and they scuttle away, muttering shit under the breath and throwing looks over their shoulders when they're far enough away that I can't catch any of them.

'Dre!' my sister wails and flings herself at her beat-up hero.

His arms hang by his sides, his eyes fixed nervously on me. I let go of his arm and nudge him forward, feeling weird about seeing my baby sister wrapped around some hooligan.

And I know the kid's a hooligan because it takes one to know one. The fact that I like him right away is a bad sign.

He runs a hand over my sister's hair, untangling pieces and pushing them away from her face. 'It's OK, babe. It's fine. I could have taken them.'

She raises one hand to his bloodied nose and cut lip, and chokes on a sob. I seriously have no idea what to think of this whole scene.

Evan walks over to me, the back of her hand brushing the back of mine. I thread my fingers through hers and hold tight. Her face turns toward mine, and she flashes a secret smile.

'Young love?' she asks lowly.

My sister is throwing herself at the kid, who's gently pushing her back and eyeing me with an anxious look that, I'm sure, is his attempt to communicate that he doesn't want any part of her PDA. Private displays of affection concerning my little sister? I'll deal with the reality. Public displays of affection? Andre and I both know that's not going to go over well.

Not in front of me anyway.

'Too young. And that kid isn't good enough for Ithaca.' I narrow my eyes and Andre puts both of his hands on my sister's shoulders and speaks to her in low, urgent tones.

'Stop scaring him.' Evan chuckles. 'Look at them. So in love. Do you remember your first love?'

She leans her head on my shoulder and I can smell the sweet burned candy smell.

I pull her into my arms and look her in the eye. 'Remember it? I'm living it right now.'

She jerks back, like she doesn't quite believe what I said.

'Your ex? The one your family talked about like you guys were engaged?'

'I've loved one girl. That's you, Evan Lennox.'

She steps back, looking at the ground and shaking her head like she can't put into words whatever it is that's running through her head.

Andre clears his throat loudly. I look away from Evan and see that my sister is seriously pouting.

'Um, I think it would be a good idea if Ithaca went back in to class. She's worried about me making it home OK. Could I maybe get a ride with you guys?'

'I am *not* going to sit in class with those assholes. I'm telling my mother that I want to switch schools.' Ithaca wipes the last few tears from under her clear green eyes. 'I want to go with you.'

Andre murmurs something to her, but she shakes her head and stamps her foot. 'No! I'm tired of sneaking around, Andre! I don't care anymore. I don't.'

Evan looks at me with raised eyebrows, and I sigh. I was looking forward to a long day rolling around in bed with my gorgeous girlfriend. It figures the one time my brother manages to stay out of trouble, my baby sister jumps into some damn star-crossed love fiasco.

'Go to school,' I tell my sister. 'I'll take him home, make sure he's got an icepack on his face and takes a few aspirin. He'll be good as new before you can sneak out with him again.'

I nod at Andre, who looks a little anxious, but tries to brush it off and act tough in front of my sister.

'I'm not going.' Ithaca plants her feet and squares her chin, and I have to bite back the world's biggest sigh. She's a stubborn, spoiled brat, and she's about to unleash all of her stupid anger on me; I'm getting the beginnings of a migraine just thinking about how this will go down. 'Why isn't *she* in school?'

'*She* has a name,' I bite back, not about to let her little tantrum make Evan feel like shit.

My wildly rude sister backs down. 'Sorry. Why isn't *Evan* at school?'

'My and my girlfriend's plans aren't your business,' I counter. Ithaca kicks the toe of her dressy little shoe into the dirt with ferocious energy. 'Look, you're in hot water. You should be begging me not to tell Mama all this, and don't even get me started on our old man. You know the rules.'

Her kicks get more ferocious.

'I *hate* the rules! I *hate* them! I'm not marrying some stupid guy Pop knows from Hungary so we can keep some dumb company in the family. I'm tired of all of our family's idiotic rules.' Her eyes are wild and her hands are balled into fists. 'I love Andre. I love him and there's nothing anyone can do about it.'

Andre looks like he's ready for the ground to open up and suck him deep into it. I try not to freak out over hearing my little sister declare her love for this guy. It's all dramatics, as usual with her, and I know the best thing I can do is just ignore it.

'All right, all right.' I hold up a hand. 'Go clean up. Get to class. You can drop out and run away with your boyfriend tomorrow, OK? I'll take him home. He needs his rest after getting his ass handed to him.' He makes a protesting noise, but I cut him off with a look he realizes means business. 'I'll give you ten minutes. Exactly. In ten minutes, I expect you' – I point to Andre – 'in my car and you' – I point to my sister – 'better have your ass in class.' She opens her mouth, but I cut in before she can argue. 'Your other option is me calling Mama and Andre's parents. If he's not in the car in ten minutes, I get on the phone.'

I grab Evan's hand, and we walk slowly back to my car. She squeezes my hand tight.

'You're a good brother.'

'Don't count on that.' I look at her sidelong and feel a lump in my throat, because I have a feeling Evan isn't going to like what I'm going to have to do to manage this situation. 'She's too attached to that kid already. I'm sure he's a nice guy and all, but she's not ready to be that serious. And he would never be accepted by my family.' Evan's mouth swings open, but I push ahead, 'I know it's harsh. But I can see how this will all pan out. I gotta do what I do.'

'What is that again?' Her voice is low and accusatory.

She tries to pry her hand away, but I hold tighter.

'What needs to be done.'

I don't want her to see what I'm about to do,

because I know it's going to look cruel, but in the end? In the end, it's a quick way to finish this without it dragging on.

'What needs to be done?' She turns her head, her dark hair whipping into her face with the rising wind. 'They're two kids in love. What exactly needs to be done?'

'My family won't approve. They'll drive Andre away. Ithaca will wind up hurting more. Even if my family did approve, the girls in my family don't date until the parents allow it. Ithaca has to focus on school and her future. Not this guy.'

Evan looks at me, her eyes bright with fury.

'This guy?' she repeats, throwing my words back at me. 'So, if someone doesn't meet the Youngblood standards, they just get thrown to the side?' Her voice shakes, and she twists hard to get away from me.

'Evan.' I pull her close, run a finger along her jaw and try to meet her eyes, but she keeps them to the side. Her nostrils flare. 'This isn't about me and you. I don't care what they think of you. We're different, OK?'

She shakes her head, whipping her dark hair.

'No. Not OK. Not OK at all. How, exactly, am I different than Andre?' she asks, her voice a knife staking in my ribs over and over with every bitter word.

'I mean, I'm a little older. A little more refined. Maybe I'm the right color?'

'It's not like that,' I grind out. 'Remy's daughter is half African-American. We have no problems with that—'

'Oh, I'm sorry, I didn't know,' she cuts in. 'I didn't get the Youngblood handbook. I have no idea what's good enough for you and your family. I would assume I'm not. Andre's not. Who meets your standards anyway? And who the *hell* are all of you to have these standards?'

I try to slow her down, quiet her, but she slaps my hands away and points a finger at me.

'No! No, I will *not* be quiet about this! Last night, I thought for a few minutes that we could be together in spite of your crazy family. That maybe we had a chance. But no one has a chance, do they? And I get it, OK, I get it! Andre and Ithaca are just kids in love. They'd probably break up in a few months over something dumb anyway. That isn't my point.' She gasps and bites her lip. 'That isn't my point.' Her words come out shaky and sad. 'What chance do we really have? Tell me the truth, Winch. Because I love you so much. I do. But is this just you dragging out the inevitable? Because if you know we won't last anyway, tell me and we'll end it now.'

She looks back at Ithaca and Andre, twisted around

each other, kissing like it's the last time they'll ever see each other.

And I choke on that thought. Because I realize that my sister knows me. And she probably realizes, somewhere deep down, that this is the last time she'll see this guy she thinks she loves so completely.

'Evan, you're overreacting. You and me—'

'Is there?' she interrupts. 'I thought there was. This entire time, you and me, we've always just been a pipedream, haven't we, Winch? Tell me.' Her voice is thick and her eyes are full of tears.

'No.' I hold her at the shoulders hard. 'We're not. We're different.'

She shakes her head. 'Impossible.' She points back at my sister and her boyfriend. 'Tell me. Tell me your super sensible plan for those kids.'

I swallow hard, ashamed again about the decisions I have to make. But I have to. I have to make these decisions. They're not easy, and I don't always like doing it, but I have to.

'I'll offer him a couple of thousand, enough to make life easy on him for a while, and then tell him that he's banned from seeing her again. He won't want the money, because he's a good kid, but I'll make him take it for his mom or grandma or whoever he cares about. He'll feel guilty. He'll be scared. If he comes around again, I'll scare him off. He'll leave her alone, and my parents will find someone who will make her happy in the long run.'

She's shaking her head, her eyes squeezed shut.

I reach out to her, but she smacks my hand away.

'I know,' I plead, begging her to understand. 'It seems harsh. It seems mean. It's what's best, Evan. It's how my family does things.'

'It's the most disgusting thing I've ever heard,' Evan says quietly, her head bowed, her arms crossed tight over her chest. 'You've lived around it for so long, it's the way you think now. You don't even question it. But you justify an awful lot for them. There's no way . . .' She looks up at me, her eyes brimming with tears that spear at my heart. 'There's no way you can actually believe this is a good thing. Are you that brainwashed?'

I hate that Evan is quietly crying. I hate that my sister is looking across the field, her hand pressed to her mouth. I hate that Andre is walking toward me like a gladiator about to enter the arena, and I'm the monster he's got to fight.

I hate that they can't see the situation for what it is. That they're all blaming me for doing what's expected of me, the job no one else will take. I hate that my family put me in this position.

We get into the car, Evan silent with fury, Andre

silent with resignation, me silent with frustration. Evan speaks first.

'I understand that you're going to do what you think is right, Winch. But I have to, too. Drop me at my grandparents' house. I can't be around you right now.'

Evan 13

'Believe it or not, it wound up being too much drama even for Evan Lennox.'

I force myself to sigh dramatically, mostly to drown out the sound of Brenna's gasp of frustration. We're well into hour three of our Evan-and-Winch Relationship Dissection Marathon, and we're both grossly worn out.

'I just ... I just don't believe you,' she cries, her voice high pitched in preparation for a full-blown reality protest. 'You guys had so many obstacles to get through, but you were getting through them. Giving up now just feels—' She breaks off and lets out an aggravated moan.

'It was too much, Bren. It was too much! It never even got started, and then it just kept getting messed up. We'd take a step forward and fifteen backward. Every amazing day would end with a crazy, stupid night. Every magical night would spin out into some weird, panic-filled day. Even I'm not this dramatic, and I can't watch him self-destruct. I'm not going to do it. I'm just going to get through my last few weeks of community service with him, and that's it. Winchester Youngblood and I are from two very different worlds. We won't even have to try to avoid each other.'

I squeeze the tears out of my voice and focus on the college applications I'm filing neatly in color-coordinated folders. 'You were against me and Winch being together, remember? You said that you had a bad feeling. That he wasn't good enough. Why aren't you ever on my side when I need you to be?' I plead, plopping down in my rolling chair.

Bren *tsks* like she's my overworked governess. 'Because once in a while, I'm actually wrong. And because I know how miserable you are. I can hear it. It's breaking my heart.'

I smile at her tendency to hyperbolize when things get bad. In the background, the chime of the doorbell echoes into my room and my grandmother's voice calls my name.

'Someone's here.' My heart constricts and sings one steady, happy, hopeful song: *Winch, Winch, Winch.*

Brenna squeals with delight. 'I knew he'd come! Call me later!'

I take a second to smooth my hair before I sprint down the hall and run at ankle-breaking speed down the stairs to . . .

No one.

Gramma is holding an enormous bouquet in all buttery yellows and golds and creams.

'Who in the world sent these, honey? Someone who knows flowers, that's for sure. Are these from Eastmann's? They are absolutely gorgeous! Do you have a secret admirer, Evan? Is it Marguerite Holinger's grandson? Did you hit it off after you two disappeared at the art show?'

I'm listening to my grandmother's questions without really hearing them and looking at the stark writing on the thick vellum card she left on the side table for me:

You were right. About everything. And I don't expect another chance. But you deserve an apology. These are the beginning.
I love you.

I force the sugared-up tween hopping from foot to foot in my heart to cut her happy dance short.

I've heard Winchester Youngblood's promises before. And I know exactly why reading this one breaks my heart all over again.

He actually believes he can keep his promise.

Even if it's not possible.

'They must be from Kieren,' I lie. Gramma's head

whips up and she studies me with slitted eyes, icy blue and deeply suspicious.

'I know you're lying like a rug, sweetheart.' She takes out a vase and begins a complicated process of arranging each long-stemmed, fragrant bloom. 'I don't like seeing that gorgeous face in a frown. Spill the beans.'

I pick up a piece of broken leaf and twirl it between my fingers.

'Was my mother always so weak?'

It seems like I've changed the subject, but I'm only asking questions to support the Winchester Youngblood case that's gone to court in my head. Unfortunately, I'm having a hard time knowing if I'm on the prosecution or the defense. Or maybe I'm the judge? Or jury?

Or executioner?

Gramma takes a deep, flower-sweet lungful of air and plumps the blossoms in the vase.

'Yes.' My grandmother is only rarely so direct. And never so brief.

I wait for more, but when no more comes, I ask, 'Did you think she'd be a terrible mother?'

'She's not,' she snaps, her silvery bob swinging around her chin as she jerks another flower with enough force to snap the stem.

She puts the discarded tulip to the side, the creamy

petals bright with a single stripe of orange down the middle. I run my finger over the color, ashamed at speaking ill of my own mother, and understanding my grandmother's fierce loyalty.

Family loyalty that turns a blind eye to all evils? It's part of my birthright and one reason it was easy to be with Winch despite his yo-yoing family obligations.

'I apologize.' I pluck the petals off the tulip, leaving the tall, exposed pistil naked in the center, and whack the side of the desk with the torn flower. 'I know my mother tried to be better.'

Gramma's fingers rest on the vase.

'I wish that was the truth.' She braces her hands on the marble tabletop, her gold rings clicking against the surface. 'Your mama was a lovely girl. Lovely. But she wanted what she wanted. And she wanted things to be easy.'

My grandmother looks at me, her light eyes swirling with hurt I can't fully understand. 'You can't have it both ways. If she was going to marry your daddy, it was going to be work. I told her that. And, the thing is, your mama wasn't cut out for work.'

Her sigh starts deep in her chest. 'I'm not passing judgment. Your granddaddy and I were prepared to set her up for a life of leisure and ease. We knew our child well and wanted her to be happy, have a happy life. She would have done well with a nice young man from a good family. One of our choosing. But . . . she was stubborn. And it just broke her world apart when things with your father didn't work the way she anticipated.'

I've already had my wrist slapped for speaking against my mother, and I understand. My grandmother loves her fiercely, which is probably part of the reason my mother has always gotten away with such awful behavior; her own mother is always on hand to sweep her problems up, and her daughter has always known how to stand on her own two feet.

'So, you think it's better to be with someone who makes sense? Not necessarily someone you love, but know is from a different world?'

The coolness seeps out of her eyes and she goes back to work making the already gorgeous flowers into something harmonious and artistic.

'I think your mother should have married someone who made sense. I think your parents couldn't overcome all the difficulties true love seems to come booby-trapped with. But the two of us?' She winks at me. 'Well, we're cut from a different cloth altogether.'

I inch closer, until the smell of fresh flowers mingles with the heady, rich scent of my grandmother's perfume. 'Did you want to marry someone who didn't make sense?'

'Good Lord, what kind of question is that?'

Gramma exclaims, her mouth quirked in a half-smile. 'Your fool of a granddaddy still doesn't make sense, and that should be obvious to a smart girl like you.'

She lifts her eyes from the petals, and they shine with a young dreaminess. 'He was so far on the wrong side of the tracks, no one even warned us away from each other. A romance between me, the daughter of one of the oldest, richest families in Savannah, and Lee Early. Even he thought it was a joke, and that's how he wooed me. No one from my life or his could wrap their head around the idea of the two of us together, so we went unnoticed practically under their noses.'

'But ... I don't understand? Granddaddy is famous. The Early name is famous. Everyone knows him. Everyone is afraid of him!'

My grandfather is every inch a perfect Southern gentleman and respected businessman, and I remember back to the night of the party with Jace. All Winch had to do was say my grandfather's name, and Jace disappeared without a word of argument.

'Well *now* they do, love.' Gramma's smile is every shade of triumphant. 'But it's fifty years since we met and started building our life together. The world is a different place now, and we're completely different people. Back then, I had a hard time convincing him he'd have any future other than the one he thought fate handed him. Now?' Her chuckle shakes the most delicate flowers. 'Now that man would forget he was ever humble, young, gorgeous-as-all-get-out Lee Early, factory worker and part-time sharecropper with nothing but his charm and work ethic to get him where he needed to be. That's why I'm around. When he gets low, I retell the story of how he got where he is. And when he gets too full of himself, I remind him what a huge debt he owes his patient, brilliant wife for his success.'

My grandparents' story is so beautiful and romantic, it almost blots out the backbone-lacking tale of my parents' marital failure.

'What did your family say? What did Grand-daddy's family say?'

For the first time, my grandmother's smile falters. She shakes her head and squares her shoulders, but I don't miss the glint of tears she does a really good job of hiding.

'When you're young and strong-willed, you have to know that you'll wind up upsetting the people who love you. My parents were mad as hornets, of course, and they predicted the failure of our marriage and our future unhappiness every time we saw them until we came to our senses and stopped seeing them.' She plucks stray leaves that don't meet her exacting bouquet standards. 'But I loved your grandfather. Loved him with my whole heart, and we decided that the love we felt was going to have to be enough. Whoever couldn't accept it would have to move aside. I can't lie to you, love. It hurt. Sometimes I questioned if the hurt was worth it. But in my heart?' She puts one hand on her silk blouse, just above her heart. 'I knew. I knew I made the right decision.'

'It must have been hard.' My words are pressed small.

'Nothing as good as what we have comes easy.' She squeezes my shoulder and kisses my forehead, then presses the vase of flowers into my hands.

I take them up the stairs and re-read his too-short note a thousand times. I lie on the bed and stare at the ceiling. I call Brenna and tell her all about my grandparents and the flowers and, of course, she tells me to call him, but I can't yet.

I think about what my grandmother said as I squirm in my kilt in world history at St Anne's the next day. I think about it when I fill out my college applications, and I think about it while I take long, hot showers and cry against the cool white tiles.

I miss him in a million ways every day. Part of me is grateful we only got a single night together, and part of me is so damn full of regret that I didn't grab and yank and claw for more when I had the chance.

I miss talking to him. I miss the sweet, slow smile that was so hard to pry out. I miss his honesty, his caring, his tough, in-control, always-loving ways. I know I have it bad when seeing Gramma's chicken and rooster salt-and-pepper shakers makes me get a big lump in my throat because any happy couple, even little ceramic condiment-holding ones, makes me weepy.

But I keep going back to the way Gramma talked about her heart.

How sure she was.

How much they lost.

How much it hurt.

The thing is, my grandparents were strong enough and in love enough that their life together trumped their losses.

And there's the crux of my problem with Winch.

He loves his family. I tried to accept the way they are. I secretly hoped I'd fit in. I wondered if he might walk away. But nothing worked; nothing was going to work. His family and I couldn't accept each other, and I'd never ask him to choose.

I kept coming back, over and over again, to the reality of our situation: part of me would always love him, but we would never work.

'That's it?' Brenna's voice crumples with defeat. I unbutton the hideous yellow uniform blouse and toss it and my plaid skirt into the hamper. I slide on pajamas and gather my knees to my chest and the phone to my ear.

'I've thought about it all week, Brenna. It's done. There never really was a way for it to work, but I couldn't accept that.' I press my forehead to my knees and clamp my eyelids tight against the tears. 'Now I can.'

'You're an idiot,' she cries. 'You have to try to make this work!'

'You told me it wouldn't have worked. I should have listened to you from the beginning and saved myself all of this pain now.'

I burrow under my covers and peek out at the creamy flowers, wilted and drooping. I'll have to throw them out soon, but my heart clutches at the thought of getting rid of his last gift to me.

'I was an idiot,' she protests. I can hear her clicking hangers up in her closet, thumping things from place to place. She's frustration-cleaning. All sounds suddenly stop, and her voice brightens like she's had a revelation. 'Tomorrow is Saturday. You still have community service.'

The knot that's been tying itself tighter and tighter in my stomach since the last time I saw him pulls again. 'He might be there. Maybe not. I never replied to his note.'

'He didn't text or call?' Brenna asks, but she knows the answer. As much as I've tried not to obsess about this, Brenna is the one person I've unloaded ever

Winch-related detail of my life to. 'You guys are so weird. It's almost like you're torturing yourselves. Just call him.'

'No. Can't. It would just be more stupid promises he can't keep and me getting my expectations up. I have to face reality, Bren, even if it hurts. And trust me, it hurts like crazy. Like a thousand paper cuts in a lemon-juice bath.'

I run my hand over the cool, empty expanse of my bed, then up and down the warm, empty curves of my own body.

'You *do* want to see him, though. You're not that insane, right?' She's begging because she believes in true love and beating all obstacles and love conquering everything.

It's not that I don't believe. I can see the beautiful kind of love my grandparents fought for right in front of my face. But that's a love between two people. Not two people and one crazy, controlling family.

'I do. I want to call him. I want to be with him. But you don't understand, Bren. Every single time I think his family is as crazy as they can get, they up their insanity level. Without a break. And I had to stand there and watch while Winch got the crap beaten out of him.'

My breath hitches for a second, and I have to grit my teeth together and push back the images of all that blood and Winch's battered body, and everyone sitting around that goddamn table not caring about what had happened to him.

'He takes the fall for Remy over and over. And when his little sister got a boyfriend, it wasn't just like they'd give him the cold shoulder and try to keep them from getting too close. There was a freaking pay-off scheme, Brenna! And he told me so calmly, you know? Like he wasn't remotely shocked and didn't think it was weird. Which is weird, right? Tell me I'm not just gunning for best drama in a dysfunctional relationship?'

'It's weird.' She blows out a long breath. 'You know I had to deal with it with Jake. When his family came around with all their money? And it's still kind of a thing, because his inheritance gets handed over at the end of this year. And it's not just, like, enough to buy a car. It's like a trust fund. Like a serious trust fund. But it's not just money that's scary. It's that power, I guess?'

I brace the bottom of my feet on the footboard of my bed and rub my thumb and forefinger against my temples.

'Yep. The control? The millions of strings that are so attached. And it was that way with my parents, you know? Money turned into something that basically screwed up our life, and they let it. But it's worse with

Winch because, with Jake, he can just take the money and give his family the finger. With Winch, it's all about his family. It's all about loyalty and doing anything for them. It's just worse because their money means that they have a lot of power. They ask him to do crazy, crazy things. Bren, if he gets in legal trouble again, he is going to jail, no questions. The judge at our hearing? She wasn't playing around. And his brother is a total loose cannon. He's not just going to calm down.'

I try to regulate my deep, shaky breaths.

'You're so worried about him. You care so much.' Brenna is just stating facts, but they get to the very core of me. I press my fist to my mouth and almost lose hold of my self-control when she asks, 'Why don't you just talk to him? Isn't there anything you can do? Isn't there anything . . . you can say? I can hear how much you love him.'

'I love him so much,' I rasp out. 'And that's why the one thing I refuse to do is watch him ruin his life and lose himself. If he's going to throw away his future and get sucked under, that's his decision. I refuse to watch him do it.'

'Oh, sweetie.' Brenna's voice is warm and soft as a hug.

Only because she's my best friend and she's seen me through everything and back again, I cry without caring that she can hear. First muffled little sniffles, then full-blown belly sobs.

I cry in front of her because I sure as hell won't do it in front of the boy I love and have to let go of. She stays on the line until I'm wrung out, sodden, and calm. Her sweet words are the last thing I hear before I disconnect and sink into a long, black, dreamless sleep.

Winch 13

Andre didn't take the money.

I moved the amount up a few times, especially once I saw the falling-down trailer he was going back to. I knew my dad would be happy to have the money paid and the situation swept under the rug.

Ithaca? It would take awhile, and I predicted a lot of threats of 'never forgiving' us, but eventually, she'd realize it was for her own good and life would move on. It wasn't always romantic and easy.

That was the thing that Evan didn't get.

The day of the fight, the day after the perfect night I spent in Evan's arms, Andre had stared at his hands in the backseat of my car for a few minutes after turning down more money than I know the kid's entire family had seen in a year.

I was pissed off because I'd dropped Evan at her grandparents' house after breaking every promise, right along with her heart. And there wasn't a damn thing I could do about it. I just wanted this punk out of my car, and I wanted to stop fucking up every single time I tried to make things work with Evan.

Not so much to ask for, right?

'I love her.' Andre interrupted my run of self-loathing. He lifted his eyes, dark and totally belligerent, and glared at me from the backseat.

'You're what? Seventeen?'

I flicked my eyes, focused and controlled from years of experience, to the reflection of his seething ones in the rearview mirror.

'Eighteen in three days.'

He crossed his arms over his chest.

'All right. She's gonna be seventeen in four months. You two are babies still, OK? You'll meet other people. You'll get over this.'

I tossed the words at him, and they came out harsher than I meant them to. What did this kid know about love and loss and screwing it all up?

'You have no idea.' His mouth twisted in a sneer that was half rage, half pity. 'The way you dropped your girl off like that? I would never have left Ithaca that way.'

'You have no idea what goes on between me and Evan.' My voice cut out, cold with warning.

'I know she was upset and you let her go. I know she had things to say to you, and you didn't listen. Ithaca and I aren't like that. I care about what she thinks and how she feels. I'm going to be there for her, no matter what.'

The look on his face was ballsier than I would have expected in response to my stare-down, and it irritated the shit out of me.

'You think you know a single fucking thing about how life works? I have more people to look out for than you could imagine. I have more responsibility than you could know, and I've had it since I was younger than you are now. I can't just drop everything because of the way I feel. I have people depending on me.'

My blood pressure was definitely on the rise, and the look of total disrespect in the little douchebag's eyes wasn't helping me keep my cool.

He popped the door open and gave me a last look, one full of bravado.

'Tell your family I wouldn't take a damn cent from any one of them. And I know you got a lot of people to worry about, but you can subtract Ithaca from your little list. Because *I'll* be the one taking care of that girl for the rest of my life.'

He slid out of the backseat and slammed the car door, strutting into his rickety trailer without a backward glance in my direction.

I drove home with a bad taste in my mouth and thought about what that little shit said for hours. Days. The entire long week.

I thought about it when I drove past Evan's house, trying to catch a glimpse through her bedroom window like some sad stalker.

I thought about it when I picked up the phone to call her a dozen times, but never did.

I'm still thinking about it when I go to pick up Remy, drunk, fresh from a brawl, shirtless, and shoeless, passed out in front of some dive.

I watch my brother chatter to himself, curl into the fetal position, and weep into the seat of my car. He needs help. He needs some kind of rehab or something, but I know my parents will never say yes to letting anyone outside of the family in, not even a counselor or therapist. Every priest we know is too caught up in my family's glory and too swayed by the crazy amounts of money and stained glass and new robes the Youngblood family donates to ever interfere, even if my brother's life is at stake.

When I get home, my father shoos Colt, all wide-eyed and shaky, back to the den and helps me heft Remy into his room. My father looks at Remy, a slobbering, sobbing, shaking, skeletal version of himself and says, 'Tell your mother to make a pot of strong coffee and let's get out of here so he can sleep it off.'

No one says anything else about it, not even when Remy pukes so long and hard, it finally comes up blood. My parents have a hushed argument in the kitchen that ends with my father's firm 'no' and my mother's tearful acceptance.

My dad comes to my room, his eyes bloodshot and the lines in his face deep. 'Call about getting the carpet in Remington's room replaced tomorrow. Top priority.'

'Yes, sir.' I watch his back as he leaves me in my room.

Carpet.

Top priority.

Days go by and I argue with myself – Evan and Andre's words screaming in my head – and I wake up with a pretty clear realization.

The kid was right.

Evan was right.

I've been kidding myself for a long time.

I also realize I have no clue what to do to fix this whole damn mess. It was easy for me to let go of Evan because I told myself it was for her own good.

Really, it was so I didn't have to face some hard truths. And, of course, just when I resolve to do things right, the chaos dominoes start tipping over and everything conspires against me.

It starts with Ithaca barging into my room twenty minutes before community service.

'What the hell did you say to him?' she screams, her face so distorted with bald fury, she looks almost ugly.

'Say to who? Calm down.'

I move forward, attempt to put my hands on her shoulders, but she jumps back like I'm a venomous snake.

'Calm down? Fuck off!' Her voice carries through the entire house.

Benelli cracks her door open and peeks out.

'What's going on?' she asks, her voice low. 'Ithy, what's wrong, sweetheart?'

Ithaca throws herself into our sister's arms and weeps, Benelli looks at me with her eyebrows furrowed, and Colt opens his door and crowds the hallway.

'Andre Ortiz enlisted in the army.' Colt pushes his dark hair out of his eyes, and I'd rather take an arms-held-back beating than have to face the look of disappointment he's shooting my way.

Ithaca's sobs are muffled in Benelli's shoulder. Benelli looks from Colt to me and back. 'Oh no. The skateboard boy?'

Ithaca wrenches her head from Benelli and points an accusing finger at her. 'You're laughing at me? You? Out of everyone in this entire fucked-up family, I thought you would understand, Bee! I thought you'd get how much this hurts!'

My sisters glare at each other, powerful secrets tossing between them that could drown us all.

'I do understand. I wasn't making a joke.' Benelli's voice is so urgent and nervous. I wonder what she's hiding. 'It's not the end of the world, sweetie. He's a smart guy. He'll do fine.'

My little sister shoves her hands in all that pretty gold hair, now tangled and wild-looking. 'Josh Ranson's brother died in Afghanistan a few months ago. Jessica Lister's brother got his leg and hand blown off.' The sobs start low and deep in her throat. 'He's not cut out for this! He got accepted by an art school in Philadelphia. And I told him he could get loans and grants. We were filling out all the paper-work. Then he said he needed to take care of me, and he went off and just signed up. And you can't undo that. The recruiters make you sign a contract.' She whirls around and jumps at me, her fists hammering at my chest. 'What did you say to him? What did you say when you dropped him off that day?'

'Nothing,' I lie. 'Lots of young guys join the army, Ithaca. Especially when they don't have much going for them.'

Her mouth drops open and her green eyes flash. 'You think he didn't have much going for him? Really? You? The guy whose job is being Pop's puppet?'

'Ithaca,' Benelli hisses. 'That's enough.' Her tone goes gentle when Ithaca's lips tremble and she slides into a heap on the floor. My sisters kneel, side by side. 'It's OK, baby. Stop crying. Andre will be fine. You'll be fine. It's going to be OK.'

Ithaca's face swings up, her eyes hollowed. 'What did you say to him, Winch? Stop lying all the time and tell me.'

'I didn't tell him to join the fucking army, that's for sure.' Colt snorts and Benelli and I both shoot him a look. 'You got something to say?'

It's like all this intense rage and upset and anger flashes on his face for a quick second, but he shuts it down and goes neutral.

Seeing my little brother employ my tactics gives me a peculiar twist of self-loathing I really didn't need today.

Colt shakes his head. 'No. I don't have anything to say to you.'

Benelli stands her full height, hands on her hips, face all pink from pissed-off rage. 'You know what? You two better learn some goddamn respect, OK? Winch does things every day neither one of you would even want to think about. He does things for all of us. He didn't get to go to some cushy private school. He didn't get to run around and play ball and go on dates. So if either one of you has something to say about how much he's messing with your little lives, maybe you should do it after you thank him.'

The fury in her voice silences the twins. They both stare at the floor.

I don't know what to say. I'm glad Benelli stood up for me, but I don't want their thanks. Our baby brother and sister are right. Maybe they can see it for what it is in a way Benelli and I can't.

Before I can answer anything, Remy stumbles out of his room, and all four of us face our older brother.

His lips are ringed with crusted blood. His skin is yellowish, sagging on his face, and sculpted close to his bones like a skeleton's. He's been going downhill for a while, but maybe I just never let myself notice how bad it was getting. He looks like a vampire or a zombie, or some other pieced-together creature from a horror movie.

'What's up, chickens?' he slurs, lumbering down the hallway on unsteady feet. 'Ya'll were so loud, you woke me up.'

Benelli's lips tuck into a tight line, Ithaca looks at him with clear terror, and Colt can barely keep the disgust at bay.

'Remington, you need a shower, some hot soup, and to get back in bed. I'll tell Mama to start you some lunch.' Benelli looks as grimly determined as a captain in the army marching her troops to certain death.

'No rest for the wicked, baby.' Remy sniffs under his armpit. 'No rest, but yes to a shower.'

It would have been something we would have all laughed about not that long ago. When did Remy stop being our favorite comic relief and turn into a macabre reminder of every single thing that's so fucked-up about our family?

'Why are you all so damn serious?' His eyes attempt to focus on one of our faces, then the next, and the next. He can't stop himself from rocking back on his heels and swiveling in a wide circle. 'Someone die?'

You died.

I know the same thought is at the forefront of all our brains. We all knew he'd been bad for a while, but his downward spiral has speeded up in the last few weeks. How did he turn into this reanimated corpse version of himself right in front of our eyes?

'No.' Benelli's voice is gentle as a nanny's. 'Come on. You need food.'

'He needs help,' Ithaca says, watching Benelli help Remy walk down the hall on unsteady legs like he's ninety.

'That's Winch's job. Right?' Colt slides a glare my way, his mouth working back and forth like he's wondering if he should spit out the words pressed in his mouth. And then he does. My pacifist brother sure as shit knows how to kick me when I'm low down. 'By the way, I forgot to say *thank you.*'

He stalks to his room and slams his door.

'This family is so seriously fucked up,' Ithaca mutters and slams her door too.

I'm alone in the hallway, a headache grinding through my skull, a feeling of complete despair eating at my gut.

And I'm late for community service.

By the time I pull up at the center, they're already dismissing people who put in hours this morning.

'Mr Youngblood.' The officer in charge frowns when I check in. 'We don't tolerate late arrivals.'

'I'm very sorry, ma'am. I'll do whatever you need. This won't happen again.'

I scan the area for Evan, and should be glad I don't see her.

I made so many promises I could never begin to keep, I feel like a huge loser. I feel like I have no right to ask anything of her when I've basically given her nothing. I haven't even had the guts to call and check on her.

I get handed a shovel and pointed in the direction of a smoldering garbage pit. I shovel through the debris and ash and keep the fire going strong. I want Evan.

I think about her constantly. If I'm honest with myself, I've hardly thought about anything else for days, since she got out of my car and walked up the steps to her grandparents' house.

I dream about her. I wake up hard and ready, wanting her with every uncontrolled shred of my body.

I look for her every time I stand up with a shovelful of smoldering garbage.

I don't deserve her. I've wasted second and third chances with her.

I've been an idiot.

But none of that stops me from wanting her so badly it aches.

I'm sick of doing the right thing and ignoring all the desire that's built up inside me. I want her. I want her in every way possible.

I shovel and choke until it's time to leave, and I'm completely covered in grime. No amount of standing under the dribbling hose is going to wash this all off.

'You wanna come out with a couple of the guys? Play some pool, drink some beers?' Rolo never usually invites me to go anywhere, but most of the time, I'm calm and laid-back. Today I've been a furious dickhead and, unfortunately, Rolo took the brunt of my asshole behavior. I guess he figures I could use a drink or five.

'Thanks, man.' I try to hand his handkerchief back, but he waves it off. 'Look, I'm sorry I was an asshole to work with today. I'm just having a whole thing with Evan and my family.'

I've never been big on sharing how I feel, and

it's just as awkward as I thought it might be.

Rolo switches his weight from foot to foot. 'I'm sorry, bro. That sucks.'

He's not inviting me to tell him anything else, but the words just kind of spill out. 'I love her, you know?' He nods. 'But my family . . . they ask a lot of me. And it's been coming between us.'

'You still work for your old man?'

Rolo runs the weakly dribbling water over his arms and passes the hose my way again.

It's stupid to even pretend that it's going to help get me clean, but I drizzle the water over my skin so I have an excuse to stand here and hash this all out with him.

'Yeah. I do. I just . . . it's complicated, you know, because it's work and all, but it's more family.'

'Oh, I get it.' Rolo rubs a dirty handkerchief over his face and neck, taking the black soot down to a dull gray. 'Family helps you every time you need a hand, but they cross every damn line, too.'

That's it.

'Exactly. And I'm just trying to figure out how much I owe them and how much I can take for myself, I guess.'

I thought the filth couldn't be washed off, but even the tepid, tricking water is taking the grime away, layer by minuscule layer.

'Well, you know, family is good and all. You need them. But you gotta do your own thing. Remember, at some point your dad was just his father's son, too. And he had to grow up and be his own man. I'm gonna bet that didn't happen without some shit going down, right?'

Rolo yanks his sweaty shirt back over his head.

I put mine back on, too, and think about my father and grandfather. I barely knew my father's father. What little I gathered from family visits to Hungary was that he ruled the family with an iron fist, and my father was more than happy to take his shares and control of the family business across the Atlantic to start something on his own.

'I never really thought about that,' I admit. 'Listen, thanks for the invite, but I think I better go find Evan and get things back under control.'

'Do what you have to do. Maybe some other time?'

I grab his hand in a rough mix of a slap and a shake. 'Yeah. Definitely. Soon.'

Driving to Evan's house, I feel more lost than I ever have in my entire life.

A few weeks ago, I knew exactly where I was going and what I was doing. Now every single thing I thought I knew for sure has been shaken. I don't know how I feel about my family, my future, my place, my beliefs.

The only thing I know for sure is that Evan has helped me change everything and, whatever the hell my future might hold, I want her in it.

I get to her house and go right to the front door. I stink. I'm dirty as hell. I won't make a remotely decent first impression if one of her grandparents opens the door, but I don't care. I'm on the verge of exploding, finding a new path, forging a new way, and I need her at my side.

I can't do this without her.

A woman with silver hair opens the door and presses a hand covered with tons of rings to her chest when she sees me. She looks over my shoulder, like she's trying to see if I've got my gang behind me, ready to jump her, and then she looks back at me with unapologetic suspicion.

'Can I help you?'

'My name is Winchester Youngblood. I'm here to see Evan, ma'am. If she isn't busy.'

I wish I'd gone home to change and have a shower. But 'home' is relative at the moment, and the only place that feels like somewhere I belong is wherever Evan is. I know how I look, I know how I sound, but my head's been spinning for weeks, and I know, I know without a doubt, that seeing her will calm things down, put things right.

'Evan is about to get ready to go on a date.' She

pulls the door half closed and forces me back down the marble stairs. 'A date with a gentleman who doesn't yank her young heart back and forth without a second thought. Shame on you.'

She shakes a finger in my face, her light-blue eyes full of fury, just like Evan's when she gets upset. 'I know who you are, and I know what you've done to my granddaughter. I'm well aware that she may come off as a tough little cookie, but that couldn't be further from the truth. She has a delicate heart that's been used and abused more than it should have been in one young life. And your behavior just supports her idea that she's not good enough. That she's not worthy of being loved.'

'Ma'am, I know what I did. I know the mistakes I made. I'm here to—'

'I can imagine exactly what you're here for,' she interrupts, her mouth pressed tight. 'And I suspect you'll be back again if you have a mind to be, no matter what I say to you now. But listen to me. Listen to me right now. If you love her, if you even care about her a little, leave her alone. The two of you don't have what it takes to go the distance. She needs someone strong. Someone sure. That isn't you, son.'

She gives me a long, dismissive look, steps back into the doorway, frowns, and clicks the door shut.

I consider my options. I could call her. Just dial her number and connect.

Or I could be dramatic and scream up to Evan, call her out and get her to come to her window, and then explain it all to her. That I want to be with her. That I love her. That I'm finally, truly ready to change.

I could leave. I could leave and let her have whatever life she'll have with whatever guy she's going on a date with.

Just when I'm about to jump the fence into the back garden, my phone rings, the song rock-heavy and melancholy. It's Colt.

'What do you need?' I answer, my eyes still locked on her curtains, which haven't so much as fluttered. Does she know I'm here? Does she even care?

'Uh, Winch?' His voice is low, like he's whispering into the phone, like he doesn't want anyone to know he's calling.

The temperature of my blood dives.

I wanted to walk away from all of this, wanted to do better for Evan, but I know for sure that whatever he's asking for, it's not going to be easy to turn him down.

Walking away isn't simple. Even when you're taking baby steps.

'Winch? You there?' His words shake.

'I'm here. Tell me.'

'It's Alayah. And Remy. They're ... uh, they're gone. And he was in bad shape.'

I'm back in my car in a few short seconds, the engine revved so loud, I finally see her, pulling the curtain aside and stepping on the balcony.

Just in time to watch me pull away.

Evan 14

'Tell him I can't go,' I repeat to Gramma as I attempt to gently push past her and get to my car.

I stuck by the promise I made to myself, and I haven't contacted Winch or sought him out. His path to self-destruction might be on a fast-as-hell crash-course, but I'm not about to station myself in the cheering section.

But he came to the house. Maybe because things really *are* different. Maybe because, this time, he *did* change. Maybe.

I don't know, but I need to find out. I'm an idiot to hold out hope, but I do. Something in me just can't let go of the idea that this will work itself out, even if I know I'm stupid to expect that.

'Evan, no. Evan, listen to me. Evan!'

The sharp jerk of my name from her lips roots me to the spot right by the front door, my hand on the door-knob. I look at her and twist my hands around my keys.

'I have to go to him.'

I'm ashamed at how my voice wobbles.

She shakes her head and tucks a piece of my hair back into my ponytail. I'd been in the middle of straightening it when I heard Winch's car pull out like crazy. When I came out of my room, Gramma told me that he'd come here for me. And she told me that she sent him away.

Now my heart is desperate in my chest, like a bird crashing into a window over and over again, confused that it can't get to what it sees and wants, and willing to kill itself in the attempt to remedy that.

'You do not have to go to that boy. Evan. Listen to me.' She smooths her hands over my hair and down onto my neck. 'You do not have to throw everything away for any boy. Or for your parents. Or for those backstabbing friends. Or the teachers who gave up on you.' Her voice is sopping wet and about to overflow. 'Please hear me out. Your mother never would listen, but you and I are the same, and I know you can understand this, love. Listen.'

I swallow hard and decide listening will be the quickest option. I'm not about to run from this house and leave my grandmother standing in the hall. Respect for her is coded into my anatomy. But so is general disobedience, and it kicks inside me, ready to burst through the door and find Winch. Find him and tell him . . . what, I don't know, and, frankly, I don't care.

I don't care if it's desperate, I don't care if it's all just the same damn merry-go-round of pain and disappointment. I want him. I want him so badly, and I need him.

I need him, even if needing him is the worst idea in the world.

I'm tired of fighting it, trying to make sense out of all the bad and good that has defined our relationship so far.

'I'm listening.'

My ears can hear her, anyway. But my heart and mind are already racing out the door ahead of this conversation, hoping to catch up with him, wanting to be back with him.

'You're chasing him and he wants to run, darling. If he isn't attached to you now, he never will be. Listen to me.'

Her voice is so desperate, I look up and resolve to listen. Really listen.

She takes a deep breath in. 'Love, I've watched you grow up amid all this chaos. And Granddaddy and I tried to do right by you, but we don't always know what to make of things. Look how we parented our fool daughter. We were never mad at you for getting into trouble. You have violent emotions. I know too well how that is. But listen to me: you need to let go of this one.'

'Gramma,' I begin, and it sounds like I'm about to recite some kind of speech even though this is all off the cuff of my crazed heart. 'I love him. Really, I do. And we can make it work. Like you said, I have what it takes to be strong. I have what it takes to make this all happen . . .'

I trail off and watch her shake her head back and forth. 'It isn't you, love. It isn't you I doubt. It's him. If he's so easily swayed, it will be your mother and father all over again. He never stood up for their love. There were always distractions, Evan. You remember?'

I swallow hard. 'But it was the races with Daddy. It was gambling. A vice. This is family.'

'Family.' She rolls the word on her tongue. 'Darling, family can be the very devil in disguise. More powerful than any drug, more alluring than any sin. They can demand a loyalty that will rip your heart out and chew it up without the thought of an apology. You don't need to say a word, but I want you to think about what he's done for them. What they may ask him to do in the future. I know the Youngbloods by reputation, and I'd caution you strongly before you took up with one.'

'But he's—'

Gramma puts a hand up. 'Evan Lennox, I'm the last

woman in the world who'd judge a man by his name. But I do know how to weigh a man's actions. And his actions make your daddy's habit of gambling on the horses seem very tame. I'm begging you, do not open your arms to the heartache your mother put up with for so long.'

The warpath drum of my heart has slowed, and she puts her hands on my shoulders. 'Tonight's date might be a blip in your radar. Or it might be a step in the direction of a lifelong, rewarding love. All I'm asking is that you open your heart and let go of this boy who's had you so twisted.'

'But he loves me, Gramma.'

The words come out shakily as I try not to dissolve into tears.

'I have no doubt at all that his feelings for you are strong. But if his actions don't measure up to his intentions, you're better off without him. Your grand-daddy and I have kept our mouths shut for a few weeks now. But we decided to say our piece, and now I've said it and feel better. Your passions have ruled your head and heart for a long time now, sweetie. And it's brought you nothing but heartache. Let go of this one and open up to the possibility of something new. Something better.'

She runs her fingers through my hair, gently un-doing the tangles.

My throat feels closed up. My eyes burn. My heart is a lump in my chest, empty. Winch roared away before he got a chance to talk to me. I slide my phone out of my pocket.

No text. No message. No missed call.

He gave up on me, again.

He probably got a call from Remy. Again.

The pattern will never end, no matter how much he wants it to.

Because his intentions don't match his actions.

I've given him so many chances, opened my heart to him, and had him open his to me. But if he doesn't choose me, choose us, there's nothing I can do. There's no way I can right this. Slowly, I will my stomach to unclench. I kiss my grandmother on the side of her mouth.

'I love you. You're right. First step. Tonight, I take my first step.' I manage to say it without crying. Mostly because I shut down completely. 'Now, if you will excuse me, my hair is a mess, and I have to fix it.'

Gramma beams and I walk up the stairs, head high, turn into my bathroom, soak a washrag in cold water, set my phone alarm for five minutes, and then cry thick, shaky, moaning sobs into the cloth until the beep sounds.

It was the same amount of time I gave Winch on

our first date. I should have walked away when that alarm first sounded. I didn't then, but I will now. I have to.

I sit at my dressing table and fix my hair, put on my make-up, and just when I brush the eighteenth coat of mascara on my eyelashes, the doorbell chimes. I hear Granddaddy answer and exchange hearty, manly words with the guy who's waiting downstairs. He's some son of some colleague of my grandfather's, and Granddaddy called him a 'go-getter', which is basically the very highest praise he ever gives anyone. So this guy must be something special.

But he's not Winchester Youngblood.

I hang my silky robe on the hook in my closet and slide into a simple green dress that I've always liked but never loved. Maybe that's just because I've never given it a fair chance. I dab a last coat of lip gloss on and head down the stairs in dangerously high pink heels with little bows at the toe, perfectly adorable, and a good way to lift my spirits every time Winchester invades my thoughts. All I have to do to buoy my mood a tiny bit is look down at my fabulously outfitted feet.

The guy, Callum Long, stands with a bouquet of mixed flowers, maybe more gorgeous than any Winch got for me. I take them from his hands and bury my nose in the petals, but I don't inhale the sweet aroma, because there's a line between playing along to mend my tattered heart and taking a sledgehammer to the last brittle pieces. I'm not strong enough to jump that line yet.

'You kids look smart together.' Granddaddy beams, hooking his thumbs through his red braces.

I wish, right then, that he'd had the opportunity to meet Winchester. I wish he'd been able to take him aside and smoke a cigar on the porch with him. Maybe he would have opened up about his story, how he left his family and struck out on his own. Maybe Winch would have told Granddaddy his problems. If anyone can fix any problem, it's my grandfather.

But I was so wrapped up in just figuring Winch and me out while we were together, I never considered having him over.

Now it's nothing but the dust of old regrets, and I need to shake it off.

I kiss Granddaddy on the cheek and let him pull me into a long, gruff hug.

'You take care of her, Callum,' my grandfather threatens with a wag of his finger.

Callum's voice is rich and low, with just that bit of a country-boy drawl that always uncoils something deep and sweet in me.

'Of course, sir. I won't let her out of my sight for a single second. Are you ready, Evan?'

His light eyes flick up and down me quickly, clearly pleased with what he sees.

There's a kick of delicious warmth in my stomach, exactly what I would have expected from having a good-looking, tall, sweet-eyed boy looking me over.

It's just not anything close to the inferno I feel when Winch looks me over.

'Let me say goodbye to my grandmother,' I stall, but Gramma is bustling in to take my bouquet and arrange it in a vase, just like she did with Winch's.

This time she's all smiles and kisses and pats on my backside, telling us to be good and have fun. She looks happy. She looks relieved.

'Your granddaddy and I will be out late, but I won't be surprised if you come home after us!' She winks at me.

I wish I felt a sliver of her enthusiasm.

Callum opens the door of his sleek sports car for me, and I sit on the leather seat and smile and make inane conversation as we weave into downtown traffic and head to a fancy restaurant I used to go to with Rabin, but it was called something else then. I hated the lamb chops. They were overcooked.

And just like that, it's like life has been dimmed, and I'm back to remembering less than delicious meals and less than amazing boyfriends. Small talk is hard to keep up, and everything feels distracted and distracting.

Callum orders a bottle of wine for us, and this place is swanky enough that they don't ask for my ID or seem to care if I drink. The sweet drizzle of the bubbly white is crisp and dulling at the same time. He's talking about his engineering classes, and, to be fair, it's not his fault he's being so boring. I've hardly done more than sip my wine, smile, and nod at him.

I can barely taste the food when it finally comes, and, though I force myself to have dessert and walk downtown a little with Callum, I can't will myself to hang around for a drive to a party.

'I'd love to. I would.' I act as best I can all wide eyes and emphatic nods. 'But I'm just really tired. I had community service this morning and it was a long day. You understand, right?'

I bat my lashes and his sweet smile is a relief. He's not going to push the issue.

'Of course, darlin'. St John's had crazy community service requirements when I was a senior, too. On the plus side, it looks amazing on college applications.'

His smile is so sympathetic, I don't bother to correct him and let him know that this particular community service will do nothing at all to attract colleges toward me.

The drive home is quiet, and I give Callum a chaste kiss at my front door, hoping it will communicate nothing more than my tepid appreciation for this night. This date. This first step that is, I hope, not going to be a reflection of how bland and lukewarm life devoid of Winch will be.

I watch him walk back to his car, and I turn into the empty house. Gramma and Granddaddy have never set a solid curfew before, but tonight all time limits were waived because, I think, they hoped I'd fling myself back into a social life and some semblance of happiness.

Even though the dinner felt like it lasted for hours, it's only been a scant two. Saturday night looms long and empty. I walk upstairs and fall back on my bed, not bothering to change out of my dress.

I decided, after looking in the plush bathroom's gilded mirror at the restaurant, that I really don't love the dress. Or maybe I was just caught up in the theme of the entire night: blah.

I text Brenna, and she texts back such an excited stream of questions, I wind up just tapping a message to let her know that I'm having so much fun, I'll have to fill her in later.

Brenna has been rooting for my happiness, however it comes, like a frantically hopeful cheerleader, and dishing all the depressing details of my latest social failure just feels like too much effort at this point.

I do my best to switch off my brain as the dark rolls

in and the house goes utterly, depressingly silent. I've gone blank. Erased. Empty. It's the only way I can be if I want to survive without sobbing over Winch and all we could have had, now lost for good.

But no matter how hard I work to shut my brain down, my body aches for him in the dark. I crave comfort that goes way beyond warm baths, soft pajamas, creamy chocolate truffles; those are shallow, non-essentials. I need his touch, his hold, his love.

I know I can't have it. I know the need will have to eventually melt away. But tonight, in the dark of my room, I'm not convinced I can live without it.

And then I hear the hiccupping roar of an engine. It's Saturday night. It could be any stupid showoff on a date. There's a way bigger chance it isn't him than that it is.

A yell shatters the quiet of the night.

'Evan!'

I sit up, shocked. Because it's him. It's Winch. But not the way I know him. I get up and run to the balcony outside my room, ignoring the slight bite of a chill on my skin. It takes my eyes a long few seconds to adjust in the dark, but when I finally see Winch, shock seizes me.

'Winch?' I ask, not sure the loping, staggering figure below could be my cool, collected, always-in-control Winch.

'Evan!' He yells like he didn't hear my voice. He looks up and squints, then trips over a potted plant. The ceramic pot crashes and I hear the heavy thud of his body crashing into the dirt and his guttural curses. 'Evan!'

His yell is impatient this time, and I raise my voice, glancing nervously at my neighbor's house. He's going to wake the entire damn street up.

Even as I think this, a thick, sweet happiness swirls through me. I have no idea why he's here or what he wants, but I'm completely thrilled that he's down there, waiting for me.

'Wait, Winch! I'm coming down.'

'No!' he protests, but I ignore him and fly down the hall and stairs, through the kitchen and out the back door that leads me into the gardens and his arms.

He folds me in his embrace, but staggers back and has to lean on me to keep from falling over.

'Evan.' His voice, always so strong and calm, comes out like a whimper around my name. 'I've missed you so damn much. You don't know . . . you have no idea how much I wanted you.'

His mouth is nuzzling near my ear, and I turn my face so our lips can meet, momentarily shocked by the stench of liquor on him. One kiss has my head spinning, and I feel like I downed a viciously hot shot of whatever he drank.

I ignore his drunkenness and kiss harder, balling my hands in the fabric of his T-shirt, pulling his hard, lean body close to mine. He wraps his arms around me and kisses back like this kiss is his final request. His hands roam everywhere, pressing against my skin and stopping to squeeze while he murmurs sexy pleas in another language.

'I want you. Now,' I plead, using the full force of my willpower to pull away from him and drag him behind me.

He stumbles along, trying to talk to me, trying to talk me out of this, maybe, so I refuse to slow down or listen. I just power forward, into the house, up the stairs to my room and onto my bed, pulling him down next to me. He smells sooty and sweaty, nothing like the clean and polished Winch I'm used to.

'I love you,' I insist, hoping to throw up the one roadblock he won't dare smash through.

It works. My words still the protest that I know was on his lips.

'I love you,' he says instead of whatever he was going to say to argue us out of this tangled, sweet perfection. 'I have to tell you something . . . I have to tell you—'

I clamp a hand over his mouth, his lips and breath warm and ready on my palm. 'I want to be with you. Now.'

I slide my hand down below the waistband of his pants, skim along the elastic of his boxer briefs and listen to the hiss of his breath as I cup him, smooth, hot, and hard, against the palm of my hand.

'I love you, and I don't really care what you're going to say. I want you. I want you so badly, Winch. Don't say no to me. You've said no to a million things I've asked for. Not this time, OK?'

'You're gonna regret this.' He leans his forehead on mine and squeezes his hands at my hips hard. 'Please, hear me out, Evan. Please let me tell you what—'

'Stop.' I kiss his lips, hungry for the taste of him, the taste I can never get enough of. I rip my mouth away. 'I'm not an idiot. Whatever you're going to tell me, I know it will be bad, OK? Maybe it will even be bad enough to end everything permanently. But before I hear it, I want this. I want right now, and when it's done, I swear to you, I will never regret being with you right now. Please. Please, Winch. I love you.'

He groans and blows a long, hard breath against my neck, then swallows so his throat goes tight, and nods.

'I love you, too. Never doubt that, OK? Never doubt that.'

Then, in the dark of my room, Winch strips my clothes off with efficient ease, no fear or reluctance. His hands run over my body, cradling my skin, caressing every inch of me with a finality I don't want to ponder too long.

My silky green dress is puddled next to us on the floor, my flimsy underthings twisted in the sheets. I tug his clothes off, careful of the bruises that still purple his body, slowly turning a dingy green around the edges. When we're both naked, our hands running up and down over the hot skin of each other's bodies, he whispers against my ear, a long, shaky string of sentences in a language I don't need to be fluent in to understand.

He's saying goodbye.

My brain realizes it, but my heart rejects it completely. And my body is convinced it can change his mind.

My kisses are quick and light while his voice rumbles against my ears, but they pick up and press harder when he falls silent. I lick and nip with my tongue and teeth and, when I lay my hands on his chest, I can feel the frantic beat of his heart.

Frantic because of me, frantic for us, frantic over love.

'Winch,' I moan, leaning over to grab for a condom, eager to draw this out, but twice as eager to be with him and capture him in an inescapable moment while he's possibly looking for a reason to stay.

His mouth slides over mine, his hands run up my

back and press into my hair, and everything goes still for a second when I straddle his hips, pressing against him and over him the same way I have with so many other guys before, but also in a way that's completely new and totally for Winch and Winch alone. I roll the condom on and press myself down on the length of his hard-on, flattening my palms on his chest as we fit together.

'I love you,' I declare, my voice rubbed raw from the confusion of never being sure with him, coupled with the pleasant pain of always trusting, no matter what.

He drags his hands down my arms, my ribs, and holds my hips tight, his teeth clenched, his head thrown back, like he's fighting against the fall. I kiss his neck, the space behind his jaw, along his stubbly chin, and pull his face up to kiss his lips, his mouth, him.

I use my hands and mouth and words to push him closer to the edge.

'Only you,' I whisper, and the rhythm of our two bodies is awkward and jerky because my eagerness is warring with his attempt to hold back. 'I know what you came here to tell me . . . it's over.'

'Evan,' he pleads, his eyes slitting open, deep blue and welled with drunken sadness.

He wraps his arms around me and buries his face in

the space between my neck and my shoulder, kissing my skin before he pulls away with a groan.

I rock harder against him, loving the full, heavy, pumping feel of his body in mine.

'Don't. Don't hold back, Winch. Let go. Let go with me.'

'I can't,' he begs. 'Evan, I can't. I promised . . . I promised not to break your heart.' His hands hold firm until he stills me. He looks right at me, his eyes bloodshot and ringed with purple bruising. 'I made a promise I couldn't keep. I took a gamble, and I shouldn't have. I thought I could leave before something like this happened. And now it has.' His voice cracks, and he lifts a hand to my face, tracing a thumb gently across my jaw. 'If I could walk away, I would. But I can't. I can't, Evan. And this one is the end.'

I have no idea what happened. Laundering? Drug trafficking? Murder? There's nothing I'd put past the Youngbloods.

But I lace his fingers through mine and shake my head. 'I'll never give up on you. I can't do it. I tried, and I can't, so I'm not going to waste my time. We're in this together, whatever it is.'

He flips me over so the long, hard weight of his body covers mine. He kisses my lips, runs his tongue along my jaw, sucks softly down my neck, and nuzzles my hair. He doesn't agree or disagree with my proclamation.

'I don't deserve you,' he chokes out, and moves against me with all the desperation of a guy who has nothing to lose.

A guy who's ready to fall because he's between a rock and a cliff's edge.

And, as his body clings close to mine and shudders right along with me, I know he thinks this is the end. That this is his last grab before the long, lonely descent.

What he doesn't realize is that I'm already standing at the bottom, waiting to catch him. And I never miss.

Winch 15

I never drink more than a beer or two, at the most. You can't keep a reputation for being level-headed when you're stumbling like an asshole. I'm a melancholy boozer, anyway, the no-fun kind of drunk who sulks in a corner until he passes out. Lala used to complain that partying with me was like hanging out with the school chaperone.

Even if I was a happier drinker, seeing someone as constantly drunk as my brother has left a bad taste in my mouth where alcohol's concerned. I'd mopped up my fair share of regurgitated Jack and Coke, and I'm at a place now where just hearing that drink order turns my stomach.

But when Colt called and I went home to my dour, straight-lipped family and they spelled out what had happened and what needed to happen, I grabbed my mother's bottle of Evan Williams and had a few shots. Then drove to Evan's house.

Not the best idea. I think Benelli wanted to stop me,

but our father held her back. He knew what a death sentence he'd just leveled on the next few years of my life. I was as good as gone, and one last night with Evan was all I was going to get, so he let me have it.

A pity-based consolation prize for the royal fucking my life was about to get.

Part of me felt like the guillotine fell a minute before I was ready to pull my neck out and walk away.

But even if a week, a month, a year or two had passed, this was a classic Remy/Winch situation, and I would have been summoned eventually.

Throwing those shots back, I fantasized about exactly what I could have said. Say a few months had gone by. Evan would be ready to graduate. She'd be headed off for college and, instead of watching her go and trying like hell to forget her burned-sugar smell, the sound of her laugh, the icy lance of her eyes, I could go, too.

Maybe apprentice to a stone mason. Maybe rig us an apartment, spend my nights kicking back, watching her gorgeous ass study while I reveled in the ache of muscles sore from a day of hard labor. Maybe get to fall into bed with her and wake up with the cling of her smell on my skin. Maybe start to build a life that didn't revolve around the buzz of my phone and a new set of crazy violent situations and court dates broken up by helpless fucking stretches of watching my brother wither into a blood-vomiting scarecrow while everyone kept their mouths shut and let it all happen.

And that string of fantasies is what broke my resolve to keep Evan out of everything. I just wanted . . . I needed one more minute with her. One more minute to hold her and tell her I loved her more than anything. I wanted the two of us to be together more than anything, before I said goodbye for good and got caught up in something so dark, it more than trumped all the petty shit I'd been involved in up to that point.

Ending up naked in her bed, her sweat-slicked, slack-limbed body soft and sweet under mine, wasn't in the plan. But my plans have been getting fucked up left and right, so maybe this was inevitable.

I try to roll over to the side, but she pulls me back, her hands running along my back, her eyes raking over my face.

'Tell me. Tell me why you think you're leaving me again. Because you're not, you know. You're not leaving without me.'

I kiss her, even though I should get up and leave. This has already gone further than it was supposed to.

'Evan . . . you have no idea how much I love you.' I push the long pieces of hair tangled at her neck back, run my hands over the smooth skin of her cheeks, rub my thumbs over her lips, brush over her eyebrows with the tips of my fingers and watch while she closes her eyes and makes a noise that sounds kind of like a cat's purr. It's a noise that instantly turns me on, fast and hard, like I didn't just have the most amazing sex with this girl ten minutes before. She makes me crazy.

And I tell her. 'You drive me nuts. In the best way. Believe me, if there was any way at all I could change things, make things right, I would do it, Evan. But I can't.'

I don't know what I expect after that little speech. One more roll in the hay before she waves goodbye? Tears? Begging?

There are a few scenarios that go through my head, but none of them match the intensity of her response.

'Are you fucking kidding me?' She sits up, half knocking me off the bed, and glares, her icy eyes pissed off as hell. 'This is it, Winch. This is it. This is the moment you step up and take control. Why does it always come to this? Why do you always back down at the last minute?'

'I'm not backing down,' I explain, my voice calm and cool as I watch her yank her underwear back on and wrestle with her lacy bra. 'I'm stepping up.'

'You're falling back,' she hisses, yanking her dress over her head. 'You're the fall guy, Winch. You're the guy they come to when no one else will stand up and take their medicine. And they come to you because you never make them stand up and take it.'

She jabs her finger at me and rips a brush through her hair, pulling it into a high ponytail. I pull my boxers and pants on and wish that she'd just clasped her hands to her chest and cried silently as I walked away.

'You have no idea what I'm facing, what my family is facing.'

'Really?' she challenges, and her eyes spark because she knows without a doubt that she has me completely beat. 'Really? I don't know? I don't know what it's like to watch my family falling apart? Losing the home I grew up in? Getting kicked out of school? Watching my ex act like a disgusting pig? I don't know what it's like to go a little nuts when my entire world crashes around my shoulders, and instead of drinking it off or getting away with a slap on the wrist, I wind up with a criminal record? I don't know? Because I think I do know exactly what you're looking at, and worse, and I'm calling your fucking bluff. You need to get a backbone!'

'I need a backbone?' The whiskey and sex and hopelessness and fear all swirl together and explode back out. 'I need a backbone?'

The sound of my own yell shocks me into silence, but Evan doesn't cower or draw back. Her look of anger melts away, and a huge smile spreads across her face.

'That's it. That's it, Winch. Let. The. Hell. Go,' she whispers, nodding her encouragement. 'Let go.'

'Fine!' I snap, yanking my shirt over my head. 'You want me to let go? You want it! Fucking fine, Evan. How's this for you? My douchebag brother just got himself into some deep shit, OK? He took Alayah, my niece. He violated a court agreement to limited visitation and took her, and he wound up getting drunk with her in the house. He hired some high-school girl to babysit, so Alayah is fine. But the girl answered his phone, since it never stopped ringing and he'd passed out. It was Delphine, and she threatened to call the cops if the girl didn't put Remy on the goddamn phone, but she couldn't, since my shit-for-brains brother was passed out. Benelli got there before Delphine showed up, and now my family wants me to take the fall, because otherwise, Remy could lose custody of Alayah and none of us would be able to see her again. So what the fuck am I supposed to say?' I scream, my last word echoing, my chest rising and falling, and a tremendous, splitting head-ache crushing down in my skull.

Evan stalks the two or three feet between us and sticks her beautiful face so close to mine, I can see every curling black eyelash around her blue eyes. 'No.'

'No?'

I can smell her skin, I know what her lips feel like, and I want to jump over everything and kiss her, hard and long, so I can forget this all, finally.

'No,' she repeats. 'Tell them "no".'

'Did you not just listen to what I said?' I ask. 'He'll lose custody of Alayah. No one will be able to see her.'

'Good,' she says, grabbing me by the shirtfront. 'Stop buying into their bullshit and think about this like a rational person for once, Winch. Does your brother deserve custody of that little girl?'

Obvious as it may seem, the thought had never occurred to me. He's my brother. Alayah is his daughter. They're both my blood. The word is out of my mouth before I have a chance to process.

'No.'

'Tell me what needs to happen, Winch. Not what your family is telling you to do. What needs to happen?'

Her hands unfist from my shirt and she wraps her arms around me.

I cup her shoulders with my hands and squeeze. 'Remy needs help.'

'OK. Like what?' she asks.

I take a deep breath and say what needs more than just to be said. I say what needs to happen.

'Remy needs rehab or counseling or something. Or he's gonna kill himself. My parents need to stop covering for him. I need to stop covering for him.'

'OK. Good. So how do we do this?' Her words are soft and sure.

'Do what?' I'm lost in the smell of her, the feel of her curves, the sound of her voice. How can I miss someone so badly when we're in the same room?

'Get Remy into a rehab? Stage an intervention? Get you fired from your position as Youngblood family fall guy?'

She tries to ask it all with bravado, but she swallows so hard, I know she's afraid of what I'll say.

And I want to thank her. I want to rewind time. I want to hold Remy's breakdown off, just so I could have a few days of living out the dream of all those fantasies.

'Evan, I know it seems like it should be that easy, but it's compli—'

'Shut the fuck up!' she yells. Shock presses my words back down my throat. 'Fine! Fine, you want this to be goodbye? You wanna end this, Winch, then end it with me. But if you think this is the worst that will happen with your family, you're delusional. Remy is going to kill himself, and maybe his daughter or girlfriend or someone else in the process. He's out of control, and you know it. If you don't step in, maybe you deserve to do time. Because you're as good as guilty for anything he does.'

'Evan—'

She's snapped right back to the rage that propelled her off the bed and straight at my jugular before.

'Don't! Don't try to rationalize! I tried ignoring it! I tried accepting it! I tried letting you handle it! Nothing worked and nothing will until you're ready. And if you're not ready to do this, you're sure as hell not ready to be with me and fight for us!'

She straightens her shoulders and juts her chin out, her rage replaced by something way sadder.

I realize she's about to steal my goodbye.

And I have a second.

A split second where my life can continue to career out of control while I sit back and watch. I'll keep my family happy, in a way, but lose Evan and, most likely, Remy.

Because she's right of course. He's going to kill himself, and I might as well be holding the bottle or the steering wheel or the knife or whatever it's going to take to finally break him.

'Fine,' I say, and she pulls her bottom lip in and chews, ready for this to be it, after one hell of a fight.

But I'm a Youngblood.

We don't give up that easily.

'So what do you think, smartass? How do I do this intervention shit?' I reach for her hand, and her eyes fly up to my face, surprised and ecstatic.

409

'Winch!'

She pulls me into her arms, and I kiss her, scared as hell, but ready to change the path that's been running me to nothing good for way too long. I'm ready to change my path with her, even if it scares the shit out of me. Even if I know it's not going to be pretty.

'First we need allies. We need your family on board. We can go see them tomorrow.'

I feel like suggesting we run away, hop a plane to anywhere, start a whole new life over in some foreign place, because starting fresh seems a thousand times better than facing down my family and what's sure to be their refusal to hear me out or let me go.

But Evan looks so hopeful, I trick myself into thinking for a minute that it all might work out. And then she says the one thing that really matters.

'No matter what, I'm here for you.'

So I get ready to let go and free-fall in the scariest jump of my life. But she's with me. So I swallow my fear and do it.

Evan 15

This is only the second time I've even been to the Youngblood house, but there's this feeling of foreboding I can't shake. Like maybe this is the last time. I know, deep inside me, that whatever goes down tonight, things are about to change in a huge way. My palms are slicked with sweat, and I feel a dizzy, light-headed rush in my head when I look at Winch. I can tell he's nervous, too, and I get why. His family is huge and beyond intimidating.

But I'm here for him. And I'm going to fight for him. If he falls, I'll be at his side to pick him up. It may be the first time anyone's ever bothered to do that for him. I kiss him before we go in, and he pulls me close, deepening the kiss until we're creeping into the kind of territory it won't be easy to get back from without some serious backseat action.

'Winch. Are you nervous?' I ask, pulling away, my lips sore and desperate for more of what they can't have.

Well, can't have right now.

He shakes his head, but doesn't say anything to me. We get out of the car and make our way slowly up to the house. When we get inside, his family is seated around the huge, food-laden dinner table. There's no one besides his siblings and parents, which I know is pretty unusual since, according to Winch's stories, the dinner table at their house is usually a meeting place for just about everyone in their entire extended family. Everyone looks up when we walk in. Mrs Youngblood pulls her napkin off her lap and places it on the table when she stands.

'Winchester, you should have called before you brought your friend over. I'm not prepared to entertain tonight.'

Her eyes, the same navy blue as Winch's, snap and crackle with a savagery that shocks me. Everyone else's eyes focus on the colossal assortment of food spread on the table in front of them.

It's just a tiny thing. Hardly worth noticing. I've been snubbed by nastier people in ruder ways. But there's something about this whole scenario, this entire put-down that's being disguised by a huge lie as plain as the banquet on their damn table, and I've had it.

'You are full of shit,' I announce.

I feel Winch tense. I realize he was about to speak

up on my behalf, and is shocked by my words. The eyes of every member of his family swing up at me, and all six mouths drop open. If I turned around, I bet I would see Winch's mouth hanging open, too, his eyes popped unnaturally out of their sockets.

I should shut up. I should shut up and let Winch handle this.

But I'm so sick of it all. So sick of putting a sock in it, so sick of watching this family's lies mutate and infect Winch and my chances with him. I've tried to be a lady. I've tried to keep my mouth shut and not judge and play the cool card, but it's so not me. I'm not any of that. Whatever happens today, it's going to get messy. Gloves-off, no-holds-barred messy.

'Excuse me, miss?' Winchester's father half stands, but his wife puts a hand out on his arm. He shakes it off and points a finger past me at Winch. 'This is the kind of foul-mouthed company you keep when you're running out on your own family? Your mother and I raised you to have more respect than that.'

I snort before Winch can get a word in edgewise. 'More respect? Really? You're going to talk to Winchester about respect? Respect for what? The law? The truth? Each other? Because I've never seen a damn thing but lies and disrespect as far as this family is concerned.'

Mr Youngblood's face is a shade of scarlet I didn't

imagine human skin was capable of turning. If steam blew out of his ears and fire came out of his eyeballs, I wouldn't be at all surprised.

'You have a lot of nerve, coming into my house and speaking to my family this way. Winchester, show your guest out. Now.'

His father has both hands on the table and he's breathing like his lungs are a set of giant bellows.

'No.'

The word, clear and steady from Winch's mouth, brings a gasp from every person at the table.

'Excuse me? I'm going to pretend I didn't just hear that. You take that girl back where she came from, and your mother will be waiting for your apology when you get back.'

Mr Youngblood's face has turned to granite and his eyes narrow to slits.

Mrs Youngblood has her cloth napkin pressed to her mouth. Benelli is wide-eyed and white-knuckled. Ithaca's red-rimmed, cried-out eyes look bright with surprised glee. Colt is gripping the edge of the table and shifts his mouth back and forth nervously. Remy leans woozily in his chair, either completely drunk or entirely uninterested in what's going on. Or, most likely, a little bit of both.

'I said no.' Winchester's voice is clearer, then he half chuckles, and it's a sound that isn't remotely

414

humorous. 'What Evan said is true. And it's about time someone in this house told the truth. I kind of expected the roof to fucking cave in.'

'Watch your goddamn mouth!' Mr Youngblood sputters. 'I had a feeling this whole thing was a bad idea. I had a feeling letting you get tangled up with an outsider would bring us trouble, and now here it is.' His glare focuses on me, vicious and hard, before it settles back on Winch. 'I'm gonna remind you of something. Family is forever, Winchester. You were born a Youngblood and you'll die a Youngblood. Whether or not this trash stays with you—'

Winch rushes past me and lunges at his father. I grab him behind one elbow, and Benelli jumps up and grabs his other. Colt half stands, but gets pushed back by Remy, who smacks the flat of his hand on the table. Mrs Youngblood and Ithaca jump at the sound, and everyone turns to watch Remy sway and try to collect his words.

'She's good people, Pop.' He turns his bleary eyes to me. 'She's . . . you can't do this to Winch. Can't. Cannot.'

He's clearly drunk and about to be dismissed by their father.

'Remington, sit the hell down before you pass out. This isn't about your brother's love life. This is about our family and your daughter. One wrong move could cost us everything.'

He directs his attention back to Winch, who's breathing heavily, but keeping it all together. Barely.

'He'll go to jail,' Remy argues. 'He'll do hard time. Kidnapping. That's what they'll slap him with.' He sits on the chair with a hard thump and goes a little green. 'I need to go to court.'

'This isn't a joke, Remington!' Mr Youngblood's patience is extinguished. 'You understand? Look at yourself! You're half a man at best. You won't be able to stay sober for court, and you sure as hell won't make it in jail. Winchester is smart, capable. He's a survivor. He can do this.'

'*I* can do this,' Remy says, his voice low and so forlorn it borders heavily on pathetic.

'You can shut the hell up while I run this family!' their father bellows, his lips curled back and his eyes strained dangerously out of their sockets. 'This family runs because I run it! I make decisions and you all follow my lead. The last goddamn thing we need is your stupid ass jumping in and ruining things more than they've already been ruined.'

'He needs help!' Ithaca's voice cuts through the swirling rage of her father's words.

'Ithaca. Sit down.' Mrs Youngblood's lips go tight and her eyes squint nervously.

'No!' Tears are running down her face, spilling onto the tablecloth, and she's wiping them away with the back of her hand as fast as they come. 'No! Everyone in this family just follows whatever Pop says. Well, Remy is really sick. Winch is in love, but he can't be with Evan. Colt wants to play football. I want to be with Andre. But no one gets what they want in this family except Pop, and it's not right!'

Benelli moves away from Winch's side to comfort her sister, but Ithaca throws herself out of her reach.

'Don't! You gave up on what you wanted so you could be the perfect daughter. I'm not like you. I can't just *forget* the person I love because someone tells me to. Don't you see that being perfect in this family just makes you the most fucked-up of all?'

The room erupts into a series of screams and shouts and threats as Ithaca storms away.

In the midst of it all, Remy slides out of his chair, teeth chattering, and smacks his head on the side of the table before collapsing on the floor, a slow, seeping pool of bright blood gushing from the gash at his temple and puddling around the table leg.

'Remy!' Winch's scream rises above all the chaos and he's at his brother's side in a second.

I grab my phone, poised to dial 911 when Mr Youngblood snatches it out of my hand.

'What the hell are you doing?' I yelp, trying to snatch the phone back.

He holds my phone over his head, making me jump

like some little kid being bullied on the playground until I realize how ridiculous I look and stop hopping around.

'911? Are you crazy? No authorities. No hospital. They'll do a tox screen, and he'll be in big trouble.' He tucks my phone in his pocket and puts his hands on his sobbing wife's shoulders. 'Calm down, all of you. Jazmin, go get clean towels and the bandages. Winch, lay him down so his head is tilted back. Benelli, call Campart.'

'Campart? The vet?' she asks, her eyebrows arching in surprise.

'Or Fillamin.' Their father's voice is distracted as he squats low near Remy's shaking, convulsing form.

Winch is smoothing the hair back off Remy's forehead, looking at his brother's contorted face. Remy's eyes are wild and his mouth is open like he's about to wail at any second, even though no sound is coming out at all.

'Fillamin isn't even done with nursing school.' Benelli bites her lips and looks at me.

I give her a full-on glare, laced with disgust.

I thought this family was insane, with all its lies and secrets and cover-ups. But that was before I watched them do anything at all to avoid the one thing that would save one of their own. Now, I'm positive they're criminally insane, and I know for certain that if

418

Winch goes back to them after this, there won't even be a minute's consideration.

He and I will be unequivocally done.

'Just call one of them,' Mr Youngblood snaps, grabbing a towel out of his wife's hands and putting pressure on the gash on the side of Remy's temple that's still gushing blood all over the floor.

Benelli looks at me across the dining room, and I shake my head. 'I would call 911, but your father took my phone,' I say. 'But I'm not the kind of person who'd stand around and watched someone I cared about die.'

Benelli closes her eyes and presses three numbers on her phone. The relief is instant, and a cool, black dizziness circles around me. I stagger back into the corner of the dining room, and it's like I'm in a plane that ascended too quickly. My ears clog up and I can't hear a single thing. All I can focus on are the rushed, frantic movements of the people I love, loathe, and am undecided about until a knock on the door breaks me out of my spell.

Paramedics rush in. Mr Youngblood's face is fierce and accusatory. Benelli presses her phone to her lips and watches, eyes wide, as the workers shove Winch and his parents aside and begin the frantic work of trying to save Remy's life.

The seconds tick by in violently quick succession,

but also drag like we're all set in excruciating slow motion.

They heave Remington onto a stretcher and rush out the door, Mrs Youngblood at their heels, Mr Youngblood following his wife. Winch chases after them, but the paramedic shakes his head. Not enough room in the ambulance.

I turn to Winch's siblings, huddled uncertainly in the dining room. Ithaca, who crept out from her bedroom when the screaming died down, is staring at the stain of Remington's blood.

'C'mon.' I wave them with my hand. 'Let's go make sure Remy is OK.'

'Our father will call for us when Remy's ready to have visitors.' Benelli crosses her arms and clamps her mouth in a determined line, even though her eyes race back and forth with anxious uncertainty.

Colt picks up the chair Remy knocked over when he fell.

'I want to go.' His voice is shaky.

Ithaca comes to stand next to me. 'Me too. I'm sick of waiting on everyone else to make decisions all the time.'

I walk towards Benelli and keep my words low enough that her siblings can't hear. 'You can wait for your father to call you. Just be prepared in case you don't get the call you want. Did you see him? Remy is sick. Really sick. And this might be . . . you may want to be there. In case.'

I can't bring myself to even say the words, but just hinting at them has Benelli blinking like mad, her resolve shaken.

'I'll get my purse,' she murmurs, pushing past me.

The twins file to the car, and I come to stand next to Winch, who hasn't moved a muscle since the ambulance pulled away. He's frozen still, his eyes staring at the vacant spot where he last saw his brother.

I'm afraid.

I shake because this was my idea. I pushed things. I added fuel to the fire and even threw the match that ignited this raging inferno.

I had no idea it would turn out like this.

I had no idea Remy would wind up in the back of an ambulance.

I'm afraid Winch will blame me. Will accuse me of working against his family. Will take out his pain on me. Will be unable to forgive me. Will hate me.

I put one hand on his arm, and the touch of my fingertips on the skin above his elbow shocks him out of his catatonic state. He blinks once, twice, his face a complete and total blank that makes my throat go dry.

And then he sweeps me into a huge, crushing hug, his face buried in my hair so I won't see him crying the tears I feel soaking into my skin.

I slide my arms around his waist and rub along his back. He's a few towering inches taller and pounds of packed muscle heavier than I am, but I do my best to offer him as much physical comfort as I can.

'This is my fault.' The words hiss out, and I know it's because if he speaks clearly, the sobs will make good on their clear and present threat. 'I did this to him. I put him in the hospital.'

'Shut up.' I force my voice to stay firm and rough while my hands move gently through his hair and knead at his neck. 'Shut your mouth. Don't you dare put this on your shoulders. Your brother was seriously ill. If he didn't fall today, in front of your whole family, he would have done it in private. And maybe choked on his puke or his tongue and died. Or maybe your parents would have decided not to take him to the hospital. It needed to happen exactly the way it happened. He needed medical attention, and now he's getting it.'

He pulls his mouth across my face and presses his lips to mine in a kiss that's more ravenous than romantic.

'I love you,' he says against my mouth. 'Thank God you're here. I don't know what I would have done without you. I love you, Evan.'

The relief is so intense, I sag against his body, dropping the strong girlfriend act for a long second so

I can just be with him, locked in his arms, happy in this moment when we somehow become a pair. I am the pepper to his salt, I am the cream to his coffee, I am the jelly to his peanut butter, and it feels good. It feels right.

I hope, with everything in me, that it lasts.

Benelli emerges and we file out of the house and squeeze into the car, which I drive because Winch is still shaken and edgy. Even the fact that I'm the one driving is a huge proclamation of how our relationship stands and what it means. He trusts me behind the wheel, driving his siblings, taking him to the hospital to join the rest of his family. I just watched Winch's brother have a seizure, but strangely, I feel good. Real and happy.

And nervous. I know very well how the best feeling in the world can sometimes be nothing but the prelude to disaster.

We get to the hospital, and Winch pulls on that air of command he wears so confidently.

'Winchester Youngblood, here to see my brother, Remington.' His charming smile brings out a smile on the face of the pudgy nurse behind the counter.

She's not immune to his good looks and flirtation. 'Remington Youngblood,' she repeats. 'That's some name.' They exchange another smile, and my blood boils. I know this is all about playing a game, getting

423

things done, but I still hate it. All my stupid jealousy dies down quickly when I see her face lose its flirty smile. 'Oh. Your brother is in critical care. I'm afraid I can only admit family.'

He doesn't even look back. 'We are. His family.'

'All of you? Siblings?'

I expect her to single me out, but I at least have the dark hair and light eyes the rest of them share. It's blonde Ithaca she's frowning at.

'All of us.' Winch says the next words so casually, I'm almost able to keep the shock off my face. 'My brother, my younger sisters, my wife.'

My heart races, and a mix of happiness and embarrassment makes me blush. It's a credit to the Youngblood penchant for lying that not one of them even draws an audible breath.

The nurse raises an eyebrow, but there's something about Winch that people want to believe, and in seconds, we're headed up the hushed hallway she directs us to, not making a sound other than the squeak of our sneakers on the polished linoleum.

Mr and Mrs Youngblood are at the nurses' station. Her eyes are red and bleary, and she's desperately clutching a balled-up tissue in her fist. He looks pale and gray-skinned, his paunch and thinning hair somehow more obvious in the harsh fluorescent lights. They're both incredibly stupid, selfish parents, but my hate for them melts when I see the crippling weight of their sadness. Even if their problems are their own damn fault, I have a heart.

Winch approaches his father. 'Pop, what do they say?'

'They think the seizures were caused by the mix of drugs in his system. He has concussion from hitting his head. There's been some damage to his kidneys and his liver isn't looking so good, but may be repairable.' Mr Youngblood lists Remy's ailments in a monotone.

'Can we see him?' Ithaca asks, biting her lip.

I know she's upset that she stormed out of the room before it happened, even if there wasn't a single thing she could have done to help him. Irrational guilt is something I get.

'We know we need to let him rest,' their mother says to the nurse on duty, her voice thick. 'But can his brother and sisters see him? Just for a minute?'

The nurse considers for a moment, and then concedes, 'Just for a minute.'

Winch has my hand in his, but I pull back gently. 'Not me.'

'You belong in there. Remy would have wanted it,' he argues.

His father sighs and shakes his head behind Winch's back, and his mother's eyes narrow at me.

'No. Go see your brother.' I push him to the room, and he walks over, looking back at me as he does.

As soon as he disappears into the room, his father turns to me.

'It would be best if you didn't see my son for a while,' Mr Youngblood says, straightening his back and looking down his crooked nose at me. 'We're going to have a serious family situation to deal with, and the last thing he needs is an outsider taking his attention away from what's important.'

A few weeks ago, Mr Youngblood's little speech would have been all it took to make me crumble inside and give up. But Winch and I are a unit now. Where he goes, I go. So I look both his parents in the eye, first one, then the other, and hold my hand out, palm up.

'I have no interest in what either one of you thinks I should do. Please give me my phone back before I have to report it stolen.'

His mother clicks her tongue and mutters something about 'disgusting lack of manners', and his father yanks my phone out of his pocket like it's a germ-ridden piece of crap before he slaps it into my palm.

'You're feeling high off of this right now, missy, but listen to me.' He wags a finger in my face, so close I could snap out and bite it if I wanted. And it takes everything in me to keep myself from following through with this. 'Winchester is loyal to his blood. He's misguided right now, by you, probably by what you're doing with him between the sheets.' I veer back in disgust, and his snaking smile tells me that he knows he's pushed over a line and doesn't care. 'But when that fades, he'll come back to us. He'll forget you. You should make it easy on yourself and just leave before you wind up dumped.'

My spine stiffens and my throat tightens. I have to force myself not to blink until the threat of tears is gone, and I work hard to get my voice under control so I can answer him.

'Trust me. He's never coming back to you.'

It's a bet. It's a bet on Winch that I'm willing to make even if I can't see the end result, like I always could with the horse races.

He comes out of Remy's room just then, his lips pinched and white, and the look of sadness in his eyes makes his mother flick a smile my way.

But it's me he goes to, me he folds in his arms. I grip right back, and hope that our love will be strong enough, that we'll have what it takes to make it through all of this together.

Winch 16

My stomach is twisted in knots. My parents are standing in the hallway outside my room, glaring, arms crossed, feet tapping, and the anger they're obviously feeling simmers and pollutes every ounce of space.

'This is unnecessary, son.' My father gestures to my nearly empty room. 'This is still your home. You wanna strike out on your own? OK, fine. But you don't just strip your past clean.'

I stack the boxes neatly, but I don't feel any energizing hum of defiance or righteous fury. I feel old and sapped. I feel a little like my brother must have when the hospital finally released him, spent and barely able to stand up straight.

When I went with him to sign into the long-term rehab facility, I was pretty sure it was just a hopeless attempt to stall the inevitable, and that he'd check himself out and find the closest bar. But he's stayed there, role-playing and keeping a journal and talking to a whole team of doctors.

Which is why I'm leaving.

I have to if I want my brother to live.

I have to if I want a shot at a real future for myself.

'I think it's time for a clean start, Pop.' I pull a long piece of packing tape over the closed flaps of the last box. 'Remy needs this.'

His eye twitches, and I regret saying the last words.

'Remy needs *this*? How, exactly, do you think it's possible that Remy needs not having his family together, working to get him back on his feet? Or is this going to be where you repeat all that psychobabble those quack doctors are charging me an arm and a leg to throw in my face?'

My dad's voice is so loud it brings Colt shuffling out of his room.

'Are you leaving today, Winch?' He eyes the boxes and then me. For the first time in a long time, my brother looks at me with something other than disgust; he looks proud.

A few weeks ago, I wouldn't have given a shit if Colt was proud of me or not. Now I'm glad he can look up to me for doing the one thing every Youngblood is trained never to do: walk away from the family.

'Yeah. I'm packing the last of it today, and moving into my apartment.' I turn back to my father. 'And, what the doctors say? It's not psychobabble,' I explain for the hundredth time, even though I should just drop it. I start to lift a box that's a little too big, but before I rip my back, Colt swoops in to grab the other end and grins at me. I grin back and look at my parents. 'They explained how what we do, what I do, enables Remy to do all that crazy stuff. When he gets out, he's gonna need to be so careful about things. I don't want him to fall back into bad habits.'

'How will he get well without all of us around him?' my mother asks, grabbing at the gold and ruby cross around her neck. She's been going to extra masses, praying about the whole situation. Sometimes I wonder what, exactly, she's asking God for. Most of the time, I'm glad I don't know.

'He has a support team,' I remind her. 'And I'm not out of his life forever. I'm keeping my distance for now. Just until he's back on his feet.'

'So you're planning to come back to the family, run things like you did?' My dad's face is so relieved, I feel bad for crushing his fantasy of us being one big, obedient family again.

'I have my own plans, Pop. I love you all, but it's time I did something for me.'

Colt picks up three boxes that are probably too heavy for him. 'You want me to bring these out for you?'

My little brother has always hated arguments and

fights, ever since he was a tiny kid. Lately it's been brawls day in and out around here, and since he sees another one brewing, he's eager to get away from it.

'Thanks, Colt.' I watch him leave, then turn my attention back to my parents, who look like they're in mourning when they should be happy. 'I'm going to apprentice. That's a good thing. And Remy is getting treatment. That's good, too.'

'I don't understand how all this good stuff has to come when you're both so far from this family,' my father argues. Mama puts an arm around his waist and presses her cross to her lips.

It's so obvious, I consider not answering him. But I was blindsided by my family for years. It took almost losing my brother and the girl I love to wake me up. Maybe losing me and Remy will be the wake-up call my parents need.

'Because the family isn't working the way it needs to,' I explain as patiently as I can. 'So we need some distance. I'm still your son. I still love you.'

My father looks at me for a few long beats, and I wonder if any of what happened in the past few weeks is going to sink in for him, going to change him. But he just grimaces and shakes his head. 'Yeah, well, you got a real funny way of showing us your love, son. That's for sure.'

He and my mother watch silently as Colt and I pack

the boxes into the U-Haul I rented. My sisters come out of their rooms just as we're finishing, and we all move to the front room.

So this is it.

I don't feel as good as I imagined I would. A lot has changed in a short space of time. I'm glad I'm moving on, but even with all the shit, there was still a lot I loved about being so close to my family. Evan's 'Sometimes, Always, Never' game flashes through my brain.

I'll always love my family.

I'll see them sometimes.

I'll never be under their thumb again.

But never being under their thumb means that I'll be shut out. There will be secrets I'm not told, there will be problems I don't help solve. I'll miss the down-time, the fun time, the family dinners and UFC fights and masses that are all I've known my whole life. I feel like I'm having an organ transplant. Even though I'm taking out what's poisoning me, I'm still losing a piece of myself. And it aches.

We do the requisite hugging and well-wishing, more so with my siblings than my parents, who look aged and shell-shocked. I feel guilty, but not guilty enough to stay.

And before anything is resolved in my head, before I know what I'm really doing or if it's really a good idea, I'm driving away. It doesn't take long to get to where I need to be, but this is the goodbye that's really going to hurt. Luckily, it's still a day or two away.

The door to Evan's grandparents' house swings open and Mr and Mrs Early give me a lukewarm greeting.

'Winchester,' Mr Early says, gripping my hand too hard and staring me down with a warning glare. For someone who resembles a cross between Colonel Sanders and Santa Claus, this guy is pretty intimidating.

'Evan is up in her room.' Mrs Early still hasn't forgiven me for being the persistent suitor they couldn't get rid of. She wanted me to disappear, let Evan date some nice boy from one of the families they knew. But I wasn't about to let that happen.

'Thank you, ma'am.' I give her my most charming smile, but she freezes me out. It must be something in Evan's bloodline that makes such scary women.

I start up the stairs and find Evan sitting at her dressing table, putting on the last of her make-up while her best friend chatters to her on speakerphone. '. . . Nothing to worry about, sweets. He's going to be in a program, OK? A stone masonry program or whatever. Not to totally buy into the gender stereotype, but realistically, how many girls could there possibly be in a school like that? And that's beside the point. He has you. What guy in his right mind would ever pursue any other girl when he has you?' Brenna's voice is bossy but caring. I love that she's got Evan's back.

I come up behind Evan and kiss her neck. She gets a big blob of black eye make-up on her cheek. 'Winch!' she squeals. 'Don't sneak up on me when I'm putting on mascara. I could have poked my eye out!'

'Stop being so sexy and I won't be tempted.' I grab a tissue and make a move to try and wipe it off, but she springs back in horror, takes out a container of round cotton things and goes to work getting the gunk off. 'Hey, Brenna. I like your advice.'

'Hey, Winch!' Brenna says, and although I've never met her, I can almost picture her bouncing in her chair. 'I know, right? Your girlfriend is so smart, but she's kind of being an idiot about this.'

'You just keep reminding her she's got nothing to worry about, OK?' Evan turns to me, the mascara blob gone, and kisses me full on the mouth. I immediately want her, but I can't have her. Not yet.

'I will. Have a safe trip, Winch. And good luck with the, uh, stonework!'

'Thanks, Bren,' I say, unable to keep down a sheepish smile. I'm excited about this. All of this. My new life, my new job. I can't wait.

Evan grabs the phone and takes it off speaker so she can whisper whatever crazy girl secrets she's telling her friend. I sit down and wait. When she hangs up, she immediately straddles my lap and presses against me.

'Not here,' I say when her hand cups my dick, already completely hard.

'We can be so quick,' she says as she nibbles my earlobe. 'I've missed you.'

I stifle a groan. 'If Lee Early caught us, he'd put a bullet through my brains, no question. I can't even believe you convinced them to let you stay over with me.'

She leans back, her arms linked around my neck. 'Yeah, it wasn't easy. But I've been on good behavior, my community service is all done, and I think they love you. I mean, they're still pissed as hell at you for dragging your feet. But now that they know you, they love you as much as I do. Well, almost as much.' She grinds on my lap and smiles this wicked smile that just turns me on more.

'Stop it before I need a cold shower.' I kiss her and move her firmly off me, trying to focus on anything that will make my dick chill out enough so that I can speak to her grandparents without needing to keep something in front of my pants at all times.

I mentally focus on baseball stats, gather her bags, and we head down to say another round of goodbyes, but these are way less drama-filled, both because the Earlys are more easy-going people and because this is all good for them. Evan will only be gone two days, and then I'll drive her back. I will stay hundreds of miles away, indefinitely. It's as perfect as they could have hoped for.

'Why did the only school that offered a stonemason apprenticeship have to be seven hours away?' Evan grumbles as we buckle into the truck.

'It's the best school for the kind of stonework I want to do,' I remind her. 'I want to be good at this. I want to start to make a life for us, Evan.'

'How do you always manage to say exactly the thing that makes me feel better?' She rolls her window down and lets the cool wind whip through the cabin as we start up. 'Are you sure you can drive this thing?'

'Are you insulting my driving skills? I'm practically a professional driver.' I make sure I double-check my blind spots after bragging to her. I'd been driving a sleek little car for so long, my ability to maneuver something this big is rusty, and I need to give it my full attention.

By the time we're two hours or two thousand radio station changes in, Evan starts to poke at the thing that's been making me have minor panic attacks about every fifteen minutes.

'You look nervous.' She passes me a piece of gum, but I shake my head and hold the steering wheel tight, eyes fixed on a road I've never traveled down before.

'I've never really done this kind of stuff. I might suck,' I admit out loud. As soon as I say the words to her, a little bit of the edge wears off.

She turns in her seat and takes off her sunglasses. 'You will be amazing. You'll be the top apprentice at the school. No one works harder than you do, Winch.'

A long minute ticks by before I get up the guts to add, 'I've never lived away from my family.'

She unbuckles her seatbelt and slides across the bench seat, buckling the center lap belt over her curvy hips before she leans her head on my shoulder. 'It's scary.'

She doesn't go on or give me some speech about how much better off I'll be without them or why it's good that I'm finally doing something on my own. She gets that I just want to feel scared and sad and nervous as fucking hell for a minute.

I can only admit it to her. I'm not used to feeling nerves like this, not about my own choices and future, anyway.

'I don't know what my father will do,' I tell her. 'He's relied on me so much. I do so many things for the business. I'm afraid Colt will get pulled in, or he'll ask Remy before he's ready, and it will all get screwed up.' I tighten my hands around the steering wheel. She rubs my arm in a slow, comforting path from my elbow to my wrist, over and over.

'And I'm afraid for Andre, you know?' I add, even though I know I'm just being an irrational ass. Evan nods and I keep talking, letting out all the anxiety I usually keep bottled up. 'Why the hell didn't he take the damn money? He'd be in art school now, not suited up for boot camp. He's tough and all, but I don't know if he's cut out for all of that.'

'I hear you.' She wraps an arm around my waist and squeezes.

'And I'm scared for Benelli. Ithaca told us all how she had some guy, someone she loved that she gave up on. What if he's "the one", you know? I can't imagine giving up on the one. I'd be lost without you.'

Evan rubs her face on my arm and kisses my bicep, sighing deeply.

'Am I crazy for worrying about all this?' I ask.

She shakes her head. 'You worry because you care about them. You care because you're an amazing person. But I think you should have a little faith in them. You guys are strong people, you know? And you all have to fight your own battles. No one could have done this for you, Winch. You had to decide to fight for us and your future, even though it was hard. Your brothers and sisters will have to make their own decisions too, and live with them.' She nestles down next to me. 'And I'll be around. I can always stop by and help if anyone needs it. I'll keep an eye on them.'

That makes my heart thump kick-drum loud in my chest. Even after all the hell my family put her through, Evan still offered to help them. For me. I love her for that. I love her for a million reasons, but especially for that.

'I love you, you know that?' I turn and kiss the top of her head.

She moves closer to me. 'You better,' she says around a long yawn. 'I love you, too.'

She's asleep before I can communicate any more worries, so I just let them all run through my brain, sharp and real, sad and bittersweet. Even though it hurts to do it, I'm glad. I'm glad I can feel it all and let it go, because I'm ready to move on.

I glance down at the phone balanced on the dashboard. It doesn't ring any more. I had the number changed and I didn't give it to anyone for a while. By the time I leaked it out, the people who'd tried to call while I was unavailable had found other sources, and my family knew that I wasn't at their beck and call anymore.

The end of that life isn't easy to accept. It had been mine for so long, it had become comfortable to me. I understood who I was and how I belonged, even if I didn't like it.

Now?

There's so much risk, so much to lose. I'm not the

one who's going to fix everything, I won't be the hero who comes by and sweeps up everyone else's messes. My life as a fall guy is getting put further behind me every single day. Now I'm going to have to live on my own terms, clean up my own messes, and have my own adventures.

It feels freeing, but at the same time a little fucking scary to live without any more excuses. To live freely. To live my own life, my own way.

With Evan at my side if I'm lucky.

I think about this through Evan's cat naps and radio station changes, her hours reading, head leaned against the window, and eventual deep sleep. Evan lifts her drowsy head when we're ten minutes away from my new place. She looks around sleepily and says, 'It looks like the ghetto.'

My laugh is nervous in my own ears. 'I have to live on a pretty small amount of money for a while.'

'Why didn't you just take the money your parents offered you?' she asks, no accusation in her voice.

I flip my eyes from my GPS to the tatty street signs that mark the roads. 'Youngblood money always comes with strings attached, Evan. You know that.'

When we pull up at the apartment, she inhales in a sharp, worried breath. 'Winch. Are you sure about this?'

I get out of the truck, walk around to open her door, and let her step into my arms. I kiss her forehead and then move my mouth down to her lips. 'Just for a little while,' I say, low, just for her ears. 'Just till I get a good job. I'm gonna do it, you know. I'm gonna move on and up before you know it. I swear.'

'I know that,' she says, her lips close to mine. 'I believe in you.'

That's all I need to hear.

I keep those words in my head as we open the door to my apartment and notice the scuttle of small brown bugs. Evan screams and pushes me back out into the street and we drive to the closest hardware store and pick up roach spray, scrub brushes, rubber gloves, buckets, soap, a whole bunch of cleaners, and lots of bleach.

When we come back, Evan goes to work like a maniac, scrubbing and spraying every surface she can reach, opening all the windows, and double scrubbing when she's already done. I bring in box after box and admire the sweet curve of her ass as she scrubs and polishes.

'Are you checking out my ass?' she asks over her shoulder.

I'm kneeling down to open a box, but I turn toward her. The place is so small, the kitchen is pretty much located in the living room, blocked by one long counter with chipped laminate. I move her way, until I'm right behind her, hands on her hips, bent low to kiss her neck. The sound of her moan rattles through me.

'I'm totally checking out your ass,' I assure her. 'I'm always checking you out.'

She glances at me over her shoulder, her eyes wide and her lower lip caught between her bottom teeth. My hands go tight on her hips and I press closer to the curve of her ass.

'So, is all this "woman scrubbing your house on her hands and knees" turning you on?' Her eyes narrow, and I see the spark of passion that I love so much in her.

'I like my woman to know her place,' I tease, and when she tries to turn and slap at me, I slide my hands up her shirt, along the soft, smooth skin of her stomach, and under the sweet swell of her tits. I lean over her, my chest pressed to her back, my lips brushing up and down her neck.

'You're a chauvinist pig,' she says, her voice hitched on a gasp.

'I'm *your* chauvinist pig,' I correct. 'Would you like to christen this apartment with your chauvinist pig boyfriend?'

I pull down on the lacy fabric of her bra until her nipples poke out, hard under my fingers. I press tighter against her and she turns in my arms, kissing my mouth.

'This apartment is still filthy,' she says, wrinkling her nose. 'I'm not doing it on this floor.'

Her hand runs down the front of my pants and rubs my dick through my jeans. I grind my teeth and work my hands faster, unclasping her bra, pressing her shirt up, flicking open the button on her shorts and yanking the zipper down.

'There must be somewhere clean enough.' I kiss her neck and down her shoulder, pulling her shirt to the side.

'There's nothing, Winch. The only things I cleaned so far are the cabinets and the counter. We didn't even bring the mattress in or go over the bedroom at all.'

Her body against mine makes my brain go cloudy, and all I can focus on is the word 'counter'. I lift her up so her legs are snug around my waist, and drop her on the scrubbed-down countertop.

'Winch,' she whispers, glancing around and biting her lip. 'We can't just do it on the counter.'

I'm busy kissing her perfect neck, working her thin shirt over her head, throwing her bra to the side. 'It's super clean,' I answer. 'I watched you scrub it down with, like, eight different cleaners.'

'It's not the cleanliness thing. It's just . . . oh. Oh, please do that . . . again.'

443

I'm not sure if she's talking about the way I just sucked her nipple into my mouth or the stroke of my thumb against the wet slide of her clit, but I do both again because she asked so sweetly and I love making her happy. She wraps her arms tight around my shoulders, moaning and breathing heavy for a minute, before she backs up and rips my shirt over my head, then reaches down to undo the button on my jeans, her breathing quick and raspy.

I pull my hand out from the leg of her shorts and she whimpers in protest. 'I thought you didn't want to do this,' I tease her.

She sucks a quick breath through her teeth and lifts her hips so I can slide her shorts and tiny thong down her legs.

'Um, shut up and ignore what I was saying.' She shivers when her skin touches the countertop. 'It's cold.'

I pull her, naked and so damn beautiful, to the edge of the countertop and closer to me.

'No worries,' I say low against her ear before I press a trail of sucking kisses down along her jaw. 'I'll warm you up.'

My hands run up her thighs, and she reaches down to grab my dick and pull with long, smooth strokes of her hand. I slide my fingers up until I'm in her, wet and hot, and she moves fast against my hand, slick and ready for me.

She presses one hand hard between my shoulder blades and tugs me to her until we're an inch away. I grab for the back pocket of my jeans, falling off my hips fast, and tear out a condom.

'I want you now,' she pants, legs spread, the hand on my back digging into my skin.

'Right now? Right on this countertop?' I ask, fitting myself against her.

She opens her half-closed eyes and pulls my mouth down to hers. 'Anywhere. Everywhere. Whenever. Just you. Always you – ooh . . .' A moan chases her words because, with one quick thrust, I'm deep inside her, pressing against her, holding her close, kissing her so I can taste her and catch the vibration of the jumbled words she's moaning and calling out.

'Evan,' I say, my voice low, my hands dragging across her soft skin. 'Come for me, baby. Come on me.'

She bites her lips and arches back, and I slide my fingers against the wet, ready bead of her clit in a light, quick press-and-pull until her breathing turns to gasps and she gets hotter and wetter against my dick.

'Come for me,' I tell her. She lifts her hips and pulls me closer with her long legs, until our bodies are pressed tight and she's grinding against me.

'Now,' she moans. One hand flies to my chest and she braces against me as her back arches and her legs squeeze tight. 'Now, now, now, Winch now!' She falls forward and shudders against me, her face pressed hard into my neck, her hands fisted in my hair.

I rock against her a few more times, and it's all I can do to hold on that long before I let go and free-fall, losing it all with her.

'Evan, goddamn, Evan, I love you so much,' I manage to get out, and then I switch to Hungarian and say all kinds of things that I want her to know.

That I love her, that I want her, that I'm never going anywhere, that she and I are going to last. That this is real. That it's forever.

She takes a few shuddering breaths and pulls back slightly, her lips grazing my cheek.

'Why do you do that?' she asks.

'Do what?' I take a deep breath, enjoying the smell of her skin and sex over the harsh stench of bleach.

'Speak another language. During sex. You always do it during sex.' She runs her hands up and down my neck and rubs her nose against my jaw, breathing in with long, deep breaths.

'I, uh, say the things I don't know if you're ready to hear yet in Hungarian. All the things I feel about you but I don't want to scare you with. So I just say them in Hungarian.' I pull back gently, take the condom off and get my pants back on, and hand her clothes.

She hooks her bra, and I take one last look at those perfect tits before they're covered in all that lace.

'So, what did you just say? I don't mind you speaking Hungarian. Honestly, it's pretty damn sexy. But I want to know everything. There's no way you can scare me away, Winch.' She hops into her thong and shorts and pulls her shirt over her head.

'Just plans. For us. For our future.' I keep it vague, because I know I can do it, but it scares the crap out of me sometimes. How much I want it. How much it will suck if it doesn't happen. If I can't make it happen.

'Tell me,' she coaxes, pressing hard against me and wriggling, just like she knows will drive me crazy.

'Not yet,' I tell her, kissing her hard, 'but soon.' And I hold her in the middle of my new place just before I start going to school to learn my new trade, where I'll get a job I'm going to be good at and a new chance at a future I assumed was doomed just a few weeks ago.

Finding Evan turned every single thing in my world around. I think I'll always be a fall guy, but I'm only falling with her, for her, into anything she wants because I know I can trust her with my future, with our future.

I just need to find the guts to say all that in English to her.

I'll do it. I know I can do it.

'So, what do we do about this dump?' I ask her, distracting myself from my fear of the future.

'Clean it,' she answers. 'Then we put all your stuff

away, then we get into bed and don't sleep. It will be a while before we see each other again, so I want to take every opportunity to get in your pants.'

She grins at me and pushes me away from the counter before she attacks it with a scrubbing brush.

'You just cleaned that,' I point out.

'Um, yeah, and then we had wild sex on it. Not very sanitary.' She glances up and raises one eyebrow. 'I appreciated all your, um, hard work before, but that doesn't excuse you from this moving-in business. Get to work. I want to have some time to get it on tonight before we crash.'

'It's sick how much I like it when you boss me around,' I tell her as I lug another box in from the truck.

'I'm a good boss.' She puts her hands on her hips and looks around, and it's hard for me to imagine a girl looking sexier than she does right now, her shirt stuck to her with sweat, her hair in a messy ponytail, her skin flushed from all her energetic scrubbing and sex. 'The kitchen is officially scrubbed down. I'm going to start on the living room.'

The next few hours fly by, and by the time it's dark the place is spotless, most of my stuff is unpacked, and we've christened the shower. Evan lies by my side on my bed and looks around the echoing, overly white space. 'It's spooky how empty it looks in here,' she whispers.

'It's not empty. We're here.' I link my hand with hers in the dark and fit her close to me on the mattress.

'What about when I leave?' Her voice shakes a little, and I pull her tighter to me.

'Then I'm here, and I wait for you.' I press my chin on the top of her head, still damp from our shower.

'And when I'm done with school?' Her voice is so quiet, I can barely hear the question.

'Then I come see you at college every chance I get. And when I graduate, I find a place by you and seduce you into moving in with me.' I run a hand up and down her body, shoulder to hip, over and over.

'And then?' she asks sleepily.

I'm about to switch to Hungarian, but I don't. I don't because I know how to let go now.

So I just say it, in English, to the girl I love, fear be damned.

'And then I save up for a ring and ask you to marry me. And then, if everything goes the way I want, you agree. And then whatever you want. As long as you're with me, I know things will be all right.'

I feel her go stiff in my arms, and I wonder if I should have just stuck to goddamn Hungarian. She's got her whole life ahead of her, and, love me or not, she may not be ready for all the things I want from her and with her. The last thing I need is for her to feel like she has to compromise on anything for me.

She sits up, and I feel my heart lurch in my chest.

'Do you mean that?' she asks. 'Do you really mean what you just said?'

Fuck.

'Yeah. Of course I mean it. I wouldn't have said it if I didn't. But I understand if you—' I sit up next to her, ready for her to say she's not ready, she's not going to rush this, that she needs time, that she's—

'I love you. I love you. And I know you didn't ask yet and don't have a ring and don't know when this will all happen, but my answer is definitely "yes".' She throws herself into my arms so hard it knocks me back on the bed, and she winds herself around me and kisses all over my face, quick and furious. 'Yes to everything. Yes to anything you think or want. Yes to us. Always. Yes. I love you.'

Her kisses invite mine, mine inspire more of hers, and I let go. I fall into her, into her crazy love, into the promise of our future, into every scary, unbelievably amazing thing I was ever nervous to dream about and now get to hold in my arms. I fall into this love, no matter how scared out of my skull I am that I might mess up or she might need space and leave me or we might face challenges together that test everything we want.

I'll spend the rest of my life falling as far and deep as my heart will let me go in love with this perfect, crazy girl who taught me to let go and hold on. I know in that minute I'll be Evan's fall guy until the day I die, and my future, for the first time in my life, is an always I can't wait to fall into.

Acknowledgments:

This is the coolest section in a book, because it's where an author gets to give smooches to all the people who helped her along the way and let those people know how appreciated they are! I'm very smoochful, and know how lucky that makes me.

Thank you to my husband and daughter. I always promise I'm going to write during school/work hours and be fully present at all other times. I break that promise daily, and they love me anyway. And feed me and nudge me toward the shower and help with the chores I always mean to do, but forget because my characters are distracting me! They are my heart, and I don't know what I'd do without them.

Thank you to my amazing fam who always pitch in to cheer me on, act like I'm more famous and wealthy than I'll ever be, and give me crazy help and advice anytime I need it. Or don't. But that's the beautiful thing, isn't it? I love them more than I can express. And I'm a wordy, expressive girl!

To my sweet, loving friends who read and tell me what's good and/or crazy in my book. Particular love to Steph, who has to put up with me because I won't go away; Katie, who has to put up with me because we're sisters; and Tamar, who has to put up with me as payback for all the years I tortured/loved her in college.

To the enormously cool team at Dystel and Goderich, so many thanks. Thank you to Jane for giving me the coolest call (straight from NYC) that set my career on a whole new path. Thank you to Lauren, who always goes the distance and a hundred times beyond, and who held my hand and cheered me on through many exciting new experiences. Every single person I've interacted with from the agency has made me beyond grateful that I get to be a part of this team. I am so incredibly proud to be represented by a group of forward-thinking, brave, brilliant professionals who have such awesome humor and incredible enthusiasm for books and writers.

To the passionate, amazing team at Random House UK, who took a chance on me and have been the most encouraging book lovers and author supporters. Thank you to Lauren Buckland for that lovely introductory email (that seemed a little surreal when I opened it) and for picking up *Fall Guy*. Thank you to Carmen McCullough, whose emails I always look forward to, and who has gushed with me over the design team's amazing covers and worked with me through edits and questions and particulars with incredible patience and humor. I so appreciate the help and support of every single person who has embraced me so generously. You guys are seriously beyond rad!

A huge, colossal, ever-loving thank you to the group of authors who are my herd of wild, magical, talented unicorns. They have showered me in glitter to celebrate my successes, given me virtual smooches when I'm down, and been my inspiration along every step of this amazing journey. So much love, beauties. So much love.

And huge, enormous, all-consuming love to the community of readers, bloggers, and other authors who support, inspire, share, and encourage the writing and reading of every kind of book. I'm honored to be included in the ranks of such a passionate, loving, supportive group of people who share my love of stories that transport and beautify. You. All. ROCK!

DOUBLE
The First Brenna Blixen Novel
CLUTCH

Who to choose . . . ?

Thrust back into school life after a year in Denmark,
Brenna Blixen is soon making new friends and
catching the eye of two boys with bad reputations.
There's the dark and mysterious Saxon, and
the gorgeous and sexy Jake.

They're both totally hot and totally into Brenna.

But Saxon and Jake have unresolved history, and
Brenna's caught in the middle.

It's time to make some tough choices, fast.

When Brenna Blixen is offered a trip to Paris for the
winter break, she jumps at the chance.

After a tearful goodbye with her gorgeous boyfriend,
Jake Kelly, Brenna is shocked to discover that
Saxon Maclean is also headed to the City of Love.

He's trouble and irritating as hell.
But also seriously hot.

Can Brenna resist her animal urges, or is good girl
Brenna about to turn bad . . . ?

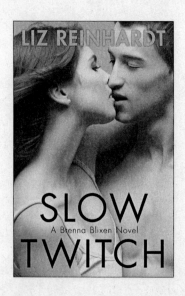

It's summer in Sussex County and things are heating up for Brenna, Jake and Saxon.

Who will end up with who, and will all that unresolved chemistry finally get put to bed?